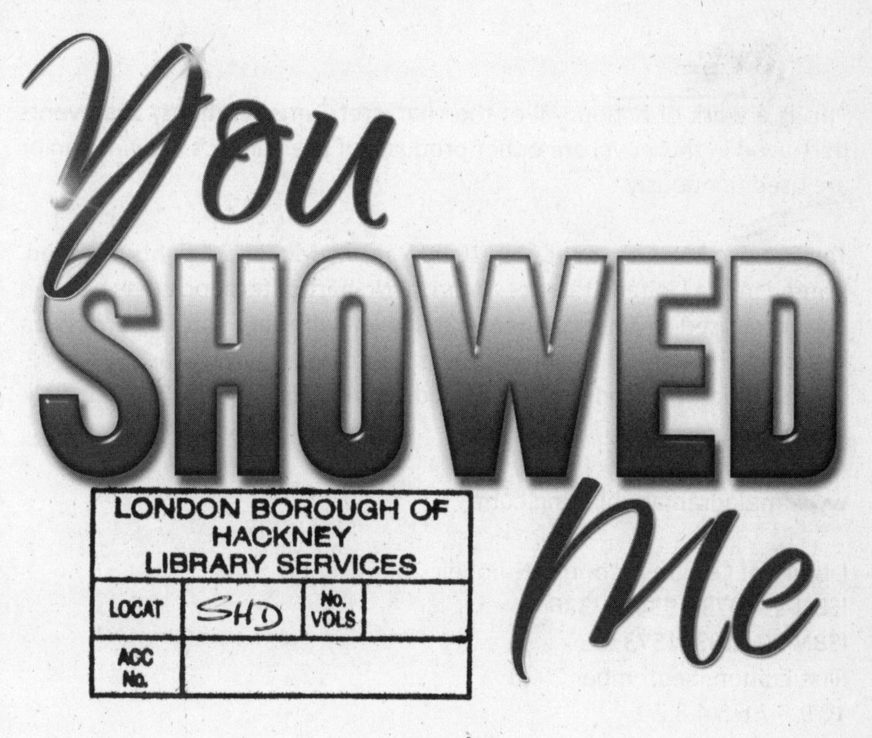




*a novel by*

*Nahisha McCoy*

This is a work of fiction. All of the characters, organizations, and events portrayed in this novel are either products of the author's imagination or are used fictitiously.



www.melodramapublishing.com

Library of Congress Control Number: 2010926186
ISBN-13: 978-1934157336
ISBN-10: 1934157333
First Edition: September 2010
10 9 8 7 6 5 4 3 2 1

Editors: Melissa Forbes, Brian Sandy, Candace K. Cottrell
Interior Design: Candace K. Cottrell

# Acknowledgments

First and foremost, I want to thank God for blessing me with this talent and giving me the strength and courage to use it. Next, I want to thank my family for believing that all things are possible. To the Fenner family, Auntie Ruthie, Uncle Robert, and Raven, thank you for always pushing me to do better, supporting my dreams, and believing in me when I didn't believe in myself. Auntie, you are my rock and foundation. I love you very much.

To my three sons, David, Nashene, and Dontae, thank you for being so patient with me as I continue to finish this book and turn my hobby into a career. I love all three of you guys. To my fiancé Dale, you are a good man, a diamond in the rough, and I appreciate you for always giving me a shoulder to cry on, an ear to hear me, and support when I need it. Don't ever change, no matter what.

To my extended family, the Watkins, you have been with me through thick and thin. Thanks for all of the cigarettes, late-night talks, laughs, and most importantly, friendship. You guys are the best.

To my boy Randy, you continued to push and challenge me at every turn to finish this book. You even went out there and started selling them on your own for me without looking for anything in return, and for that I am very grateful and appreciative. Thanks for being a true friend.

To my sisters, Vinnie, Toya, Stacey, Nay-nay, and Judy, and my nephews, Sheeky, Chocolate, Kell, and little man Jahquan, keep on keeping on. It's always good to know you guys have my back. I have nothing but love for you all.

A special thanks to my other extended family, the Fullers—Tasha, Shaunette, Nate, Steve, Mrs. Fuller, Angie, Tafira, Jason, and others. Thanks for always keeping me in your hearts and minds, especially for always making me feel like I am a part of your family.

To my girls Shafai, and Tajah, as well as the staff at the Brooklyn HIP Center, good looking-out. To the rest of the coworkers I got along with, I will miss working at the Bureau of Labs with you guys.

To Ticia, Roman, and Robbie, good looking out. Y'all are a force to be reckoned with. Ha! Ha!

To my friend Nancy Martinez thanks for always being a true friend. To Sgt. Hollingsworth, thank you for being a cool and honest supervisor. Working with you was the best. To my fallen coworker, you are missed dearly. Rest in peace Tony K. Roston. God bless!

To my good friend Al-Saadiq Banks, writer and author. Boy, if it weren't for you believing in me and supporting me mentally, I couldn't have done it. Thanks for everything.

Grandma and Bee-Bee, I wish you guys were here with me. I know you're in heaven looking down on me, and I hope I made you proud. I miss you dearly and carry you in my heart.

To everyone in Red Hook, Brooklyn, Harlem, Queens, and New Jersey, thank you for all your continued support.

To all you haters, backstabbers, liars, cheaters, connivers, and tricksters, I did it anyway.

# Prologue

Thinking about how she'd gone from being in love to just barely loving her man made Naheema Morgan disgusted with herself. She couldn't stand that she'd made it so easy for this man to come into her life and make her feel like she wasn't worth a damn. She'd allowed Mike to make her feel like she was the ugliest, vilest thing in the world.

But Naheema was far from ugly, and her attitude about life had always been far from nasty. She knew she was, and would always be, an attractive, young, vivacious African-American woman. The man above had blessed her with a five-foot two-inch frame and with the shape of an old-fashioned Coca-Cola bottle. She was designed to belong to a house of love, and not a factory full of dry knuckles. With her brown shoulder-length hair, almond-shaped, chestnut brown eyes, and soft, round face, she looked as if she'd been painted by Michelangelo for the entire world to adore. Her 36B cup breasts were the size of fresh, ripe mangoes picked straight from a farmer's market. She kept her body in perfect form, and her complexion made her look as if she had been dipped in honey and sprinkled with just the right amount of cinnamon.

Sitting in her jail cell contemplating her next move, Naheema sat down on her cot, replaying the last three years of her sorry-ass relationship. She looked out her tiny window as the colorful array of purples, pinks, and yellows glistened off the ocean water, making the prettiest rainbow, as the sun descended for the evening.

She picked up the letter that she'd just written to her ex-boyfriend.

*Dear Mike,*

*You are a bastard who abused and deceived me by doing whatever was necessary to get me to love you. You are worse than the devil himself. A least the devil had a soul. I wish that I could be there to see you die. Believe me; I know they will put you to death like the dog you are. I hope my words are the last thing you see before you burn in hell.*

*Always,*

*Naheema*

She folded the paper, placed it inside the envelope, put a stamp on it, sealed it, and placed it inside of her Bible. This was her farewell to a horrible relationship with a monster of a man. She hoped it would reached him in time.

# Chapter 1

## IN THE BEGINNING

Macy's; Fulton Street, Brooklyn, NY
May 2001

Rushing to walk out of Macy's department store, Naheema miscalculated the timing to step through the revolving doors and slammed headfirst into it. She fell back and busted her behind, sending her bags flying in every direction. She looked up, praying that no one noticed, but to her embarrassment, everyone stopped what they were doing to look over at her. She felt so stupid.

One of the male security officers ran over to her and helped her up. Naheema tried to laugh it off as she held the security guard's hand to get up from the floor. She picked up her bags and inspected them and noticed she was missing some things from the bag. The bag with her lingerie was empty.

As she continued to look around for her stuff, she noticed a brown-skinned man walking in her direction. As he got closer, she noticed he was holding something in his hand.

Naheema was so busy staring at the man walking toward her that she didn't hear the security guard asking her if she was okay. The guard finally tapped her and asked her again.

She snapped out of her daze and whispered, "Yes."

When the guard attempted to ask her again, she brushed him off. It was embarrassing enough that this man walking toward her might be holding her sexy underwear. She would be devastated if he returned it in front of the security guard.

Taking the hint, the guard walked away, and she returned her attention to the man just as he approached.

"Excuse me, miss. Is this yours?" the man asked.

Naheema wanted to respond, but this gorgeous specimen of a man standing so close to her took her breath away. She started to hyperventilate.

He smiled, took her by the arm, escorted her to the side, and sat her down. "Are you okay?" he asked.

Naheema attempted to answer, but nothing came out of her mouth.

"I'll run and get someone to help," he said, getting up.

Naheema placed her hand on his wrist and shook her finger back and forth. Finally able to calm her breathing, she answered, "Yes. That's mine, and I am feeling better." She let go of his wrist.

"I thought I was going to have to call nine-one-one for you." He smiled as he slipped her negligee into her bag.

"That won't be necessary, and thank you for being so discreet." Naheema smiled at him and stuffed the negligee deeper into the bag.

"Not a problem."

This man's Ralph Lauren cologne was driving Naheema crazy. It didn't hurt that he was sexy as hell with his soft brown eyes and deep dimples. He looked to be about six-two and weighed about 180 pounds. She could tell he was rippling with muscles from the way his clothes fit him. His Coogi jean outfit, black custom-made Bruno Magli shoes, and his Mercedes key chain screamed money.

Naheema stole little glances at him, and he smiled in return every time. With his immaculate haircut and trim, he looked as if he'd just left the barber's chair. That's when she noticed his pearl-white teeth and the smoothest skin she'd ever seen—not a blemish, pimple, or bump in sight.

"Oh, where are my manners? I'm Mike, and you are?" Mike held his hand out.

"I'm Naheema. Nice to meet you," she said, placing her hand in his to shake it.

While looking directly into her eyes, he took her hand in his, pulled them to his lips, and kissed it.

Naheema quickly pulled her hand away from him and placed it back on her lap. Her hand began tingling from the sensation of his soft, luscious lips on it. She thought to herself, *It's a sin for a man to look and feel this good.*

She looked down at his hands and saw no wedding band, but she noticed that he had excellent taste in jewelry. His pinky ring was encrusted with emeralds, and as she looked up at him, she saw the matching emerald earring in his left ear. She assumed emerald was his birthstone because it was also on the face of his Citizens watch.

"Did I offend you?"

"Oh, no. It's just that my hands were on the floor when I fell," she said, trying to hide her discomfort.

Mike smiled. "No problem."

They continued to talk for another five minutes before she realized she had to be on her way, so she began grabbing her bags and stood up. She thanked him for his help and turned to leave. As she got to the door, Mike called her back.

She turned around. "Yes."

"This may seem corny, but do you like the comedy club scene?"

"Yes, I do, but I haven't been to one in a while."

"Well, if you get some free time, give me a call. Maybe we can go to one." He reached into his back pants pocket to retrieve his business card to hand her one.

"I'll do that. Thanks." Naheema took the card and stuffed it inside of her pocketbook.

"All right then, Naheema. It was really nice meeting and talking with you." Mike held the door open for her. "Oh, and watch out for those revolving doors." He laughed.

"You are so funny," Naheema said, laughing. She left Macy's embarrassed, happy, and wet.

Naheema walked to the corner of Jay Street and saw that her bus was a block away. She crossed the street by the Lane Bryant clothing store and headed down the block to Smith Street. As she stood in front of the New York City's Housing Court building, she contemplated whether she should take out Mike's business card to look it over.

Just as she placed her bags on the ground to reach into her pocketbook for the card, the B61 pulled up. She pulled out her MetroCard and climbed on the bus.

The entire ride home, her thoughts were on Mike. From his appearance, Naheema knew he wasn't your average Joe. And from talking to him, she knew he was educated, smart, funny, and single. In fact, Mike seemed like an okay guy, and she wanted to get to know him better.

Naheema was so busy daydreaming about Mike that she missed her stop and had to get off on Wolcott Street, two blocks down.

After she made it home, her house phone rang. She dropped her bags on her bed and ran into the living room, where she grabbed the cordless phone. "Hello."

"Hey, sis. What's up? What you doing?" her sister Shaquanna asked.

"Hey, girl. I just walked in."

"From where?"

"Macy's. They had a nice sale going on, so you know I had to go and do me."

"Yeah, I sure do. If it's expensive enough for a sale, it's cheap enough for you to buy." Shaquanna laughed.

"And you know it." Naheema walked back to her bedroom. "Oh snap! Quanna, you will never guess what happened to me?"

"What?"

"Damn, girl! I said *guess*."

"You know I'm not good with guessing games, so just tell me."

Naheema whined, "All right, fine, spoilsport."

"Naheema."

Naheema began to unpack her stuff. "All right. I busted my ass inside of the store."

"You're lying."

"Girl, if I'm lying, I'm flying." Naheema laughed.

"Wow! You had to be embarrassed. You fell in Macy's during a sale." Shaquanna laughed.

"Please. Not as embarrassed as having a total stranger pick up my negligee and hand it to me."

"You're serious?" Shaquanna asked, continuing to laugh. "And knowing your freaking ass, you probably had some outrageous shit."

"No, Shaquanna, I'm not you."

"My bad, I forgot. You're a closet freak." Shaquanna said, laughing.

"Whatever. Anyway, that's not all."

"Really?"

"Once the man got close enough to hand me my stuff, I started hyperventilating," Naheema said, laughing.

"Naheema, stop playing with me." Shaquanna was laughing hysterically. "You're gonna make me piss my pants."

"I'm serious. Quanna, this man was so damn sexy, looking at him caused me to have breathing problems. Not to mention, he smelled so fucking good. Girl, he was fine as all hell."

"Well, damn! If he had you hyperventilating, he must have been something serious, especially if you stopped and talked to him."

"Shit! I had no choice. He had to sit me down so I could catch my breath." Naheema sat on her bed and started removing her sneakers.

"You're funny."

"Quanna, you had to see him. He had the smoothest brown skin, pearly white teeth, and a gorgeous smile with the deepest dimples. And his eyes, oh my goodness, his eyes were light brown. Girl, when he kissed my hand, his lips were soft and moist. I had to quickly move my hand from him. I swear I can still feel his lips on my hand."

"Damn! That's serious. Shit! You got me wet thinking about him."

"Who are you telling?"

"So how was he dressed?"

"I'll put it to you like this: If I was to hook up with him, I know damn well I would never stress about my paycheck covering my rent again."

"So did you get his number?"

"Yeah, he gave me his business card."

"Did you call him?"

Naheema looked at the phone as if she was staring Shaquanna. "Hell no!"

"Why not?"

"Are you crazy? I don't want this man to think I'm desperate."

"Naheema, please, this is the twenty-first century. Call that man, but, if you don't want to, then hook a sister up." Shaquanna laughed.

"Shut up. Look, I have to go. Are we still hanging out later?"

"I don't know. I may get stuck working a double tonight, but I'll call you and let you know."

"Okay. Love you."

"Love you too. And call that man."

Talking to Shaquanna had Naheema seriously thinking about calling Mike. She not only didn't want to come across as being desperate; she didn't want him to forget her either.

She reached into her pocketbook and pulled out his card. She looked at it and read it out loud, "Official Kuts Unisex Shop." She placed the card on her dresser inside of her jewelry box.

She put away her clothes, got undressed, walked to the bathroom, and jumped into the shower. She figured she would give Mr. Mike Williams a call tomorrow.

After dinner, Naheema walked into her living room, grabbed her black-and-white notebook and matching pen and began writing.

*Dear Diary,*

*Here I am at the age of twenty-six, and I'm still writing in diary like I'm a schoolgirl. Today I met the sexiest man I've seen in a long time. He was gorgeous. He has the most amazing smile with very gentle features. He had on an expensive Coogi outfit, with some soft, black Bruno Magli shoes. He was charming and carried himself very well. He appears to be somewhat mysterious, but had an inviting presence about him. He is well built and stands 6'2". The shape of his biceps, triceps, and deltoids were easily seen through his sweater. Being as muscular as he is, he was neither intimidating nor unnerving to be around. His hands were big as boxing gloves, but were a soft as a baby's behind.*

*Diary, I think I fell in love at first glance. If I could have gotten away with it, I would have snuck him into the ladies' room and did him right there and then, but that's not me. Well, that's it for me.*

Naheema closed her diary and carried it into her bedroom, smiling at what she'd just written. She placed the book in her top dresser drawer, closed it, and jumped into her bed.

In less than an hour, she was fast asleep and having dreams of her and Mike, playing hide-and-seek deep in the wetness of her cave.

# Chapter 2

The next morning, right before leaving for work, Naheema grabbed Mike's business card from her jewelry box and placed it in her wallet.

During her lunch break, she dialed his number.

A female answered on the second ring, "Official Kuts, how may I help you?"

"Can I speak to Mike?" Naheema asked.

"May I ask who's calling?"

"Naheema."

"Please hold."

The longer Naheema stayed on hold, the more nervous she became. It had been a while since she'd made the first move in a relationship, so she was feeling out of place making this call. She knew men had this way of thinking that if a woman made the first move, then that meant she was desperate, but she didn't feel that way about herself at all.

Young, beautiful, intelligent, and with a bachelor's degree in business administration, Naheema started working for the City of New York a year after graduating high school at the age of seventeen. On her eighteenth birthday she was hired to work for the New York City Housing Authority.

She lived with her sister Shaquanna in an apartment in Red Hook,

Brooklyn, for two years before Housing called her off their list for an apartment. By the age of twenty, she had her own apartment. Now at the age of twenty-six, she was still single and did not have any children.

Naheema knew she was far from being rich, but she wasn't broke, although there were times when she felt like she was living paycheck to paycheck. In some small way she knew that she wanted a man in her life who would be able to help her, but she knew that having a man didn't necessarily mean happiness. However, she was tired of the status quo and she was tired off using her sexual toys. Either way she knew Mike didn't know all of that, and that he might just take her calling him so soon as an act of desperation.

Just as she was about to hang up, he answered the phone, "Good afternoon. This is Mike speaking."

"Good afternoon, Mike. This is Naheema. Do you remember me?"

"I sure do." Mike laughed. "How's the head feeling?"

"Oh, so you're a comedian?"

"I'm sorry about that. Seriously, how are you doing?"

"I'm feeling fine. I just wanted to call you and thank you again for your help yesterday."

"That was no problem. Besides, it was more for my benefit."

"What do you mean by that?"

"I don't want you to think that I'm a stalker or anything, but I was sort of following you in the store."

"Really?"

"I was trying to build up the nerve to speak to you, but then fate took over, and an opportunity presented itself." Mike laughed again.

"You're really a comedian."

"Hey, well. What can I say? No, but seriously, what took you so long to call me?"

"I just met you yesterday. Besides, you could have called me."

"You didn't bless me with your number, but believe me, if I had it, I would've called you before you got to where you were going."

"I hear that."

"Naheema, can you hold on for a minute?"

"Sure."

Mike thought he had Naheema on hold, but he didn't, and she heard the conversation in the background about a female there causing problems. She heard Mike yelling, and then she heard the phone drop.

A minute or two later, he was back on the phone. "Naheema, are you at home?"

"No, I'm at work. Is everything okay?"

"No, it's not," he said, exasperated. "Do you have a number where I can call you back?"

"Yes."

"Okay, good. Give it to me."

"Okay." She read off her cell phone number to him.

They hung up, and Naheema went back to work.

Naheema's workday was coming to an end, and she hadn't heard from Mike yet. She was hoping that all was fine on his end since he'd promised to call her once he settled everything down in his shop. She shut down her computer and punched out.

She walked from Seventh Avenue and W.142nd Street to the A train on Eighth Avenue and W.145th.

While on the train, Naheema thought about the type of woman she was. She knew she was all that and more, but she couldn't understand why she kept ending up in some messed-up relationships. Every time she thought she had something good going, the skies would open up, and it would rain on her parade.

Before bumping into Mike, Naheema had just gotten out of a messy relationship with a guy she'd met in her church. They had been dating for about three months when the drama started. A younger woman came to the church claiming that the guy was the father of her unborn child. She made a scene inside of the church, jumping in the guy's face, claiming if he didn't do right by her, she was going to call the cops on him.

Later on that evening, the guy called Naheema, asking her to let him take her out so he could explain what had happened earlier. He wanted the chance to explain everything to her before she cut him off.

Against her better judgment, she agreed to go to dinner with him, but she picked the place. She wanted someplace close, in case she needed to make a hasty retreat. So they went to Applebee's on DeKalb Avenue in Brooklyn. After they were seated, and their order was made, he started to explain.

He gave Naheema a story about the young lady being the daughter of his ex-girlfriend and that the ex-girlfriend had put her daughter up to embarrassing him because he'd caught the mother sleeping around on him with his brother.

At first Naheema started to laugh in his face, but as he went on explaining, she found herself agreeing with him about how some women can be really vindictive when they feel they are not finished with a relationship, so she gave him the benefit of the doubt.

Naheema continued to see the guy, and for the next couple of weeks, their relationship seemed to be sailing smooth.

A month later, while Naheema was at work, the young lady from the church popped up at her job. Naheema was covering the receptionist board for her coworker and happened to look up and see this young lady staring down at her. Naheema was flabbergasted. Somehow, this girl found out that Naheema worked in the management office of the building in which the young lady lived.

The girl politely asked Naheema if she could speak with her. Naheema asked the young lady to give her five minutes. Once she was relieved by the receptionist, she left the office, with the young woman following closely behind.

As soon as they stepped onto the porch of the management office, the young lady started pleading her case. Then before the young lady walked away, she asked Naheema to stop seeing the guy, and warned her that, if she didn't, she was going to make her life a living hell.

Naheema laughed at the young lady's antics and went back to work.

Two days later the girl showed up at Naheema's job and made a scene. They had words and the young lady left, so Naheema assumed it was over. By the end of the week the young lady had made two more appearances at Naheema's job, making a scene, and each time the young woman was escorted off the premises by the superintendent. Naheema's manager gave her a verbal warning and informed her that, if she didn't handle the situation, she would have to eventually write her up and possibly send her for a suspension hearing.

Naheema was pissed. Enough was enough. The following week came and left without out an appearance from the young lady. Naheema knew that the young woman was just biding her time. She knew that girl wasn't giving up that easily, so she and two of her coworkers made plans to wait in the parking lot for the young lady to show up.

As the parking lot cleared out, the young woman spotted Naheema standing by the car, so she approached her, yelling and screaming, and pointing her finger in Naheema's face.

Naheema looked around to make sure there weren't any witnesses. Then she balled up her fist and punched the young woman in her face, causing blood to gush from her nose. The young woman jumped back in surprise, but was too slow to prevent the ass-whipping coming her way. Naheema grabbed the girl by the hair, wrapped her fingers deep into her extensions, and began pounding on her face.

When Naheema's coworkers broke up the fight, the young woman was missing a handful of braids and four teeth from the top row of her mouth. Naheema jumped into the car with her coworkers and pulled off, leaving the young woman crying, holding her head and her mouth, as sirens from a police cruiser sang loudly in the background.

Naheema called the guy when she made it home, cursed him out, and broke it off with him. She hung up feeling rejuvenated, but by the evening, she was concerned about being arrested for assault when she returned to work on Monday morning. She also knew she would be going to a different church come Sunday morning.

When Naheema looked up, the train was pulling into Jay Street—her stop. She got up and exited the train. She went upstairs and out of the train station to wait for the B61. While she waited for the bus, her pager beeped, letting her know she had a voice message. She walked to the corner and used the pay phone. She dialed her pager number, entered her pass code, and listened to the message.

*"Hey, Naheema, this is Mike. Sorry I'm just getting back to you. It was crazy at the shop, but give me a call when you can. I'll be waiting."*

Naheema deleted the message and just smiled. She was definitely going to call him back once she got home and settled.

She walked back over to the bus stop with a smile on her face. As she was about to stand and wait for her bus, she remembered she had to stop at the dry cleaner's for her outfit. She made a right turn on Jay and Willoughby Streets, walking up the two blocks, passing White Castle, and Burger King, thinking about what she was going to eat for dinner.

Standing on the corner of Smith Street, she waited for the light to turn green. She crossed with the crowd, silently thinking to herself, *God, I need a car.* She continued to walk up Borough Hall, past the courthouse. She was so busy in her own little world that she almost got knocked down by a couple who came running out of the courthouse in matrimonial bliss. She looked up in time to see the bride smiling away her cares.

Naheema quickly moved around the happy couple, smiling because they were smiling. She made a left turn at Borough Hall and Remsen Street and walked a half of a block before entering the dry cleaner's. She pulled her ticket from her pocketbook and handed it to the store clerk. As the woman typed her information into the system, Naheema continued to daydream about nothing.

Two minutes later, with her clothes in hand, she headed to Court Street and Atlantic Avenue to wait for the B61 to arrive.

Twenty minutes later, the bus slowly made its way to the bus stop. She stepped onto the bus, paid her fare, and took a seat. She pulled out a book that she wanted to read. It was written by one of her favorite authors—Al Saadiq Banks. She was glad that she'd purchased the book on 125th Street last week. She opened it up and began reading.

She got off the bus on Richards Street and walked down the block to King Street. As she got closer to her building, she noticed at least six police cars and two ambulances in the parking lot. She tried to continue on to her building, but a plainclothes detective stopped her and asked for her ID. She removed her license from her pocketbook and handed it to the detective, who took a good look at it and then let her pass.

Naheema got to her building and saw some of the neighborhood dealers inside of her building. She asked them what happened, and they told her that two bodies had been badly burned and thrown from the roof.

Naheema shook her head back and forth. She thanked the young drug dealer for the information and walked to the elevator. She got on and rode to her floor. She got off the elevator and noticed two guys standing in her hallway. They looked like they were nervous, which made Naheema nervous.

Just as she was about to pull out her Mace, the apartment door adjacent to her opened, and a young man that she knew from the way stepped out. She calmed down when she realized that the two men were waiting to be served. She quickly stepped to her door and entered her apartment. As she locked the door and secured the chains around the door, she took a few deep breaths before removing her purple gloves and scarf and stuffing them inside of her hat. She removed her purple knee-length coat and stuffed the hat inside of the sleeve of her coat before hanging everything up and heading to her bedroom.

She stripped out of her clothes, grabbed her towel, and headed to the bathroom to take her shower. After drying off and applying lotion to her body, she grabbed a T-shirt and a pair of boy shorts from her dresser drawer to put on. She went to the kitchen to warm up the rest of her dinner from the night before.

After she ate and cleaned up the kitchen, she grabbed her cordless phone and went back to her bedroom to call Mike. His receptionist answered and informed Naheema that Mike had stepped out of the shop. Naheema left her phone number and hung up.

Naheema turned on her television and got comfortable in bed. A little after nine p.m., she started to doze off.

An hour later, her house phone rang.

"Hello," she answered, sleep in her voice.

"Hey, Naheema. It's Mike. Did I wake you?"

"Um, no, it's okay," she said, trying to wake up.

"Are you sure? I can call back tomorrow."

"No, it's okay. What time is it anyway?" Naheema sat up in her bed to turn on her lamp.

"It's ten o'clock. It's still early," he said, laughing.

"Maybe to you, but I have to get up early."

"Tomorrow is Saturday. You have to work?"

"No, but I have a jump rope team that I work with on the weekends."

"That's nice. So is that an all-day event?"

"No. We usually practice from nine in the morning to eleven. After that, I walk them home then I go home. Why?"

"Okay, well, I would like to take you out tomorrow evening, if you're not too tired."

"Really? That sounds nice, but I would have to check my schedule. I may be washing and drying my hair at that time." Naheema laughed.

"Oh, so now you're the comedian."

"I am a jack-of-all-trades," she said, laughing.

"Okay. I liked that one. So tell me about yourself."

"What do you want to know?" Naheema asked.

"Do you have any kids? Do you have a man that I should be worried about? Things like that."

"No to both. What about you? I assume that someone like you would have a baby mother or two hidden somewhere or a wife in hiding."

"No to both. I just recently got out of a disaster, so I am a free man."

"That bad, huh?"

"Let's just say she was pretending to be everything that she wasn't. Now how come you don't have a man?"

"Let's just say that there are a lot of wolves in sheep clothing." Naheema yawned.

"Okay, I'll accept that."

Naheema and Mike continued talking into the wee hours of the morning. He told her all about himself, his dreams, his plans, and his life. She did the same.

When they finally hung up it was after three a.m. Everything she'd learned about him made her take more interest in him. She also opened up to him about her life, her dreams, and her plans, telling him where she worked, what she did with her spare time, and where she lived.

Naheema enjoyed talking to him and couldn't wait for Saturday evening to come around. She turned off her lamp and conked out for the night.

Saturday morning came and Naheema was drained. She got up and got herself together and left her apartment to coach her jump rope team. The day started off cloudy but eventually turned into a beautiful day. Once she was done, she went home. She showered, dressed, made herself some food, and grabbed her novel to finish reading it.

An hour into relaxing, there was a loud knock at her door. She threw the book on her bed and jumped up.

"One minute," she screamed, as she walked to her door. "Who is it?"

"It's a delivery," the man said.

Naheema looked through her peephole and saw a flower delivery man. She opened the door.

"Can I help you?"

"Yes. I have a delivery for Naheema Morgan. Can you sign here please?" The man handed her the clipboard.

Naheema looked down and noticed a wonderful bouquet of roses in all different colors. "Who are they from?" she asked the deliveryman, as she signed and handed back the clipboard.

"I don't know. There's a card on them. Have a wonderful day." He handed her the flowers.

"Thank you. You do the same." She closed and locked the door behind her.

Naheema was shocked. She had no clue who would be sending her flowers. She walked into her living room and sat down on her couch. She placed the vase on the table and removed the card.

*Dearest Naheema, thank you for some much-needed conversation. I couldn't stop thinking about you last night. I can't wait to see you later. Mike W.*

Naheema smiled so hard, her jaws began to hurt. She picked up the flowers and set them on the living room windowsill. She stared at the flowers in amazement. She had to call Mike to thank him for such a beautiful array of roses. She walked into her room to grab her phone, but as soon as she picked it up, it rang.

Her girl Dina Jones was on the line. Naheema and Dina were best friends from back in the days when Naheema lived in Brownsville. After high school the girls lost contact until Naheema moved to Red Hook. When they saw each other again, it was like old times. They became even closer than they were when they were younger.

"Oh, hey, Dina."

"Damn! What did I do?" Dina asked.

"Nothing. I thought you were somebody else."

"Really? Do tell," Dina said.

"Oh, it's nothing," Naheema said, playing coy.

"Naheema, please, you were too damn happy just a minute ago. So tell me who he is, and how good is his sex game?" Dina said, laughing.

"Girl, I met this fine-ass man day before yesterday while I was shopping at Macy's. We exchanged numbers and got to talking, and now I'm sitting here looking at this gorgeous bouquet of roses that he sent to me."

"Go ahead with your bad self. Shit, I can't even get a man to buy me a drink, and you got some man buying you flowers. I need to go shopping with you."

"You're stupid. What's up?" Naheema asked.

"I was just calling to say sorry about not coming over last night. I got into something and didn't finish until late."

"You mean something got into *you.*" Naheema laughed.

"Whatever," Dina said, laughing. "But, listen, if you're free tonight, we can do something then."

"Not tonight. I have a hot date."

"I hear that. Well, call me later and tell me how it went," Dina said.

"I will. Later, girl."

After they hung up, Naheema called Mike and thanked him for the flowers. He was happy that she'd received them so quickly.

Naheema heard some commotion in the background, and Mike explained that the cops were out in front of his shop, and that he would have to call her back.

She pulled her beige two-piece Donna Karan linen suit from the closet. Thankful that it was wrinkle-free, she removed it from the plastic and hung the outfit up behind her bedroom door. Then she set her alarm for six-thirty p.m. and lay down on her bed to take a nap.

When her alarm rang, she jumped up and dashed out the room into the bathroom. She took a shower, using her Body Essence shower gel, rinsed off, and turned off the shower. She climbed out of the tub, grabbed her towel, and quickly dried off.

She stepped into her bedroom and began to take inventory of her "smell-goods." She grabbed a bottle of White Diamonds perfume, removed the cap, and sprayed the perfume in her most sensual places. Then she pulled out a brown, lace bra and thong set that she'd purchased from Victoria's Secret.

After putting on her undergarments, she grabbed her FDS powder spray and sprayed between her legs and on the crotch of her thong. Quickly glancing at the clock, she noticed she had to hurry up and get dressed.

At seven-thirty p.m., Mike called Naheema's phone to let her know he was downstairs in her parking lot. She told him that she'd be down.

She grabbed her pocketbook and jacket before taking a quick glance at herself in the mirror. "Damn, girl!" she said to herself. "You look good."

She locked her door, went through the exit, and took the stairs down to the first floor to exit her building. As she got closer to the parking lot, she noticed Mike standing beside a dark blue Cadillac DeVille.

Mike looked up, and thought his eyes were playing tricks on him. *Damn, she's looking fly as hell right now,* he thought to himself. The outfit she had on made him do a double take. The way she sashayed toward him let him know that she had class, and the way she was wearing her soft beige linen fitted slacks and sheer white blouse with that beige linen vest, showed him that she had style. Her outfit was sexy, but casual, and her soft, brown skin was gorgeous. He assumed she didn't have any makeup on. Until she was up close and personal. That's when he realized her makeup was flawless.

The Lipglass made her lips look soft, full, and erotic. *Damn, I wonder what surprises she has hidden under that outfit.* Mike knew he had to make her his lady. The mere sight of her sashaying toward his car was so powerful that it caused all of the blood from his head to flow straight to his penis, giving him the erection of a lifetime.

Quickly, he began to inhale and exhale, forcing the blood to drain from his penis before she reached his car. *Shit, she going to make me want to rape that ass.*

With each step, Naheema's heart pounded in her chest as she walked closer to the car. She knew she had picked the right outfit, from the fire and lust in Mike's eyes. She could actually feel the heat from his eyes pulsate through her body as it traveled to its destination—her vagina. He continued to stare at her with such intensity that it caused her to accidentally have a small orgasm. She thought, *Thank goodness, I put on a panty liner.*

Mike walked over to her, took her hand in his, and kissed it.

Feeling like a schoolgirl, Naheema blushed.

He smiled and opened the car door to let her in. Then he walked to the driver's side and got in.

"I hope I didn't take too long."

"Not at all," he answered, staring in her eyes.

Mike couldn't help staring at Naheema. She was gorgeous. He thought about pulling her face into his and kissing her lips, but when the cabbie behind them started blowing his horn insistently, he put the keys in the ignition, started the car, and pulled off.

As they pulled out of the parking lot, he turned to her. "You are gorgeous."

"Thank you. Oh, and thank you again for those beautiful roses."

Mike licked his lips. "You're very welcome."

Naheema smiled. She was impressed with him this far. As they were crossing the Brooklyn Bridge onto the FDR Drive, the car became quiet. Too quiet for her, which made her more aware of how nervous she really was. So, she began asking questions.

"So, Mike, tell me something about yourself that I don't know."

"Like what?"

"I don't know."

"I use to be a stripper back in the day," he replied, smiling.

"Are you serious?"

"I'm serious," he said, smiling coyly. "I used to strip for the men."

"Really?"

"You better not tell nobody," he said, as he exited on 72nd Street.

"I won't," she said, trying not to laugh.

"Cool," he said, before bursting into laughter.

"Why are you laughing?" she asked, confused.

"Man, you really believe I would be a stripping at a gay club?"

"Hey, to each his own. I wasn't going to judge you, yet," she said, smiling.

"Oh, really? Well that's good to know." He smiled, and said, "Naheema, you have a beautiful smile."

"Thank you for the compliment, Mike."

"You're very welcome."

"So where do you live?" she asked, changing the subject.

"I just moved to Harlem on West 145th Street and Fifth Avenue."

"Really? Where did you live before that?"

"I was born and raised in Red Hook. What about you?"

"I was born and raised in Brownsville, but I moved around so I lived all over Brooklyn before moving to Red Hook. So what made you move?"

"My apartment was robbed. Apparently, the two guys that robbed me ended up dead, so the cops were on me for almost a year. After that I couldn't take it, so my receptionist told me about some condos they were building in Harlem. I went to look at them, fell in love with one, and the rest is history."

"I'm sorry to hear that," Naheema said. "I hope they eventually found who killed the guys."

"I don't know, and I don't want to know. I just know I had nothing to do with it." Just then, Mike pulled up to a parking garage. "Well, we're here."

"Oh wow! That was fast," Naheema said, surveying her surroundings.

Mike parked, turned off the ignition, pulled his keys out of the car, and got out. He walked to the passenger's side, opened the door, and helped Naheema out of the car. Being the man he was, he held Naheema's purse in his arm, gently grabbed her hand, and escorted her into the Shark Bar.

Since they had reservations, they were seated immediately.

Naheema really enjoyed herself. Dinner was beautiful, and the conversation flowed, never dying down.

Once dinner was over, Mike surprised Naheema with tickets to see a new play named, *I Can Do Bad, All by Myself.* She was thrilled because she'd wanted to get tickets to that play since it'd come out.

They strolled hand-in-hand to the Beacon Theatre. The play was drama all the way around. Naheema laughed and cried during the play. All in all, she had a wonderful night.

It was late when they got out of the play, so Mike took Naheema home. They rode in silence back to Brooklyn. Naheema was enjoying the scenic view outside her window and the brown sugar sitting beside her.

Mike felt Naheema staring at him, so he turned to her and smiled. "Did you enjoy yourself?"

"Yes, I had a lovely time."

Mike smiled. "I'm glad. I enjoyed myself as well."

Naheema's heart fluttered as butterflies danced inside of her stomach. She couldn't hide her satisfaction. She smiled and turned to look out the window again.

Mike reached over and changed the station to 98.7 Kiss FM, which was playing "A House Is Not a Home" by Luther Vandross.

"Ooh, that's my song," Naheema said.

Mike looked at her, smiled, and turned the volume up.

After they pulled into the parking lot of Naheema's development, Mike turned off the ignition and faced her. He grabbed her hand and pulled her closer to him.

Naheema closed her eyes and puckered up, hoping to feel his lips on hers. She felt really stupid when she felt him kiss her forehead. She opened her eyes to see Mike smiling at her.

"Would you like walk you into the building and ride with you upstairs?"

"That's okay," she said, feeling embarrassed. "I can manage. But I do appreciate the offer."

"No problem. Call my cell when you get upstairs, so I know that you made it safely into your apartment." Mike put his car in park and got out to open her door and help her out.

"I will," she said, reaching for his hand.

Mike handed her purse to her, so she took that as her cue to leave. He watched Naheema until she entered her building then he pulled off.

Naheema got on her elevator, overjoyed with her date. Mike was the perfect gentleman. He was courteous, well-mannered, respectful, and easy to talk to. The night was perfect.

As she entered her apartment, she felt like she was high. She took off her coat and threw it over her couch. She noticed the answering machine light was blinking, so she walked over to the machine and listened to her messages.

*"You have two new messages,"* the answering machine said.

She pressed play and sat down on the couch to take her shoes off.

"Hey, girl. What's up? Where you at? Call me back when you get this. This is your sister. Love you. Bye."

*"Hey, girl. What's poppin'? It's me, Dina. If you're not busy next weekend, come to my place so we can do a girls' night. I'll cook dinner and get us some drinks. Call me back."*

Naheema erased her messages, grabbed her phone, and sat down on the couch. She dialed Mike's number. He picked up after the third ring. She informed him that she'd made it upstairs safely. They talked for a minute, and then she hung up. She got up from the couch and looked at the time on the clock: one in the morning. She decided to she'd call Dina and Shaquanna back tomorrow.

After spending the night with such a sexy man, she needed to indulge herself before going to bed. She prepared a bath and then grabbed her black bag of tricks. She took out the waterproof dildo that she'd named "the Beast," placed it on the side of the tub, and stepped in.

As she sat back into the hot water, she said to the dildo, "Tonight your name will be Mike."

As she got comfortable and began to pour water over herself, Mike's face popped into her head. She closed her eyes, pretending he was there with her. She rubbed her hands over her breasts, softly pulling at her nipples, sliding her right hand down the length of her body until she touched her soft spot.

She used her left hand to squeeze and pull on her nipple, and her right hand explored her clitoris, while she pretended Mike's hands were touching her. A soft moan escaped her lips as she continued to rub her middle finger against her clit. Heat surged through her body, causing her to arch her back and slip her finger into her cave.

"Yes," she whispered as she fingered herself.

Wanting more, she reached over, grabbed the dildo, and turned it on. The dildo began to vibrate as the tip did a swivel dance. She softly inserted the vibrator into her damp cave and allowed it to explore deep into her walls.

"Yes, Mike, right there," she whispered, licking her lips and continuing to pull on her nipple.

Naheema pleased herself for the next half-hour, experiencing multiple orgasms while pretending Mike was touching her.

Completely exhausted, she drained the water from the tub, turned on the shower, and washed up. After drying off, she got into bed wearing only her birthday suit and fell asleep dreaming about Mike.

# Chapter 3

The next morning, Naheema was up by eight a.m. She woke up feeling like she'd had a booster shot. She showered, dried off, and threw on some old sweatpants and a wife-beater. Then she walked into her living room and turned on her stereo to gospel music. She walked to her kitchen and made some breakfast. After eating, she decided to do some cleaning.

Later that evening, as she was preparing her clothes for the workweek, there was another delivery. Mike had sent her another bouquet of flowers, balloons, and chocolates, thanking her for such a lovely time. She called him at his home, and they talked well into the wee hours of the morning.

After their first date, Naheema and Mike were barely able to see each other due to his schedule. He seemed to work the oddest hours, and he constantly had to go out of town on business, which left them only able to speak on the phone. Mike made it his business to call Naheema every night before she went to sleep. Their relationship blossomed over late-night phone calls.

One week turned into three weeks, and before Naheema realized it, she was falling for Mike. She began to seriously miss his presence more and more. While Naheema was at work one day, Mike phoned her. It was an half an hour before the end of her day.

"Good evening, Drew Hamilton Houses, manager's office, Ms. Morgan speaking, how may I help you?" she asked, pissed that a tenant was calling at this time.

"Yes, can I speak with the manager? I've been waiting all day for someone to fix this sink and nobody's showed up yet," Mike teased in a deep voice.

"The manager is gone for the day, but if you leave your information with me, I can have her call you back," she said, trying to rush the person off the phone.

"No, I will not. As a matter of fact, I'm on my way to the management office right now."

She began to smile as she realized who it was. "Well, we are closed, so you might as well leave your information and I can make sure that she returns your call, or you can call emergency services after five p.m. and they can send maintenance out to help you."

"I don't believe you. I'm out front," Mike said in his own voice.

"Mike, stop playing with me." She laughed.

"I almost had you, didn't I?" he asked.

"For a little while."

"I miss you," he said.

"Really?"

"Yes, really."

"So when are you coming back into town?"

"In an hour or two," he replied.

"Cool. I can't wait to see you," she said, smiling from ear to ear.

"Me either. Listen, I'll call you when I reach Red Hook."

"Ok. Talk to you later."

"You too, sexy."

Just hearing the sound of Mike's voice had her wet in her thongs. She turned everything off, walked to the back of the office, and swiped her ID card. It registered that she was out. She closed the door and screamed downstairs to let the superintendant know that she was leaving, and then she exited the side of the building. As she fumbled in her pocketbook, she bumped into someone standing at the end of the gate. As she lifted her head to look up and apologize, she was shocked to be staring in the deep, hazel brown eyes of Mike. He was holding roses and a teddy bear in his arms.

"Surprise," he said, in his bedroom voice.

"Oh my god, you are so wrong for this," she said, smiling.

"What, you don't like it? I can leave and come back later on," he said, standing to the side.

"You better not," she said, reaching for the flowers and teddy bear.

Mike handed them to her and began slowly walking to his car. She followed. He opened her door, and she placed her stuff in the back seat. She pushed the seat back and turned around to feel Mike's soft, luscious, lips pressed against hers. After a second and getting over the initial shock, she began to kiss him back. When they pulled away from each other, Naheema's legs felt like lead. She stumbled a bit before he held her and helped her into the car. He slammed the door shut and stepped off the curb into the street thinking, *It's a wrap. She's mine now.*

Then he climbed into the car.

They went to dinner and to see a movie. After that he drove her home and rode upstairs with her. Mike was the perfect gentleman, although the beast within was burning to come out. He knew he had to calm himself. He didn't want to rush her before the time was right. They kissed one last time before he left. Naheema closed her apartment door and stood behind it for about five minutes. She was falling for Mike and she was falling hard.

The weekend went by quickly. Mike and Naheema went out to dinner and went to a poetry reading on Saturday. Sunday came and she cooked dinner for the two of them. She was ready to take him into her bedroom but he declined. She was hurt that he didn't accept. He saw the pain in her face, but explained to her that he wanted to make sure that their first night together would be something that she would never forget.

She was awestruck by his sensitivity and respect for her. That night was an uneventful one for Naheema because while she lay thirsting for Mike's touch, Mike was on the other side of town, getting relieved.

The week came to another end, Naheema and Mike made plans to spend the weekend together. But by the time that Friday evening came, Mike had to cancel due to an emergency of some kind. Naheema was a little skeptical about all of these out-of-town emergencies, but she pushed the feelings to the side because she knew that every time they went out on a date, Mike made her feel like a queen, and she never had to worry about paying for anything. His attention to detail was a godsend. He constantly complimented her while on their dates, and after every date, she received flowers. He was everything she wanted in a man—considerate, funny, intelligent, handsome, debonair, gentlemanly, and very attentive.

After five months of going out to eat, to the theaters, and dancing, he decided to surprise her and make dinner for her at his condo.

A little after six p.m., she heard a knock at the door. She went to the door, looked through the peephole, and noticed a tall, light-skinned brother with dreads standing at her door.

"Can I help you?" she asked, looking through her peephole.

The guy said, "Yes, I'm looking for Naheema Morgan."

"Who are you?" she asked, afraid to open up the door.

"My name is Randy. I'm a friend of Mike's. He asked me to deliver something to you." The guy lifted his arms up and showed her a bag of some sort.

With the chain still on the door, she cracked it open and noticed that Randy was holding two bags from Macy's. She removed the chain from the door and opened it. Randy handed her the bags and a small jewelry box, and she thanked him and took the bags. She locked her door and headed into the living room, where she turned the volume down on the television, sat down on the couch, and began opening the bags.

Naheema was in shock as she pulled out a pair of open-toe, black-and-silver Chanel heels. Then she pulled out a sexy black spaghetti strap dress by Donna Karan. She laid the dress against the couch and stared at the outfit in awe. She reached back into the bag and pulled out a silver-and-black shawl that matched the shoes perfectly. From the look of the dress, she knew it would fit her to a T.

She pushed the empty bag to the side and grabbed the second bag, which was from Victoria's Secret. Slowly, she pulled out an off-white lace lingerie set with matching garter belts. She knew this set was expensive because she'd picked it up first the day of the sale, until she saw the two-hundred-dollar price tag.

Naheema didn't know what to think or do. Mike had truly outdone himself. But she was still a little confused as to why he would buy her all this stuff. She continued to look through the bag, noticing that the rest of the stuff inside of the bag was for an overnight stay. She pushed that to the side and grabbed the jewelry box. Her hands began to shake, and her heart rate began to race.

She slipped the ribbon off the jewelry box, cracked it open, and started screaming. The box fell to the floor as she jumped up and down screaming like a lunatic. Inside were 14-kt. white gold diamond earrings. Naheema calmed down before picking the box off the floor. Inside was a card with a note.

*I hope that everything is to your liking. I hope you don't think this is too forward, but I am really feeling you, Ms. Morgan, and I hope that the feelings are mutual. If you should accept my gifts, then be dressed and ready to leave your apartment by eight-thirty p.m. There will be a gray Mercedes LS waiting outside for you to escort you to your destination for the weekend. However, if you feel that the gifts are too much, and you should find yourself returning them, I will understand. But the car will still be out front waiting for you to come for dinner.*

*Sincerely,*

*Mike W*

Naheema couldn't believe her luck. Meeting a man like him was more than she could have expected. She liked pretty much everything and wanted more. She knew that she was ready for a commitment, and she hoped that these gifts were a sign from Mike that he wanted the same. Mike had been nothing but a gentleman. She wanted to finally be able to feel him inside her wetness. Although Mike was everything a woman wanted in a man, Naheema was skeptical and didn't know if this was all an act. She still at times felt like he was hiding something. She looked at everything once again, and pushed that thought from her mind. Tonight was the night.

She grabbed everything off the couch, ran into her bedroom, and laid everything across her bed. She looked at the time. If she was going to accept the date, then she only had an hour and a half to be ready.

She walked to her bathroom and turned on the shower. She walked back into her room, looked at her hair in the mirror, and was glad to see that her hair was still holding up. She grabbed her scarf to cover her head. Before jumping in the shower, she called her sister and told her about the gifts and the note, and that she had to cancel their plans.

"What do you mean, you have to cancel?" Shaquanna asked.

"Look, girl, tonight is the night that I let Mike make me a woman." She laughed.

"What? You mean you haven't let homeboy rip your back out? You got to be kidding me?" Shaquanna asked.

"Girl, I been trying, but he was refusing," Naheema said.

"You sure he's not an undercover brother?" her sister asked, laughing.

"Hell no. Mike is all man," Naheema said, defiantly.

"Really? Do tell. I thought you didn't give up the pussy."

"Damn, Quanna, don't be so nasty with it."

"Naheema, please. This is me."

"Well, I'll find out tonight," Naheema answered matter-of-factly.

"I hope so since you cancelling our plans. I hope for your sake, he's not a two-minute lover, using you to hide his undercover." Shaquanna laughed.

"Shut up. You are stupid," Naheema said, laughing at her sister, and they talked for a couple of minutes more before they hung up.

Naheema walked to the bathroom, jumped in the shower, and turned on the radio. "I Wanna Sex You Up" by Color Me Badd was playing. She sang along as she lathered her body with her strawberries and cream shower gel.

She felt a tingling sensation run through her body as she rubbed the sponge against her neck and pretended her fingers were Mike's. Moving the sponge gently down her neck, she squeezed softly, caressing her shoulders, massaging herself with soft, even strokes. She then closed her eyes, threw her head back, and felt the soap suds slide between her breasts. As her hands began to wander, the sponge dropped out of her hand and into the tub. She caressed her nipples gently, stroking and pulling on them.

While her left hand was stroking her nipples, she slipped her right hand down to her clit and separated her lips. She used her middle finger to softly stroke her clit, causing heat to cover her loins, and continued to play with herself until she released.

She washed herself a second time, shaved under her arms and between her legs, turned the shower off, got out, dried off, lotioned up, and exited the bathroom.

She entered her bedroom and looked at the time again. Forty minutes left. She put on the lingerie Mike bought her and took her time getting dressed.

With ten minutes left, she put on a light touch of mascara, blush, and her Lipglass. She sprayed herself with some White Diamonds perfume. She checked her purse to make sure she had everything then looked in the mirror to check her appearance. She was more than pleased with the sight before her, so she left her bedroom, walked through the living room, and exited her apartment.

Naheema walked out of her building and saw the car waiting for her. She was surprised to see Randy, the delivery guy, holding the car door open for her. Randy smiled as he helped her into the car.

As they were pulling off, Naheema made a comment to him about being a jack-of-all-trades, and he just laughed.

The ride into Manhattan was a smooth one, which was very surprising because the BQE and the FDR Drive are usually backed up with cars going into the city on a Friday evening.

Naheema and Randy had a nice conversation during the ride. She found out that he'd met Mike some years ago during a time when he was going through some hardships. Randy told her about his little sister being murdered and how Mike had helped him find out who did it. After that Randy and Mike had been as tight as brothers.

Naheema told Randy a little bit about herself and how she'd met Mike. When there was nothing more to talk about, she stared out the window.

Randy pulled into the right lane and exited on W. 145th Street. He drove up one block, made a right turn onto Fifth Avenue, and pulled up to a gate. A guard came out, and Randy showed him some type of ID. The guard walked back to the gate, made a call, and then buzzed them in.

Naheema was in awe of the condo complex where Mike lived. They drove in and drove around a beautiful stoned water fountain before pulling into a parking garage.

Randy parked the car, got out, and opened the door for Naheema. He held her hand as she climbed out of the car. She looked around expecting to see Mike, but she didn't. Randy handed her a key card and directed her to the elevator. She slipped the card in the slot and waited two seconds before the elevator door opened. She stepped inside, waiting for Randy.

He stepped in, used a key to turn the elevator to unlock the floor, and then stepped back out. She looked at him confused, but all he said to her was, "Enjoy your night."

Naheema rode the elevator up to the third floor, which apparently was the top floor.

Mike's condo looked like something out of *Cribs* on MTV. A cream-colored plush carpet covered the foyer floors that gave way to tan-colored marble floors leading straight to a set of glass, crowned

French doors. On the wall to her left hung a large portrait of Mike sitting on his throne in a cream-and-brown, double-breasted, pin-striped suit, a brown fedora, and holding a cane. Under the picture sat a white baby grand piano.

As she stepped farther into the dining room, she saw a red brick fireplace and an 82-inch flat-screen Samsung television built into the wall above it. Naheema was speechless. His place was immaculate.

There was a brown leather sofa set strategically placed around the room, and portraits of African families, statues, and plants everywhere. When she looked up, she was surprised to see a hand-carved wooden statue suspended from the ceilings with pieces of crystal chandeliers dangling as well. To her left was a winding staircase of black metal, so she removed her heels and climbed the steps.

On the second floor, jazz music was playing in the background as she walked toward the living room. Again she was floored by the beautiful colors, paintings, and designs around the room. She figured Mike must have paid someone to come and decorate his place for him. She left the living room as the aroma of Italian food floated through the air, causing her stomach to rumble. The food smelled wonderful, and she was hungry, but she wanted to finish looking around.

She entered a day room and walked across to the double glass doors, and stepped out onto the patio, which overlooked the highway.

As she enjoyed the view, Mike tried to sneak up behind her, but his cologne gave him away. She knew he was in the room with her, but she pretended she didn't.

He walked up behind her and gave her a tight hug. Then he turned her around to face him and gave her a kiss on the lips.

"I'm glad that you came and that you accepted the gifts."

"Well, I almost sent everything back, but a little birdie changed my mind."

"Well, tell the little birdie I said, 'Thank you.'" Mike smiled. "Let me get a look at you."

Naheema stepped back and did a slow, sexy turn for him to take her all in. "Do you like?"

"Damn, girl! You are wearing the hell out of that dress."

"I am, aren't I?"

"I'm glad it was the right size."

"Yes, it was. As a matter of fact, how did you know what size I wore?"

"From the lingerie," he said, as he held her hand and led her into his den.

"Really?" she asked, following him.

"Yes, but let's talk about that later. How was your ride?"

"It was wonderful. I don't know how to thank you for this."

"You don't have to. Naheema, I want us to be exclusive. You are a gorgeous woman, and I want you all to myself," he said, helping her to the couch.

"Thank you."

"So I can take that as a yes?"

"Yes, Mike."

"Great!"

"What smells so good?"

"Oh, that's my special. It's almost done, so why don't you get comfortable in the living room? I'll be right back."

"Okay."

Mike got up and left the living room with Naheema following behind him. She entered the living room, placed her shoes on the mat, and placed her shawl on the coat rack. Then she sat down on his plush suede sofa.

Mike came back holding a tray with a bottle of Peter Michael

Le Moulin Rouge red wine and two wineglasses. He set the tray on the table, grabbed the chilled bottle, and poured them some wine. He picked up the glasses, handed one to Naheema, and made a toast. "To us, sharing a happy and healthy future," he said.

"To us." She tapped her glass against his and took a sip.

Mike looked her in the eyes and knew he had to kiss her. She was sexy as hell, sitting there looking flawless.

The way he was staring at her made Naheema a little nervous, so she finished her glass of wine first.

Mike took another sip from his glass before placing it on top of a coaster. He removed her glass from her hand, leaned over, and passionately kissed her.

Naheema was a little surprised, but recovered quickly and began to return the kiss to him with as much passion.

Mike began to rub her leg as he laid her back onto the couch.

"I want you, Nah," he whispered in her ear before kissing her long and hard. Slowly, he began to pull away from her embrace.

Naheema's eyes were still closed, and her mouth puckered. Even though he had moved away, she still felt his lips lingering on hers, until she opened her eyes and saw that he was staring at her. She was embarrassed, but the look he gave her let her know that there was no reason to be embarrassed, because he didn't want to stop.

She sat up as he poured her another glass of wine. The wine was taking an effect on her, and she began to get really comfortable.

They sat there in lust, talking about nothing and everything, trying to settle their hormones. Mike massaged her feet, ankles, and calves as they talked.

Ten minutes later, he got up, washed his hands, and prepared their plates. He made stringozzi pasta with baby artichokes and Italian sausages. He refilled both of their wineglasses and said grace before they dug into their dinner. And Naheema ate everything on her plate.

Mike began to clear the dishes and prepare for their dessert. He brought out a deliciously soft and tasty chocolate chestnut cake that he made.

Mike cleaned up the kitchen and escorted Naheema back into the living room. He changed the CD, and Angie Stone's soulful voice played in the background. He held out his hand to help her up from the couch so they could slow-dance to the music.

To say she was enjoying herself was an understatement. She felt like she was on cloud nine. They shared another passionate kiss before he led her back to the sofa, where she placed her legs on his so he could massage her feet and calves again.

Little by little his hands moved higher up her thighs. His hands were so soft, yet masculine. It felt good to her as she closed her eyes and laid her head back against the sofa, as Mike continued to tease her with his touches. She opened her eyes when she felt his hand caress her face. They kissed long and hard.

When they finally pulled apart, the look in his eyes let her know he was ready. He got up, took her hand in his, and escorted her to his bedroom.

As she entered his bedroom, her mouth fell open. His room was designed to look like a tropical island, and there were mirrors placed on the ceiling directly over his bed. For a minute, Naheema felt like she was in paradise. There was a huge aquarium built into his wall with all different kinds of sharks. He had flat-screen television hooked up to each corner of his bed, and a sheer black net hung from the ceiling over the bed, which took up most of the room and had a silky red robe lying across it. And he had red, white, and pink rose petals thrown about on the floor, from the bedroom entrance leading to the bed, and there was a trail of white roses leading to the bathroom.

Mike led her to the bed. He turned to her. "I hope you don't mind." He motioned his head toward the robe. "I'm hoping you would stay the weekend with me."

"That's . . . that's . . . Wow!"

"Make yourself comfortable. My home is your home," Mike said, and disappeared into the bathroom.

Naheema entered the bedroom and admired the view. She stepped to his closet and opened it. The size and depth of his closet could have fit her entire apartment inside, furniture and all. On the left side of his closet were a bunch of suits, some with the price tags on them. She looked at three of them and almost choked at the price. One suit cost over two thousand dollars, and two others cost over three thousand apiece. In the center of the closet he kept all of his jeans, sweat suits, slacks, and shirts, and to the left were racks and racks of sneakers, shoes, and boots.

Naheema knew at that moment that Mike was doing more than what he told her he did. She knew in her heart that he was a dealer. There was no way he could have all of this by just owning one unisex shop in the hood.

While she was still looking around his closet, Mike walked up behind her, holding their refilled glasses of wine. "Like it?"

"Oh! You scared the hell out of me," Naheema said, jumping and almost spilling the glass in his hand.

"I'm sorry. I didn't mean to," he said, handing her the glass.

"It's all right." She took the glass and sipped.

"I took the liberty of running a bubble bath for you."

"Thank you."

"Come on. Let me get you in the water while it's still hot." Mike grabbed her hand and led her out of the closet.

"Your shop must be doing extremely well, if you don't mind me saying."

"It is, but I also do other things on the side."

"Oh, okay."

Naheema stepped into the bathroom and was blown away by the Jacuzzi. The bathroom smelled of fresh vanilla, and the mahogany base of the off-white marble tub had the letters *M.W.* in script on it. White rose petals were thrown all around the Jacuzzi and in the water. She stepped closer and saw a set of jet massagers inside the Jacuzzi.

Just as Mike tapped her on the shoulder to hand her the robe, his house phone rang. "Give me a minute," he said, and left the bathroom.

Naheema quickly undressed and stepped inside. The water felt so good against her skin. She sat down and allowed the massagers to take her away. She finished her glass and lay back and closed her eyes.

Immediately her eyes popped open when she heard Mike yelling and threatening someone on the phone in the background. She sat straight up to try and hear what was being said, but the yelling and screaming stopped just as quickly as it started. She brushed it off, closed her eyes again, and went back to relaxing.

She was so busy enjoying the massage that she didn't hear Mike come into the bathroom.

"Hey, you all right in there?" He held out yet another full glass of red wine.

"Ooh! You scared me. I didn't hear you come in." She took the glass from him.

"Sorry about that. I didn't mean to scare you," he said, as he sat on the edge of the Jacuzzi.

"That's okay. Is everything okay with you?" Naheema felt like she'd had a couple too many glasses of wine. She was feeling nice.

"Of course." Mike took the sponge to dip it into the water. "Why wouldn't it be?"

"Oh. No. I just assumed that something was wrong when you got the phone call."

"Oh, that. It's one of the barbers," Mike said nonchalantly. "He has a lot of drama. He's been late with paying for his chair."

"Oh."

Mike poured some gel onto the sponge and began to wash Naheema's shoulders.

"Umm!" she moaned. "That feels good."

Mike slid his hands into the water and squeezed the water out of the sponge onto her neck and shoulders.

He began squeezing her breasts and slowly and softly caressing her body until he was on his knees and working his hands between her legs. Using his index finger, he massaged her clit in a circular motion, sticking his middle finger in and out of her.

With her back arched, Naheema closed her eyes and was ready to explode, but Mike stopped right before she could release. She opened her eyes to look at him.

He just smiled. "Not yet," he said, grabbing the sponge to finish washing her off.

Naheema wanted to scream at him for playing with her, but she stayed calm.

Mike got up grabbed the towel from the rack then reached his hand out to Naheema to stand up. She grabbed his hand and got out of the Jacuzzi.

He tenderly dried her off and draped the silk kimono over her. Then he led her back into the bedroom and laid her across his bed.

"Roll onto your stomach."

She did as he asked.

"Close your eyes and just enjoy," he said, pouring hot oil onto her skin.

The warm liquid spilling down her back caused her to shudder.

Mike began rubbing the oil into her skin, starting at the base of her neck, gently rubbing and squeezing the tension out of it. He moved on to her shoulders, applying a little more pressure, down her back, and to her buttocks.

Naheema was squirming from his touch. She received the shock of her life when she felt his tongue licking her from the crack of her behind to her hole. Mike had lifted her up from behind and began to perform the freakiest tongue dance with her clit; the first time in a long time she'd had this happen to her. And she released immediately.

She thought he was finished, but then she smelled a coconut scent, then felt something wet and hot touch her anus. Before she knew what was happening, Mike had entered the back door, and surprisingly, it didn't hurt. Whatever he put on her numbed the area and allowed her to enjoy it.

She began gyrating her hips to match his rhythm, turning him on. Mike was surprised. He didn't expect her to work her body the way she did.

He worked her until he was about to release. Then he pulled out, removed the condom, put on another one, and then flipped her over. He lay flat on his stomach and began to eat Naheema again.

Naheema was trying to get away from him, so she started pulling herself up to the edge of the bed.

Mike noticed what she was trying to do, so he stopped eating and caught her by her hips just as she was hanging off the bed by her hands. He quickly entered her and began to perform a "Jamaican wine" deep in her walls.

"Oh God! Yes! Mike! Oh God! Right there!"

Mike continued his sexual dance inside of her. Naheema continued to moan. Mike noticed her eyes were starting to roll back into her head, so that was his cue to go harder.

With each thrust, Naheema screamed, "Oh God! Oh God! Oh God!"

Simultaneously, they both screamed, "I'm coming!"

Naheema came so hard her ears were popping like she was on an airplane.

Mike didn't want to release so soon, but Naheema's vagina was so tight and wet that he couldn't help himself. He peeked at the clock over his fish tank and realized that they had been sexing for an hour and a half. He held on to the condom before sliding out of her and helped her back onto the bed. Then he got up and walked to the bathroom.

Naheema was in pure ecstasy. Mike did his thing, and she was feeling the effects. As she lay there trying to recuperate, she heard the shower turn on.

She must have dozed off, because she didn't remember when Mike came out of the shower. All she felt was a soft, warm cloth touching between her legs. She opened her eyes and saw Mike heading back into the bathroom, and that was it.

Mike entered the bathroom, drying off. He dropped the towel, walked over to his dresser, removed a pair of black silk boxers, and slipped them on. He closed the drawer and opened another. He removed a pair of dark green silk pajama pants, slipped them on, and closed the drawer shut. He picked up the towel, threw it over his shoulder, and walked to the bed to check up on Naheema. Realizing that she was asleep, he pulled the quilt over her, blew out the candles, and took the damp towel back into the bathroom to dump it in the hamper.

As he walked back into the room, he realized that he could get used to having Naheema in his bed. So far, she was everything that he would want in a woman. Single, young, gorgeous, no children, a good job, and a place to call her own. He was really getting tired of dealing with these chickenheads. It seemed like every chick he met was either on public assistance or had a couple of kids with baby daddy issues. But they all had the same idea in mind: sleep with a baller and get out of the projects.

Naheema was different to him. She had an air of confidence about her. She wasn't high maintenance, but she knew what she wanted and that's what he liked about her. She seemed like she was almost reserved, but he knew women like that, and if history had a way of repeating itself, he knew that he was going to have to break that out of her.

Sitting there thinking about her as she slept, he finished his first glass of wine and poured another. She stirred when he set his glass down on the nightstand.

"Hey, aren't you coming to bed?" she whispered.

"Yeah, in a minute."

"Is everything okay?"

"Yeah, I'm good. I'm just over here enjoying the view of my sleeping beauty," he said, smiling at her. "Go on back to sleep. I'll be there in a few. I have to make some phone calls before I lay down for the night."

"Okay," she said, yawning. Naheema could barely keep her eyes open.

Mike got up from the sofa, walked over to the bed, and kissed her on her forehead. She rolled onto her side and dozed off again. He sat back down, thinking to himself, *I could really get used to this shit here.*

He continued to sip on his drink as he thought long and hard about if he was ready to give up the game. But he'd had this thought many of nights and came to the same conclusion. *Shit, I'm not ready to give up fast money just that quick,* he thought.

He knew he wasn't ready to give up his other life just yet, but he knew when the time came, he wanted her standing beside him.

*Damn, I hope she'll last that long,* he thought to himself as he finished the second glass. Then it hit him that he'd turned his cell phone off after the call he took while she was in the tub. He placed his glass on the nightstand, got up, walked over to his closet, grabbed his matching robe, slipped on his slippers, and left the bedroom, closing the door behind him. He entered his living room and grabbed his cell phone off the table. He turned it on and waited for the phone to power up. Instantly his phone started beeping. He opened and saw that he had eight messages. He knew that there was trouble because six of the messages were from one of his runners in Red Hook.

Mike got a bottle of orange juice from the refrigerator, walked to his dining room, and sat down on a chair. He took a few deep breaths then checked his messages.

"Yo, Mike, pick up. It's urgent."

Mike deleted the message.

"Yo, Mike. We have a serious situation. Call me back."

He deleted the message again. From past experience, the young man knew not to leave the reason for the calls on Mike's voicemail, so the next four messages were basically the same.

The last three messages were from Randy telling him to call him back, like yesterday. Mike deleted those messages and hung up his phone. He picked up his Nextel and began returning calls. The first number he called was picked up by voicemail. He didn't leave a message.

When he called the next number, a female answered, "Hello?"

"Yo, put Man-Man on the phone."

"Who the hell is this?"

"Mike."

She stuttered, "Oh. I'm sorry. Hold on."

Man-Man picked up the phone and told Mike about another shoot-out on the avenue, due to the chick from the shop a week ago.

He informed Mike that she got picked up and started telling five-O where the spots were on the avenue.

"What the fuck you mean? She snitching?" Mike screamed, forgetting about Naheema in the bedroom.

"Five-O ran up inside of Tamika's house and took everybody and everything inside," Man-Man explained.

"Where the fuck is Randy?" Mike screamed.

"I don't know. I chirped his cell, but it's busy."

"Fuck! What they got?"

Man-Man sighed. "Everything. The new shipment, the guns, and the money."

"Yo, get everybody together and meet me at the spot."

"Now?"

"What the fuck did you just ask me?"

"Nothing. We'll be there," Man-Man said, realizing his mistake.

"Everybody, or you're gonna be held responsible for people not showing up." Mike disconnected the call.

Mike got up and began pacing his floor. This was the second time in a month that his spots were raided and Randy was nowhere to be found. There was going to be hell to pay for a screw-up of this caliber. So far, he just lost over twenty pounds of weed, twenty kilos of crack, and more than forty thousand in cash. Every one of them were in for the surprise of a lifetime. Nobody was gonna make any money until his money was replaced.

He picked up the Nextel again and sent an urgent alert to Randy with the code 031. He looked at the time. It was now two thirty a.m. He sent another text to Randy with the code for the time to meet up, 0430, and the address and apartment, 422-05.

Two minutes later, Mike received a text from Randy letting him know he'd be there. Mike walked to the bedroom, opened the closet, and grabbed his clothes. He got dressed, grabbed the extra set of keys off the dresser, and left his condo.

Naheema was fast asleep and didn't have a clue that she was now in Mike's condo all alone.

# Chapter 4

Since it was late, Mike took Harlem River Drive to Brooklyn. As he drove, he realized Red Hook's scenery was changing. They were starting to build hotels and condominiums on the run-down lots. He was beginning to second-guess his move, until he made a right turn onto Columbia Street. The contrast was like night and day. On the outskirts of the projects, it was a ghost town. The lights in houses were out, while the residents and owners inside slept peacefully, not worrying about all of the drama going on directly across the street.

Meanwhile, as soon as you entered the projects, it was like being transported to another world. Young guys were standing on every corner. The prostitutes were holding down their block on Huntington Street by P.S. 27, as their pimps held court inside the projects.

Mike continued to slowly drive down Columbia Street, because somebody's child was liable to run out into the street without looking and become a victim. As he drove past Lorraine Street, he noticed one of his workers standing on the block talking to a young honey. That pissed him off, because he knew he told Man-Man to get everybody to "the honeycomb."

He pulled over and parked his car. He rolled down the passenger window and whistled for the young girl to come over to the car. When she got to the window, he told her to tell the young man that he had five minutes to get to Mike's spot, and that he was already late. Mike then pulled a wad of money out of his pocket and slipped a hundred-dollar bill from it and handed it to the girl. She walked off with an extra bounce in her step to deliver the message.

The young man looked up and caught Mike's eyes as he was pulling away from the curb. Mike watched in his rear-view mirror as the young cat gathered his work and money before getting into his car.

Mike pulled up to the parking lot of the honeycomb and parked. He got out and surveyed the block. It was really quiet, which made him uncomfortable. He hit the button on his keys to lock the car and set the alarm. He made his way over to the building, pulled out his master key, and went inside.

The building smelled of hot piss and shit. Mike held his breath as he got on the elevator, and exhaled only when he got off on the fourth floor. He took the steps to the fifth floor to check the stairwells for anyone lurking.

As he walked up to the fifth floor, he got pissed off. The entire floor smelled of weed. "These muthafuckas are so stupid," he said to himself. He knew he was going to have to make an example out of somebody.

He walked over to the door and started to knock, but something told him that if they were stupid enough to have the hallway smelling like weed, then the apartment door was unlocked. He turned the knob and entered the apartment.

Everybody inside stopped what they were doing and looked up, pure fear registering on their faces. Mike loved it. Seeing the fear made his blow flow. He locked the door, walked into the living room, and went straight for the radio.

One of the young men started to say something, but Mike put his hand up to stop him, and the young man got quiet.

Mike turned on the radio and turned the volume up. As the music blared, he looked over to Randy and shook his head.

Randy got up, walked to the back room, and grabbed the bags out of the room. He brought them into the living room and threw them on the floor in the middle of the room. Then he walked into the kitchen, grabbed a chair, and placed that into the middle of the room.

As Randy was setting up, Mike said, "Somebody better tell me what the fuck happened and how it happened." He looked around the room at all of the workers.

Nobody said anything. "So I'm talking to my fucking self?"

Still, nobody replied. Mike continued to look around the room at each person, loving the feeling of their fear. Just as he was about to speak again, the young man from outside entered the apartment. Mike walked over to the young man and grabbed him by the neck. Then he dragged him over to the chair and sat him down in it. "Now, this will be the last time I ask what the fuck happened out there today."

Since Man-Man was in charge of that particular worker, he spoke up and told Mike what happened. When he was done with the story, Mike motioned for Randy to come. Randy walked over to the Man-Man and broke his nose.

"Aagh!" Man-Man screamed, dropping to his knees.

"How many times did I tell your dumb ass to stop letting these muthafuckas bring they hoes to the spot? How many times?" he yelled, pointing at Man-Man.

"A lot," they answered in unison.

"Now I'm out of twenty thousand in work and cash because you little muthafuckas couldn't handle some bitch. Is that what y'all trying to tell me?"

Man-Man tried to explain again, but Mike shut him down. "Didn't I tell your ass to have all of these muthafuckas off the block before I got here?"

"Yes," Man-Man answered.

"So what the fuck happened then?"

Before Man-Man could explain, Randy hit him again.

"Go clean yourself up and get back over here. You have a job to do."

Mike looked at Randy, and Randy followed Man-Man to the bathroom.

When they came back into the living room, Randy walked over to Mike, who nodded for him to handle the young man in the chair. Randy went to the young man and began to tie him to the chair. The boy in the chair realized what was about to happen and began to beg and plead.

"Don't cry now. You wasn't crying in the streets. Man up." Mike turned back to the rest to the boys and said, "This will be a lesson to all of you. When I tell you to handle something, you will do it."

Mike pulled Randy to the side and told him to have Man-Man take care of the boy. Then he told him to strip the boy naked, take whatever he had on him, and give it to another one of the boys after everything was done. Mike told Randy to wrap the boy in plastic, take him over the roof to the other building, and burn his body.

Mike informed Randy that he was taking a walk. He told Randy to chirp him when it was done.

Mike looked around at everybody one last time. He put a smile on his face and said, "Oh yeah, y'all little fuckas are going to make up that loss." Then he walked out, slamming the door behind him in rage.

As he stood in the hallway, he overheard the young man screaming for dear life. He smiled, took the steps down, and exited the building.

Naheema was in Manhattan sleeping peacefully. She rolled over to grab for Mike and realized that his side of the bed was empty and cold. She called out to him but didn't get a response. She got up and looked at the clock. The time read five-forty a.m. She got up and looked around for her cell phone. She remembered she'd left it in her pocketbook, so she reached over on the nightstand and dug inside until she found it.

As she sat up in the bed to turn it on, her vagina started pulsing. A smile spread across her face as she thought about what Mike had done to her. Her cell phone vibrated, letting her know that she had messages. She ignored them and dialed Mike's number.

"Hello."

"Hey, where are you?" she asked.

"Oh, I had to run to the shop."

"Is everything okay?"

"Yeah, the alarm went off, and I got a call from the company. I had to run out and check everything. It was a false alarm. The circuit breaker shorted out, which activated the alarm."

"How long have you been gone?"

"Not long. I should be leaving here in another half an hour. Are you all right?"

"Yeah, I was a little scared when I rolled over and didn't feel you in bed."

"I'm sorry. I'll make it up to you."

"You sure will." Naheema laughed.

"No problem, but get some rest. I'll be there before you know it."

"Okay, I'll try."

Naheema began checking her messages. Her sister Shaquanna left her two messages, asking her about her date. Her friend Shadina—Dina for short—called also. Shadina left a message asking about the girls' night and if they were still going to do it. Naheema ended her call, placed her phone on the nightstand, and lay back down. Within five minutes she was asleep.

Back in Brooklyn, the deed was done, and in the morning, the news about a dead child burned beyond recognition would be all over Red Hook.

While Mike was smoking his cigarette, Randy came out of the building wearing a different velour track suit and walked to Mike's car.

Mike took the last pull from his cigarette before dropping it to the ground. He stepped on it and picked up the butt. "Take a ride with me," he said.

"No doubt."

Mike and Randy opened the car doors and got in. Mike reached inside his glove compartment and grabbed two baggies. He threw one at Randy and said, "Roll up." Then he took the other baggie and placed the cigarette butt in it. He put that baggie back into the glove compartment.

While Randy rolled up a blunt, Mike turned the ignition, put the car in reverse, backed up, and pulled out.

They rode in silence until Mike entered the BQE going back to the Brooklyn Bridge.

"What's up with the disappearing act?" Mike asked as he entered the FDR drive.

"Sorry about that. My girl and her mother got into some shit," Randy lied. "And she called me crying and shit. I had to pick her up and take her to my crib."

"Everything all right?"

"Yeah, man. It's cool now." Randy took a pull from the blunt.

"All right, 'cause I need you to be on your game. We can't take another hit like tonight." Mike pulled off the highway on Fifty-Ninth Street.

"I got you."

"Now for business. How much do we have left?" Mike asked.

"Not enough to get through the week. Your boy had over three thousand in his pocket before we took care of him, and the rest of them together had about ten thousand in the spot." Randy passed the blunt to Mike.

"All right. Take the thirteen and go get some more trees. Have them fools in the back on Richards Street set up and bag up half. Leave the other half as is 'cause we gonna sell them like that to make up the loss." Mike parked the car on Sixty-Third Street and First Avenue in front of Randy's car shop.

"No doubt," Randy said, unlocking the door to get out. "I'll hit you when it's all done." He got out of the car and walked to the back of his shop.

When Mike got upstairs, it was already going on six-thirty in the morning. He walked into the room and checked on Naheema, who was still sleeping.

He walked into the bathroom, stripped, turned on the shower, and jumped in. He washed, dried off, and got into the bed with her.

Naheema felt his body, and she moved back into him. He wrapped his arms around her and drifted off to sleep.

# Chapter 5

While Mike and Naheema were at his place sleeping peacefully, Randy was inside the car shop removing the wire from his body. He walked inside and whistled, letting the other detectives know he was alone. To the person on the outside, the car store looked like a regular car shop, but it was a front for an undercover operation.

He walked around the counter and pushed his way through the wall. This room was like a mini "cop central." The detectives had all kinds of video and audio surveillance equipment hooked up all over the place.

Randy walked over to his partner, Detective Shawn Wilson, and handed him the wire. "Did you hear what this fool wanted me to do to that kid? I swear I can't take this anymore. I'm ready to put a bullet in his head. We have to hurry up and put this case to bed."

"Calm down," Shawn told him. "You've been in this for a little over two years, and you finally got him to trust you. Don't worry. It'll be over soon enough. We just need a little more on him so when we get him, he'll want to deal, and then we can have his connect."

Randy slammed his fist on the desk. "Man, that's bullshit, and you know it. Everybody in here knows that punk ass ain't got the balls to do this shit himself. If we tag his ass tomorrow, his bitch ass will be screaming, 'Let's make a deal,' so stop lying to me."

"Partner, come on. Just a little while longer." Shawn got from the chair to stretch his legs. "By the way, what did you do with that young man?"

"What the fuck do you think I did?" Randy said, removing his gun from his waist and placing it on the table. "I scared the shit out of him and had our informant in the next building hold him in her apartment until I can get him out."

Shawn sat back down and began to rewind the tape. "All right. That's good. But what about the body he's expecting to read about on the news?"

"Don't worry, he'll get his story. I already called the news to report a body being found on the roof of the building."

"How is that possible without a body?" his partner asked, confused.

"Just trust me. Oh, yeah, we need to re-up tomorrow." Randy threw the money on the table.

"Shit. Who's going? Is he sending one of the workers?"

Randy began smiling. "No. It's my turn to go shopping."

"Gotdammit!" Shawn yelled. "I need to call this in." Then he turned to the other detectives and began yelling out orders.

Randy just laughed. He knew in his heart that he couldn't do this anymore. He knew he had to take down the guy who murdered his sister. He walked out of the surveillance room and went into the bathroom. He closed the door and turned the faucet on blast. As he sat on the toilet, he began to think about that fateful night.

Randy's little sister was always a fast ass when it came to the opposite sex. He'd tried his best to help his mother raise her, but there was only so much he could do. They were five years apart, so while he was at college, his sister was home with their mother, running wild.

When he graduated college and came back home, he found out his mother had a loser boyfriend who'd gotten her hooked on crack and was having sex with his sister. Randy beat his mother's boyfriend to within an inch of his life and then kicked him out. And his mother cursed him every way from Sunday.

He tried his best to get some type of control over his seventeen-year-old sister, but she wasn't having any of that.

Before Randy's mother had kicked him out, she screamed, "Mike is going to kill her." Thanks to his mother he now knew the name of the kid that his sister was selling weed for. He decided he was going to handle her when she came home.

Later that night, his sister walked in the door high and drunk. It hurt Randy's heart to see her that way. He immediately started in on her, and they argued back and forth.

He followed her into her bedroom, where they began shoving and pushing one another. She punched him in the face, and he shoved her hard against the dresser, knocking down the drawers inside it. When he went to help her up, he noticed two pounds of marijuana and a gun on the floor beside the dresser. He lost it.

His sister began fighting him as he picked everything up and began tossing it out the window. She looked at him and began to cry.

He told her, "Everything gonna be okay."

The next day, while he was taking the NYPD exam in Canarsie High School, his sister was at home trying to explain to Mike what had happened to his work.

By the time Randy made it home, his sister had been dead on top of the roof for five hours. He later learned that she had been raped, severely beaten, tortured, and burned alive on the rooftop. Randy lost his mind.

For three months he tried finding out who had done this to his sister, and for three months, his mother couldn't stand the sight of him. She finally kicked him out.

Randy moved to Queens with his aunt. While there, he found out that he'd passed the NYPD exam.

Three months later he passed the academy and was officially an officer working out of the 75th Precinct on Sutter Avenue, where he worked for three years before taking the detective exam and passing it.

He worked in the homicide division for two years, taking down several high-profile drug dealers. He enjoyed his time on the team, but he had a plan. He wanted in Narcotics, so when an opening came up, he put in for it. After waiting three months, he was finally transferred over to the narcotics division, where he worked for another two years, making a bunch of arrest and raids.

He received letters of commendation from the commissioner, which came with a request to work for a special unit within the department. This particular unit was a new task force that the commissioner wanted to combat the serious drug trade and drug-related murder rate that was skyrocketing in the Red Hook section of Brooklyn. These detectives were going to work closely with the FBI's narcotics division, and they were to only correspond with the FBI. He accepted and was immediately transferred to the 76th Precinct on Union Street.

After a year of due diligence and excellent undercover work, Randy found out who was responsible for the death of his baby sister by accident. He was on an assignment to get close to this guy named Mike. The name didn't register with him until the first day of his assignment.

His assignment was to play a drug dealer who was arrested for distribution of crack cocaine and marijuana. His story was that he took a deal, saying he was using the drug, and that's how he ended up in the rehab center. He stuck to that story the entire three months he spent in the rehab, where he met the infamous Mike.

After meeting Mike, Randy realized he finally met the man of the year, so he worked his way into Mike's little organization. An incident happened, and Randy made it disappear.

Later that night, Mike and Randy got drunk together, and that's when Mike told him a story about a young woman who used to work for him. Mike explained how the girl's mother was on drugs and her brother was away in college and how she needed to make her own money, so he put her on to work for him. Her mother's apartment was a stash house for Mike.

Randy wanted to kill Mike. He continued to listen to Mike tell him how he went to get his drugs from the young lady, but she started trying to explain how her brother found it and threw it away. As Mike laughed about how afraid the girl was, Randy's heart began pacing a mile a minute.

Mike said that he had to make an example out of the girl because he didn't want anybody in his crew to see him as a weak leader and try to take him on. Mike went on telling his story and laughing about it. He explained how he beat her and had his workers drag her to the roof to rape and sodomize her as she screamed for her life. He laughed about how he watched them enjoy themselves. After his boys was finished getting off on her, he pissed on her body before pouring gasoline on her and setting her on fire with the lighter she'd had engraved for him.

When everything was said and done, Randy went home and cried like a baby. At that moment, he made a promise to his sister to avenge her death. Listening to Mike laugh as he told that story turned Randy heartless, so he was more than thrilled to know that he, Randy Simms, Detective Second-Grade, would be the one to send Mike to his death. And, for a moment, that eased his pain.

Saturday afternoon, Naheema woke up to Mike's head between her legs. Mike's tongue felt like it had its own brain. Naheema felt like the skies opened up as she released orgasm after orgasm.

When Mike was finished, he got up and walked into the bathroom.

Naheema wanted to go back to sleep, but she heard Mike calling out to her.

"Are you going to join me?"

"Yes, I'll be right there." She got up and walked to the bathroom.

Naheema was drained, but Mike was just beginning. He soaped up her sponge as she soaked her body under the hot water. She turned her back to him, and he began to wash her back, massaging her muscles as he scrubbed her body.

Naheema's brain was screaming for him to stop, but her body was telling him that she wanted him to finish, and he continued to massage and squeeze parts of her back, causing her to shake uncontrollably. She couldn't believe that she could come, just from Mike massaging her back. She never knew the nerve endings in her back could cause her to have an orgasm.

Mike smiled, because he wasn't finished with her. He massaged her neck, working his way down to her back. As he began washing her ass, she backed up, standing only an inch from his manhood. Mike wanted to bend her over and give it to her right there, but he controlled himself. He wanted to enjoy this just as much as she did. Ever so softly, he massaged in between her behind, moving the sponge to the front of her vagina. As the sponge got closer to her opening, he slipped his middle finger deep inside of her.

Naheema jumped from his touch. She wasn't expecting that.

Mike whispered in her ear, "I hope I didn't scare you."

"Um, um . . ."

Mike dropped the sponge from his hand and switched fingers, so that his thumb was pushing back against her clitoris, and his middle finger went into her asshole.

"Oh, my God!" she screamed.

"I hope you like," Mike whispered.

Naheema couldn't respond. Her brain went blank, and she couldn't form words. Her body began to shake, and her legs felt like lead as her juices squirted out of her. That had never happened to her.

Mike bent her over and reached on the windowpane to grab the open condom pack. He removed the condom and placed it over his swollen manhood.

Just as Naheema was about to stand up straight, she felt him push deep inside of her cave. "Oh! God! Oh my God!" she screamed.

At first Mike was wining slowly, hitting her walls, applying a little pressure. When he felt like she could handle it, he started pounding her insides out.

Each time he pulled out of her, he pushed in farther and farther. It felt like he was touching her lungs, because she was having a hard time breathing.

Mike sexed her in that position until he was ready to release. He stopped and pulled out, which confused her. He turned her around to face him and lifted her up. She wrapped her legs around his waist as he pounded away at her until her release.

"Aah, aah, I'm coming," he moaned.

As he released, Naheema released as well.

They washed up, dried off, and left the bathroom.

While Mike was making breakfast for them, Naheema turned on the television and her phone to check her voice messages. As soon as her phone powered up, it rang.

"Hello."

"Bitch, how the hell you gonna disappear and then turn your cell phone off?" her sister asked.

"Damn! I was about to call you."

"Whatever. When the hell are you coming home?" Shaquanna asked.

"Why? I'm grown." Naheema laughed.

"Don't play with me. Anyway, how was it?" Shaquanna asked, getting down to the real reason she called.

"How was what?"

"Bitch, stop playing. I want details."

"Look, I'll tell you when I get home."

"Oh, so it's like that? Shit, he must have put it on you, for you to be all tight-lipped about him. So when are we going to meet this Mike character?"

"Soon. Look, I'll call you back later."

"Oh yeah, before you go, turn on the news," Shaquanna said.

"Why?"

"They found another body on the roof on the avenue."

"Damn! Do you know who it is?" Naheema grabbed the remote control and turned the television to Channel Eleven news.

"It's—"

"Wait. Hold on, it's on now." Naheema turned the volume up.

*"Breaking news. This just in. A body was found badly burned on the rooftop of a project building in Red Hook, Brooklyn. The body found was none other than a sixteen-year-old black male named Jermaine Jarvis. Stay tuned for more on this report."*

"Oh, my god!" Naheema screamed. "That's Dina's cousin!"

Mike heard Naheema yelling and ran back into the bedroom to

find her on the bed in tears. He ran over to her and noticed her phone in her hand.

"What's wrong? What happened?" He grabbed her into his arms.

Naheema just cried as her sister was screaming through the phone.

Mike picked up the phone and spoke to Shaquanna, who explained to him why Naheema was crying. He thanked her and hung up Naheema's phone. Mike held Naheema in his arms, comforting her until she stopped crying.

"I have to call her to see if she is okay."

Mike gave her phone back to her.

She dialed Dina's number, and after two rings she answered.

"Oh. Dina, did you hear? I am so sorry." Naheema began to cry.

"Yes, I know. My mother called me this morning. It's okay. I'm doing okay. My aunt's not doing so well, though."

"Damn! When you speak to her, tell her that I'm sorry for her loss," Naheema said, wiping the tears away.

"Thanks, Naheema, I will. But, listen, let me call you back. I have to take my mother over to my aunt's."

"All right. Well, if you need anything, please call me."

"Okay. Later."

"Later."

Naheema continued to cry. She explained to Mike that she used to babysit Dina's cousin when he was a baby, and she fell in love with him.

Mike took her cell phone from her hand, turned the power off, and laid her back on the bed. He placed the quilt over her and went into the kitchen to make her some tea. He gave it to her, and then he sat with her until she dozed off.

While Naheema slept, Mike made a few phone calls. His first call was to Randy concerning the news on the television. Then he asked him about the re-up. Randy told him everything went smoothly, and they talked for a few more minutes.

Mike walked back into the bedroom to check on Naheema. She was still asleep. He felt bad a little for spiking her tea, but he needed her to take a nap so he could step out for a while to handle some personal business.

As he got dressed, his cell phone rang.

"What's up?"

"Hey, baby," Chyna cooed. "I miss you."

"Yeah? That's good to know."

"What are you doing?"

"I'm getting dressed. Why? What's good?" Mike slipped his feet inside of his boots.

"I want to see you."

"Good. 'Cause I'm on my way to check you too." He took one last look at Naheema before leaving the bedroom.

"All right then. I'll be waiting."

"Good. Later."

He grabbed his keys and looked around the apartment. Then he set the alarm and left. He rode the elevator down, jumped on his bike, and pulled out.

# Chapter 6

Mike exited the BQE at Church Avenue, made a left turn on Beverly, and rode straight to East 18th Street. He rode to the second house on the right and parked his bike in the driveway. He walked to the steps and entered the house, where Chyna was upstairs, laying on her bed naked and patiently awaiting his arrival.

He walked into the room, put his helmet on her dresser, and walked over to the bed to sit down.

"Did you miss me?" Chyna asked, climbing on her knees to remove his jacket.

"What do you think?" Mike started kicking off his boots.

"Good, 'cause what I have planned for us tonight is going to be out of this world." Chyna stepped off the bed to go hang up his jacket.

"Really? That's too bad," he said, rotating his neck around.

"Why?"

Chyna stood directly in front of him, licking her lips, sliding her hands down her neck and onto her breasts, rubbing and caressing her nipples. Then she slid her right hand down to her pussy and started fingering herself.

" 'Cause I have some business that I need to handle, so I can't stay the night." Mike stared at Chyna finger-fucking herself. He wanted to explode. He pulled her closer to him.

Chyna removed her hands. "Damn, Mike! This shit is ridiculous. Every time you come over here, you got to leave. What am I? Your personal Friday-night special?"

"Come on, now. You know that's not true. You know I have a business to run, so let's not go there. Let's just enjoy the time we have right now."

Mike silenced her, lifting her right leg onto the bed and rubbing the gold dick, from the chain wrapped around her waist, against her clit.

Chyna started moaning. She loved when he used her toys.

Just when she was about to stop him, he put his head between her legs and fucked her with his tongue. Softly, he licked her pussy from the bottom to the top.

As he reached her clitoris, he started nibbling on the tip. Chyna's head went back, her eyes rolling back into her head.

Mike became an octopus, using his left hand to guide the gold penis in and out of her cave, while using his right hand to squeeze her behind. He teased her by licking the opening of her wetness, gliding his tongue up and down the walls of her kitty-cat, and listening to her purr as he sucked and nibbled on her clit.

"Oh. Yeah, daddy. Just like that," Chyna moaned. "You going to make me come."

Mike liked when she moaned. He sucked hard on her clit, which caused her to scream.

"*¡Sí, papi! ¡Sí, papi!*" Then she released.

Chyna wanted more. She pulled her leg off the bed and pushed Mike back onto the bed. She began stripping his clothes off of him. She climbed on top of him to get ready.

Just as she was about to sit on his rock-hard erection, he pushed her off.

"Don't play yourself. Get the fucking condom!"

"Aww, baby, come on," she whined. "I want to feel you in me."

"And you will, just as soon as you get that."

She tried another way to get his mind off wearing a condom, sliding down the length of his body to face his manhood.

She reached for the peach oil from her nightstand and poured over his body, starting with his chest, rubbing down his stomach, and ending at his dick.

She began licking his balls, sucking them into her warm and wet mouth, one ball at a time. Then she licked the shaft of the balls up the vein of his penis until she reached the tip. Slowly, teasing the head, licking her tongue around the head before stuffing his manhood deep into the back of her throat as she flexed her throat muscles to swallow him.

Mike moaned, "I'm about to come, Chyna."

She sucked him a little more until she knew he was ready to explode. Then she stopped and climbed on top of him.

"Why you stopped?"

She just smiled as she sat on top of him, grinding her waist. "You want more?"

"Stop playing with me," he said, grinding to match her pace.

She lifted up, just enough to slip his penis inside of her.

"Aagh!" they moaned together.

She continued her assault on his manhood, grinding faster as he pumped harder. Just as she was climaxing, he pushed her off and flipped her on her stomach. He spread her ass cheeks apart and pushed himself deep into her asshole.

Chyna gave a little moan and started to take the back shots like a champ, so Mike continued to ride her like a bat out of hell.

After several minutes, Mike pulled out and released on her back, smearing her ass with the rest of his come, and Chyna fell flat on the bed with Mike lying on top of her.

"Damn, girl! You're trying to kill me?" he said, rolling off of her.

"No, I'm just trying to change your mind about leaving me tonight."

Chyna was tired of being Mike's sideline ho. She wanted more and was willing to do what she had to do to get it.

Just as she was about to make a comment, Mike's cell phone rang. He reached over to his pants and pulled the phone out, but before he could answer it, it stopped ringing. He put the phone on the nightstand and rolled over to face her.

"Look, I know that I've been really busy, but I promise you it's going to get better." Mike sat up on the bed.

"You said that before," she said, unlocking the gold penis from her waist.

"I'm going to make it up to you in about two weeks."

"Yeah?" she said, getting happy.

"Yeah. As a matter of fact"—Mike reached into his pants pocket and pulled out a roll of money— "Look, it's five thousand here." He quickly thought of a lie. "Take this and go shopping. I want you to pick up some bathing suits for the next two weeks. I'm going to take you to the Bahamas."

"Aye, *papi*, I love you so much." She grabbed the money out of his hand and kissed him.

"Turn on the shower for me."

Chyna stuffed the money into her dresser drawer and walked out of the room to go and turn on the shower for her man. She grabbed two towels with matching washcloths and placed them on the toilet seat. She left the bathroom and went back into the bedroom.

"It's ready," she said. "I'll be in with you in one minute."

Mike got off the bed and walked past her to the bathroom. He looked at the clock on the wall in her hallway. It was eight p.m. He knew he had to hurry up and get ready to go. He didn't want Naheema to wake up again and not see him there.

He got into the shower and began to soak.

Chyna entered the bathroom and climbed into the shower with him. She grabbed the soap, and started soaping up Mike's back. She turned him around to face her and continued to wash off his body, starting with his chest, rubbing down his stomach, and ending at his dick.

Mike was hard and ready to fuck again, so Chyna got on her knees and let the water rinse the soap off his dick while she licked his balls. He leaned his head back and let the water flow over his body.

Chyna stood, licked his neck, and traveled down his chest, slowly making circles with her tongue as she reached his navel. She sucked on his navel and slid down until she was back on her knees. She licked the vein protruding from his balls to the head of his dick, slowly teasing the head, placing her tongue around the head.

"Mmm! Mmm!" Mike moaned. "I'm about to come!"

Chyna sucked and sucked. Then when he was about to explode, she deep-throated him and swallowed all of his little soldiers.

Mike was drained from this adventure. He finished washing up, rinsed off, and got out of the shower.

Chyna got out right after him, and they both got dressed.

Later, she walked him to the door and watched him climb onto his bike and pull off.

# Chapter 7

Mike was back at his place within the hour. Randy had called him to inform him that everything was okay and that the money was now in the bank in the shop's accounts.

Naheema finally woke up while Mike was making dinner for them. He was really concerned about her, but she assured him that she was fine. She snuggled tighter in his arms, cuddled against his bare chest, feeling the warmth of safety engulf her. The mattress felt soft and endearing under her body, but she felt lying against his stiff frame and using his arm as a pillow was much more comfortable and preferable, as they fell fast asleep.

With the sun shining brightly through the blinds, Naheema woke up to Mike having his breakfast between her legs. After ravishing her spot, he grabbed her arms and pulled her toward him.

At the contact of their skin, a mixture of emotions shot straight into her system: desire, lust, and excitement. Everywhere he touched, she felt a sizzling burning feeling, and her breaths kept coming in shorter. From the way his hands were moving, it was pretty easy to tell that their desires were mutual. Reaching up, he pulled her deeper into the covers with him, into a never-ending abyss of pleasure and desire.

Once their lovemaking session was over, Mike got up and walked into the bathroom to turn on the shower as Naheema lay on the bed in total bliss and satisfaction. No man had ever made her body tingle the way it just had. If she didn't slow it down, she was bound to fall head over heels in love with this man.

Mike entered the bedroom in all of his glory, walked over to her, and helped her out of the bed. Hugging her from behind, he walked with her to the bathroom to get into the shower. He washed himself, and then her. He was doing everything in his power to make her his before she left to go home later. No words were exchanged between them as he rinsed her body off. Just the look of satisfaction on her face told him that he was doing a good job.

He turned the shower off, grabbed a towel for himself, and gave one to her.

Finally able to move, she began drying herself off.

They left the bathroom physically together but miles apart in their thoughts. In his mind his job for the weekend was completed, while she was still thinking about that mind-blowing sex they'd had earlier.

Mike was dressed first, so he left Naheema in the bedroom to finish dressing as he went downstairs to prepare their breakfast. Twenty minutes later, she came down to a spread of bacon, sausage, eggs, biscuits, and grits before her. He guided her to a chair and pulled it out. She sat down as he prepared her plate.

They ate in silence.

Breakfast was delicious. Naheema didn't want to leave. He made her feel so welcome and wanted. Each time she looked up from her plate, he was staring at her, which caused her heart to flutter.

After breakfast Mike cleared their dishes and cleaned up the kitchen, and Naheema got herself together. He grabbed his sweater, car keys, and her bags before punching in his password into the alarm system. They exited the apartment, taking the elevator down to his dark green Saab, where he placed her bags in the backseat.

They drove straight down Fifth Avenue and made a left turn on Madison, entering the FDR.

Naheema really enjoyed her weekend at Mike's condo. During the drive to her place, she kept stealing glances at Mike. She was falling for him, and she hoped he was feeling her too.

Loving the attention she was throwing his way, he smiled at her. The feeling of making her his woman was stronger now than ever before. She was what he wanted, and he knew that he had to make it official. He thought about how much he enjoyed holding her in his arms, but he especially liked how she felt when he was deep inside of her. When the time came, she would make a good first lady, he thought.

As they pulled into the parking lot, he turned to her and decided that she was his.

"I hope you enjoyed yourself."

"Yes, I did," she said, smiling.

"Good. I'm glad," he said, placing her hands in his. "Naheema, I really want you to be mine. Is that possible?"

"It's possible," she answered, with her heart pounding in her chest.

"Then it's official: your mine and only mine now," he said, looking at her with serious intent.

"And you, sir, are now mine."

He parked the car, turned off the engine, and got out. He walked over to her side of the car and opened the door for her. She got out and stood in front of him. He grabbed her into his arms and kissed her with passion.

Naheema was too happy to say anything. Her head was swimming. Mike held her hand and led her into her building, and they rode the elevator up to the eighth floor.

The crackhead from Friday was standing in the stair landing with the door open. When he saw Mike passing, fear registered on his face, and he took off down the stairs.

Naheema noticed it but didn't acknowledge what she'd just seen. Just as she stuck her key into her lock, the door to the apartment across from hers opened, and the young drug dealer stepped out with his head down, a bag of crack in his hands.

Mike bumped into the young man on purpose, causing the baggies to drop out of his hands.

The younger dealer yelled, "What the fuck is your problem?"

"Excuse me?"

The young man looked up and noticed Mike. He hurried and picked up the baggies, stuttering an apology to Mike before running back into the apartment.

Naheema opened her door and stepped inside. She held the door for Mike to enter, and closed and locked the door behind him. "What was that about?"

"Nothing much. I know his mother."

"Oh, okay. You can sit in the living room."

Mike followed her into her living room, liking her decoration skills. "You have a nice place. Did you decorate it yourself?"

"Yes and no. My sister and friend helped me."

"Okay. I'm feeling the color scheme."

"You can make yourself comfortable. I'm just going to drop these bags in my room."

"Take your time."

Naheema headed to her bedroom and placed the bags on her bed. She took off her shoes and placed her feet inside of her bunny slippers. She closed her room door and headed back into the living room.

Just as she was about to sit down, there was a knock at her door.

"Give me a minute to get rid of whoever this is," she said to Mike as she walked to the door. "Who is it?"

"It's your sister," Shaquanna answered.

"Damn!" Naheema whispered to herself as she unlocked the door and cracked it open. "Now is not a good time," she said through the cracked door. "How the hell did you know I was home?"

"First off, I didn't, but as I was walking into the building, that boy from over there said he saw you come in." Shaquanna pushed her way in the door.

"Aagh! Watch it!" Naheema yelled as she closed the door behind her sister.

Shaquanna walked into the living room and was floored at the sight of this gorgeous black man, but she played it off.

She walked over to him and introduced herself. "Hello. My name is Shaquanna. I'm Naheema's sister, and you are?"

"I'm Mike. Nice to meet you," he said, shaking her hand.

"Mike . . . Mike. Your last name wouldn't happen to be Williams?"

"Yes, it is."

"I know you. You own Official Kuts salon, right?" she asked, dollar signs dancing in her head.

"Yes, I do."

Naheema already knew what was going on in her sister's head. Sometimes Shaquanna could be so money-hungry.

Naheema grabbed Shaquanna by the arm and dragged her to the door. "It's time for you to go," she said, unlocking the door and opening it.

"All right. Damn! I'm going. You don't have to push." Shaquanna laughed.

"Whatever. I'll call you later." Naheema pushed her into the hallway.

"Bye. Do something that I would do." Shaquanna continued laughing as she walked to the elevator.

"Whatever." Naheema closed and locked the door. She walked back into the living room and saw Mike standing by her window. "I'm sorry about that. My sister can be a little abrasive."

"It's not a problem. But, look, I have to take off. I have some errands to run." He walked toward her door. "I'll call you later tonight."

"Mike, you don't have to leave if you don't want to. She's not coming back." Naheema laughed as she walked to the door.

"You are very funny, but no, it's not because of your sister. I really have to go," he said, reaching for the door.

"Okay," she said, standing at the door.

Mike reached in and tongue-kissed Naheema, leaving her feeling weak in the knees, breathless, horny, and woozy.

"I will call you later," he said as he released her.

Naheema nodded. She watched him go through the exit door then she closed and locked her door. She leaned up against it. Every time Mike kissed her, she felt like he was taking her breath away from her.

Naheema walked to her bedroom to start putting her stuff away, while she thought of her weekend at Mike's.

As the day turned into night, weariness over came her, so she crawled into her bed and fell fast asleep.

Mike called her, but she was too tired to answer the phone, so he left a voice message. "Hey, sexy. I figured you'd be tired. Sorry for calling so late. All right, I'll call you in the morning."

The next morning while Naheema was at work, a delivery of roses with a teddy bear was sent to her job. When she pulled out the card, Mike had written a message saying that he missed her lying next to him, but since he couldn't wake up next to her, he wanted her to have a gift from him to let her know she was on his mind.

For the rest of the day, Naheema smiled like a woman in love. Mike was stealing her heart, and she was happy to give it to him.

As the months flew by, Naheema was spending more and more time at Mike's condo. She was enjoying every minute of it. She had clothes at his place, and he had clothes at hers. At times she left for work from his condo in the city.

Naheema was getting a lot of jokes from her sister about spending so much time with her man, but she brushed it off. Naheema didn't care how her sister felt. She was happy, and that was all that mattered.

# Chapter 8

A month after their one-year anniversary, Mike surprised Naheema with two-first-class round-trip tickets to Freeport, Bahamas for five days and four nights. They stayed at the Pelican Bay resort at Lucaya, Bahamas. The first two nights was like a movie. Mike bought her an 18-kt. white gold diamond necklace and earring set, which he presented to her on the second night of their trip.

He'd made reservations for them to have dinner on the water. Naheema almost pissed her bikini when she looked down and saw stingrays swimming under them, but the hostess assured her that they weren't harmful.

They had a wonderful dinner, and while Naheema watched the sun set, Mike placed the diamond set on her neck and put the earrings in her ears. She cried as he took her in his arms and kissed her passionately. Mike was quickly becoming her everything, and she assumed she was his.

The next morning started off perfect. They went sightseeing to one of the Berry Islands, off the coast of the Bahamas. They enjoyed the food and ended up at a little hut that sold exotic alcoholic beverages made from different berries on the island. Naheema was enjoying herself, and apparently Mike was enjoying himself too.

As they partied on the beach later that night, Naheema noticed

Mike's eyes were constantly focused on a woman standing at the bar. She tried to focus her eyes on the woman, but with the amount of alcohol she'd consumed, her eyes couldn't get it together. So she let it go for the moment and went back to sipping on her piña colada.

She got up from the table and pulled Mike with her to the middle of the dance floor, where she began gyrating her hips against his body. She was feeling the music pulsating through the speakers.

But she was the only one, because Mike's attention was elsewhere.

Naheema got pissed at him and stormed off the dance floor to their table.

Mike followed her. "What the fuck is your problem?"

"You're my damn problem. You're busy staring at that he/she, while I'm standing there working my body for you on the floor." She snatched her glass from the table.

"Naheema, don't start that shit. I wasn't staring at anybody."

"Whatever," she said, getting up and pushing him to the side. "I'm going to get another drink."

"Give me." He grabbed the glass. "I'll get you a drink. I have to go to the bathroom anyway."

"Whatever." She handed him the glass and sat back down, trying to calm her nerves and put her anger in check.

Five minutes later, when she realized Mike hadn't returned, she got up to go look for him. As she walked past the hostess, she scanned the area. Not seeing him, she continued to the restroom. As she got closer, she heard voices coming from the back area, so she entered the bathroom. But it was just a bunch of drunken women.

She left the restroom and headed for the room where they were now staying. She strolled along the beach, trying to calm herself down. As she got closer to their room, she noticed the soft light flickering in the window of their bedroom. She smiled and headed toward the door.

She pulled out her key and opened the door. She called out to Mike, but he didn't respond.

She slipped out of her sandals and headed toward the bedroom. Hearing laughter, she picked up her pace. She opened the door and saw nothing. Mike was nowhere to be found, but the television was on.

She walked over to the windowpane, blew out the candle, and sat down on the bed. She turned the volume down on the television, picked up the phone, and dialed his number. His phone went straight to voicemail. She left him a message saying that she was in their room. She hung up and looked at the time. It was only twelve-thirty. She sat there for a while then decided to take a shower.

After showering and putting on some comfortable clothing, she lay across the bed and ended up falling asleep.

The sounds of a female laughing on the TV woke her up. She looked at the time, and it was now two in the morning. Mike was still not there.

She called his phone, and again it went to voicemail. She left another message then got up and went into the bathroom to freshen up.

She left the bathroom, grabbed her keys, left the room, and headed for the front desk, strolling along the beach for a minute before entering the main part of the hotel. She stepped to the desk.

"Good morning," the hostess said. "How can I help you?"

"Yes, I'm looking for my fiancé. Would you happen to remember if you saw him?"

The hostess looked at Naheema like she was crazy. "Ms. Morgan, your fiancé ordered another room."

Confused, Naheema looked at the girl. "Excuse me? No one

informed me that we changed rooms."

"I am so sorry. I set it up earlier. He came in while you all were at the party to set it up. I told my coworker to let you know, because you weren't in your room when I came to give you a key." The hostess removed a key from the shelf and handed it to Naheema.

"No problem. Thank you," Naheema said, taking the key to see what room they were now staying in.

She left the front desk and headed in the opposite direction of the old room. She was stressing out, wondering what was going through Mike's mind when she didn't come to the room. She was praying that he'd believe she was still in their old room.

As she approached the door, she heard laughter from a female coming from the room. She assumed Mike had fallen asleep with the television on.

As she got closer to the bedroom, the voice threw her for a loop. It sounded like Shaquanna's, but she was at home in New York. She pressed on.

Standing in front of the bedroom now, she heard Mike's voice but couldn't make out the words. She then pushed the door open a little, and the sight before her knocked her backwards.

She heard the "oohs" and "aahs" and walked into the bedroom afraid of what she might see. Because the room was dimly lit with two candles, she was able to make out the silhouettes, which caused her to be stuck on stupid. She stood there in full shock.

Mike was fucking some woman with blond hair from behind, and the woman held on to the bedpost for dear life. He was so busy pounding away that he didn't notice Naheema standing there.

"Aah, aah!" he moaned.

Just as he was about to release, Naheema jumped on his back and began pounding away at his head.

Mike jumped and pushed Naheema off his back, causing her to fall to the floor. He backed up and turned around, his condom-covered penis standing at attention.

Shaquanna was on the bed grabbing at her costume, and using the sheet to cover her face. *Thank goodness for the veil,* she thought to herself.

Mike yelled, "What the fuck!"

"You bastard!" Naheema screamed back, getting up from the floor to attack him again. "Who is she?" she asked, not realizing that it was her sister. She charged Mike again, throwing blows at his face.

Because he was drunk, and his shorts was down to his ankles, he slipped when Naheema punched him in the nose. Naheema saw him hit the floor, and attempted to jump over him to assault the woman on the bed.

But Mike was quick. He jumped up, fixed himself, and grabbed Naheema by the neck while Shaquanna blew out the candles. Mike dragged Naheema out of the room. Shaquanna jumped off the bed and quickly ran over to the door and locked it.

Naheema fought Mike every step of the way, but he continued to squeeze the back of her neck to get her to stop fighting.

"Get off of me!" she screamed.

"Shut the fuck up!" Mike yelled back, dragging her by the neck to the opposite end of the hotel.

As Naheema reached up to try and remove his fingers from her neck, Mike punched her in the face and knocked some of the fight out of her. The next thing she knew, she was seeing stars.

When they made it back to the old room, all hell broke loose.

Mike opened the door and threw Naheema in, and she hit the floor hard.

But that didn't stop her. She jumped up and threw a combination of punches at his face.

Mike grabbed her by the neck and slapped her down, and she hit the floor again. Mike began kicking her in the stomach and assaulting her with blows to the head and back. He beat Naheema like she stole from him.

As quickly as the beating began, it stopped. Mike, finally aware of his surroundings, looked down at the damage he'd done to Naheema's body. There was blood everywhere.

He ran into the bathroom to get a towel to clean up. He wet the towel in warm water and came back into the bedroom. He sat down next to Naheema on the floor and began to wipe away the blood from her nose.

Naheema moaned and cried in pain. "Why, Mike? Why?"

"I'm sorry, baby," he pleaded as he wiped the blood away. "Please forgive me. I don't know what got into me."

"How could you do that to us?"

"Ssh! Don't talk. Please forgive me." Mike helped her up from the floor, took off her clothes, and laid her in bed.

Naheema's body felt like it was on fire, like her ribs were broken. Her mind kept replaying the scene in the bedroom, as she began to drift in and out of sleep. Right before she went to sleep for the night, she whispered to Mike, "It's over."

Mike looked at her like she'd lost her mind. He started to say something back, but he noticed the tears falling from her eyes and knew that she was only talking through the pain. She loved him, so he knew he could fix this.

Naheema was in so much pain, her attempt at sleep proved to be futile.

She woke up in the middle of the night to find Mike missing from his spot. She attempted to get up, but the pain knocked her back down. She tried to turn over, but she couldn't move.

She knew then that what had happened to her that night wasn't a dream. She didn't know how to forgive him or even if she wanted to forgive him. She just knew that when they got back home, she was going to stay away from him for a while.

Mike walked over to the bed with a glass of water and two pills. "Here. Take this. This will help you sleep."

Naheema wanted to refuse his help, but the pain was unbearable. She took the pills and drank the glass of water.

Mike took the glass from her when she was done, placed it on the nightstand, and climbed in bed with her as she dozed off to sleep.

While Naheema and Mike slept, Shaquanna was making her way to the airport, happy that Naheema didn't see her having sex with Mike. She knew she was wrong, but after meeting Mike at Naheema's place, she had to have him. In her mind, she felt that Naheema wouldn't be able to handle Mike herself.

As she got her stuff together, she began reminiscing about the day she'd met the man they call Mike.

It was the day she popped up at Naheema's house after she'd pulled the disappearing act for the weekend. When she left Naheema's apartment, she waited downstairs by her car for Mike to leave. She pulled out her business card and wrote "call me" on the back. She held the card in her hand and waited. She didn't expect him to come down so soon after she left, but she was happy that he had.

When she saw him leave the building, she climbed into her car and waited for him to climb into his. Once he was seated in his car, she slowly pulled out of the parking lot and drove to his car. Right before he could pull out, she pulled in front of his car and cut off her engine.

Mike was about to curse her out, until he noticed it was her, and they both got out of their cars at the same time.

"I am so sorry," she said, playing stupid. "My car shut off."

"It's all right." He walked around to the front of the car. "Do you know what's wrong with your car?"

She followed him. "No, I don't. Do you mind taking a look at it for me?"

"No problem. Just lift the hood up for me."

"Sure," she said, walking back to the driver's side. Then she whispered to herself, "I can do more than that."

"What did you say?"

"Oh, nothing." Shaquanna got in the car and pulled the lever for the hood to pop open.

Mike pulled the hood up and began to check her car. He had a feeling there was nothing wrong with the car, but he pretended to take a look at it anyway.

She got out and walked over to him. She was admiring his physique. If she could have gotten away with it, she would have fucked him right there in the parking lot, but she didn't want prying eyes to see.

As Mike turned to her to tell her he didn't see anything wrong, she stepped to him, kissed him, and began massaging his dick. Mike was enjoying himself, but he pushed her away, afraid that Naheema might see them.

Shaquanna guessed what he was thinking. She stepped back in

front of him and whispered in his ear, "Her window is in the front." Then she stuck her tongue in his ear and licked it.

Mike was horny as hell, but he didn't want to let her know it. He pushed her off. "What the fuck is your problem?" he asked, stepping around her.

"You know what the fuck is my problem. I want to fuck you," she said, trying to approach him again.

"You need to chill the fuck out, for real." Mike backed away. "You know I'm with your sister."

She walked closer to him. "And? You can be with me too."

"Look, Shaquanna, I don't know what type of shit you're up to, but I'm not with it," he said, walking to the driver's side of his car.

She blocked him from entering his car. "I want you to be all up in my shit."

Shaquanna looked around and noticed a dumpster was blocking the view of Mike's car. She decided, right then and there, she was going to taste him. She dropped to her knees, unzipped his pants, and gave him a blowjob in broad daylight in the parking lot.

Mike was blown away. Shaquanna sucked him like she was a Hoover vacuum. Within minutes, he was releasing his soldiers down the back of her throat. "Aah! Aah! Damn!" was all he could say.

"It's more of that . . . when you call me," she said, as she stood up and wiped her mouth. She placed her business card in his hand before walking away. She closed the hood of her car, jumped in, and started the engine. Then she rolled down her window. "Don't forget to call me," she said before pulling off.

Shaquanna left Mike standing there, his limp manhood out in the open. He was blown away by what just happened. He thought about going back upstairs to tell Naheema about her sister, but he didn't know what she was going to say, and he damn sure didn't know how she would take it, so he fixed himself and climbed into his car. He figured he would play it by ear before saying anything.

As Shaquanna boarded the plane, she knew they would have to be more careful if they didn't want Naheema to find out about them. She'd pulled the dummy move by following them to the Bahamas. Mike had made it seem like he would be able to get some time away from Naheema while they were there, but that wasn't the case.

She sat down in her seat, removed her cell phone from her pocketbook, and called Mike. His phone went straight to voicemail.

"Mike, look I don't know what we were thinking, but we can't do it like that anymore. Don't get me wrong; I was loving every moment of it, but if Naheema had seen me, it would've been a serious situation. Well, I'm on the plane now on my way back to the city. Call me when you return. We can hook up then. Later."

She sat back to enjoy her ride. She knew in her heart that she was going to have to end it. She and Mike had been hooking up every other night since she'd given him that blowjob, sneaking time to see each other whenever they could. They'd been fucking like rabbits in heat—in their car or at hotels.

She'd even tried to get him to come to her house, but he never had the time. When they got back to the city, she was going to make sure he made the time because she was getting tired of fucking him on the go. She lay her head back and fell asleep.

While Shaquanna was in the air headed home, Naheema and Mike were waking up. Naheema's body was sore as all hell. Mike got up and tended to her every need. She wanted to finish questioning him about last night but didn't have the strength at the moment to deal with it.

Mike ordered breakfast for them. As they were waiting for their food, he went into the bathroom and turned on the whirlpool. He dropped a few salt beads into the water, along with some bubbles. Then he went back into the room to help Naheema undress. He picked her up from the bed, carried her into the bathroom, and gently placed her inside of the tub.

The water felt good on Naheema's aching body.

While she soaked, he left the bathroom and walked back to the bedroom. Just as he was about to grab his cell phone, there was a knock at the door. He opened it up and let the waiter in with the food, escorting him to the bedroom so he could set up the tray.

The guy placed the white roses on the table and began to change the linen on the beds. When he was finished, he turned to leave. Mike followed him to the door, tipped him, and locked the door.

When Mike entered the bathroom, he noticed tears falling from Naheema's eyes. "Baby, I'm so sorry. Please forgive me." He got on his knees, grabbed the sponge, and began to soak it in the water.

"Why, Mike? Why would you fuck somebody else? Who was she?" she asked, her eyes closed, and constantly replaying the scene in her head.

"I don't know who she was. I was so drunk out of my mind."

"I don't care. You are a grown man. That is no excuse for hurting me like this," she said, tears falling down her face.

"Baby, I'm so sorry. Please forgive me. I never meant to hurt you like that. I would never want to cause you pain." He squeezed water from the sponge onto her neck. "I don't know what came over me."

"That doesn't explain why you would hit me the way you did. You were wrong, not me."

"I'm sorry. When you started hitting me, I blacked out. I forgot where I was and who I was fighting."

"So it's my fault that you beat me like this?" Naheema opened her eyes to look at him.

"No, baby, it's not your fault. I'm just saying that I blacked out when you started hitting me." He poured gel on the sponge.

"I-I-I don't know what to say. I don't know what you want me to say."

"Say that you forgive me. Say that you'll let me make it up to you. Say that you won't leave me." Mike began to gently wash her body.

"I don't know if I can."

Mike washed her up then rinsed her off. He pulled the lever up so that the water would drain from the whirlpool. He helped Naheema up, grabbed the towel, dried her off, helped her out of the tub, and placed the robe around her body. He lifted her up into his arms and carried her back into the bedroom, where he removed the robe and gently laid her on the bed.

He walked over to her bags, reached in, and grabbed the oils. Then he went to the bathroom, grabbed a cup, placed the bottles of oil inside, and ran the hot water in the cup. He went back into the bedroom with the cup and placed it on the nightstand, grabbed the pitcher, filled her glass with apple juice, and handed her two pills with the juice. Naheema took the pills with juice and swallowed it.

As the pills worked their magic, Mike rolled her onto her stomach and began pouring the warm oil onto her back. He massaged her body with the oils, starting at her neck, working his way across her shoulders, then to her back. He poured more oil into his hands and began massaging her thighs, calves, ankles, and feet.

When he was done, he turned her on her back and repeated the pattern.

"Um! Um!" Naheema moaned, as Mike massaged her nipples. "Ooh!"

Mike continued to oil and massage. He trailed her stomach, kissed her navel, then massaged her legs—right then left. His hands traveled back up her legs, softly squeezing her inner thighs. He traveled a little farther up, spreading her legs, and rubbing his thumb across her clit.

Naheema moaned, "Ooh! Aah!"

Mike removed his thumb and palmed her vagina, inserting his middle finger in and out of her cave.

Naheema was about to climax. "Mike, stop. Please, stop."

But Mike continued to work the inside of her cave.

When he removed his finger, Naheema thought it was over, but then she felt his tongue dancing on her walls. He used his hand to spread open the lips, as he licked the walls of her vagina. She tried lifting her arms to push his head away, but the pills had already taken effect.

Mike licked, sucked, and nibbled on her clit until she released into his mouth. Then he continued to lick her clean.

After releasing, Naheema passed out from exhaustion.

Mike got up, grabbed his cell phone, and went into the bathroom to wash his face. He closed the door, turned on his phone, and waited for it to power up.

It registered four messages. He entered his code and listened to his messages.

One message was from Shaquanna. He listened, smiled, and deleted it.

The second was from Chyna. She cursed him out because it was supposed to be her on the trip to the Bahamas. He deleted it.

The last two messages were from Randy.

"Mike, the spot was raided last night. They got everybody downtown, so I'm heading over there now to see if these dudes are going to get bail. If anything, I'll get one of these chicks to go and bail them out."

Mike deleted that message and listened to the next one, which was left two hours later.

"Mike, bail was $1500 each, so you need to hurry your ass back to the States because it's getting hectic."

Mike deleted the message and called Randy to let him know he would be returning in the morning, and that he would take care of everything when he got home.

Early the next morning, the car was there to pick them up and take them to the airport. Naheema was able to move around a little better. She knew that once they got back home, she was going to ask Mike to go back to his place because she needed time to decide if she wanted to stay with him.

After they boarded the plane, he asked, "How are you feeling?"

"Tired."

As the flight attendant walked past, Mike asked her to bring a pillow and some water for Naheema. Then he handed Naheema two more pills and the glass of water.

Naheema swallowed the water with the pills, and a few minutes later, she was fast asleep.

Naheema was both exhausted and exhilarated to be back in New York. They walked to Mike's car, which was in a parking garage at JFK Airport.

The drive home was a quiet one. Naheema, still hurt by the events that had taken place in the Bahamas, really didn't have anything to say to Mike.

Mike was quiet as well, as he replayed the events in his mind. He didn't want to lose Naheema, but he knew he had to give her some space to get over it.

They pulled into her parking lot. He got out and grabbed her suitcase and attempted to help her into her building, but she stopped him.

"Baby, I know you're still mad, but you have to believe me when I say I am so sorry. I never meant to hurt you. I love you."

Naheema looked at him in shock. She couldn't believe he'd just professed his love to her. She didn't know what to say, but she knew she had to say something. In her heart she loved him too, but if she told him now, he would think she was over what he'd done.

"Mike, I appreciate that, I really do, but I can't say it back to you at this moment, not with the way that I'm feeling right now. I just need some space to clear my mind. I don't know if I can forget or forgive what you did to me or to this relationship. Love is not supposed to hurt." She took her suitcase from him. "I just need some time."

"Okay, that's fair enough. But I do love you, and I hope that you can forgive me."

Mike stepped in to kiss her, but she turned her face in time for him to catch her on the cheek. He knew then that it was going to take a lot more than just saying, "I love you," to win her heart again.

He stood there watching her as she walked into her building. He wanted to go after her and fuck the shit out of her, to make her see how he felt, but he knew that wasn't the right way to do it. She was different.

She wasn't like the rest of these hood rats.

He got into his car and pulled off, heading home. He made a call to Randy before jumping onto the highway, but the news he received had him making a quick U-turn. His shop had been shut down by the feds, and there was a warrant out for his arrest. Randy informed him that their lawyer had called Mike three times but kept getting the message that his voicemail was full, so the lawyer called Randy.

Mike was beyond pissed, but there was more.

Two of his main workers and some guys from Clinton Street had a shoot-out over the weekend that left two of his moneymakers dead. Now the block was crawling with NYPD detectives.

Mike told Randy that he was on his way to the spot. He hung up and called his lawyer.

The news from the lawyer was even more depressing, but it had a great outcome. Mike's lawyer informed him that because he wasn't in the country during the time of the raid, he wouldn't be accountable for the drugs found in the shop. Mike asked him how.

"A young man took the rap for hiding the drugs in the shop, telling the feds you were unaware of the drugs being there." The lawyer also went on to explain that he was now in the process of having the warrant dismissed.

Mike felt a little better. He told the lawyer he would see him on Friday with his fee, and then he hung up. He couldn't believe all the shit that had happened while he was gone. He was going to have to make some major changes in his crew, and fast.

Mike parked a block away from the spot by the corner store and bought two six-packs of Heineken. Then he made his way over to the spot.

Later on that evening Mike called Naheema and told her a little bit about his situation with the shop being shut down.

Naheema had mixed feelings about not being able to see Mike as much, but she was happy because it made it that much easier to stay true to her words. This also meant that she now had time to hang out with her sister and girlfriend.

She put in a call to Shaquanna to see about making some plans, but she got her voicemail. She then made a call to Dina to see how she was doing, and to let her know that she was back in Brooklyn, but Dina's voicemail picked up, so she left her a message.

Naheema got up from her bed and took out her clothes for the work week. Then she showered and went back into her bedroom to lotion her body. She went through her dresser drawer and grabbed a long white T-shirt to put on.

She started removing the clothes from her suitcase to put them in her hamper. When she pulled out her last negligee, the necklace and earrings Mike had given her fell out. She picked them up and stared at them, then broke down crying.

As the memory of him putting the necklace around her neck and the earrings in her ears replayed in her head, she knew she was deeply in love with Mike, and that she would eventually forgive him because he was human, and humans make mistakes. But she wasn't going to make it easy for him to get her heart completely.

Meanwhile, Mike was on the ave, flipping out. He beat one of his workers so badly that he had to be admitted to Long Island College Hospital's intensive care.

He and Randy had words also. He didn't understand how Randy could let any of this shit happen.

Randy let Mike rant and rave before letting him know that he was at fault too, and they almost came to blows. But Randy cooled it down, accepting responsibility for the incidents.

Mike didn't like it, but he let it slide for now. He knew that he was going to have to get rid of Randy because too many things were going wrong on his watch. He was disappearing too much, and when the cops came around locking dudes up, Randy could never be found. Something wasn't adding up, and Mike was becoming suspicious.

Randy had a feeling that Mike was making plans to get rid of him, so he already had some things in motion. His superiors had informed him that when they did the next raid, he had to get caught too. Tired of dealing with men like Mike, Randy wasn't feeling that. He couldn't wait for the day to come when he would sit in court and serve Mike his death sentence.

After their argument was over, Mike and Randy slapped palms, and Randy slipped Mike the key to the safe where the money was.

Mike thanked him and left the apartment. Then he got in his car and pulled off.

Randy stood there in the hallway, watching as Mike drove away.

"Your day is coming." He pointed his finger at the car like he was pulling a trigger.

# Chapter 9

A week went by before Naheema heard from Mike. She wasn't sure if she was ready to forgive him for that horrible vacation, but she did miss him. Even though she had not answered any of his calls, she did receive all of his gifts. Mike sent flowers, chocolates, and bears. She gave all of the chocolates and flowers away, but she did keep the bears. Mike was growing tired of this game Naheema was playing, but he knew he had to make it right with her. He was not going to lose her.

He decided that he was going to just show up to her job and take her out. Naheema was happy to see Mike parked in front of her job. They hugged and kissed like two people in love. Mike took Naheema to dinner and afterwards they headed to her place, where they made love well into the morning.

Naheema was happy she'd decided to give Mike another chance.

For two months, Mike and Naheema made up. They had sex in every corner of her apartment, going two and three times a day. He'd just about moved most of his clothing into her place. He was over there so much that Naheema made him a copy of her apartment key so she didn't have to constantly leave her keys with him.

After two months of sexing each other crazy, they finally decided to take a little break. Friday came, and they went out to dinner, but it was cut short because Naheema starting getting nauseous from the smell of various foods. Mike stopped at the store and bought her a ginger ale, then took her home. They showered and climbed into bed.

At three in the morning, Mike's cell phone started beeping. He grabbed it, looked at the message, and turned the phone off.

At nine the next morning, there was loud banging at the door.

Naheema jumped up, put on her robe, and headed to the door. She screamed, "Who the hell is it?" as the person continued to knock at the door.

Naheema looked through the peephole and saw Shaquanna standing there. She unlocked the door and opened it.

"What the fuck is your problem? Knocking like you lost your damn mind." Naheema blocked Shaquanna from entering the apartment.

"Naheema, please. I always knock like that. I don't know why you're flipping now," she said, pushing her way in. "Move! Damn! I know your man is here. I saw y'all come in last night, so don't even trip."

"So if you know that, then why are you knocking like you're the cops?" Naheema asked, closing and locking the apartment door.

"Girl, please stop tripping. I had to pee, so I came here because Dina is not at home." Shaquanna speed-walked to the bathroom.

"Whatever." Naheema sat down on the couch.

Shaquanna noticed that Naheema couldn't see her, so she snuck a peek at Mike, who was lying stark naked on the bed. "Damn!" she whispered to herself.

Mike heard her and looked up. Shaquanna smiled, but the look on his face let her know she was fucking up. She sucked her teeth at him and went into the bathroom.

Naheema heard her sister sucking her teeth and assumed she was doing it at her. "I know damn well you're not sucking your yellow-ass teeth at me."

Before leaving the bathroom, Shaquanna noticed Mike's Polo cologne on the space saver, and a smile spread across her face. She grabbed the cologne, sprayed some between her breasts, and put it back.

"I know you heard me," Naheema said.

"Heard what? I just got out the bathroom."

"Whatever."

"Anyway, I'm getting ready to go. I know you're busy, but I'll come through later."

"All right," Naheema said, getting up from the couch. "Oh, is Dina still having the sex party tonight?"

Before Shaquanna could answer, Mike came in the living room, a towel wrapped around his waist. "What sex party?" he asked, as he entered. "Good morning, Shaquanna."

"Morning, Mike." Shaquanna stared at the towel.

Naheema noticed what her sister was looking at and pushed her toward the apartment door. She unlocked the door, opened it, and pushed her into the hallway.

"What you do that for?"

"You know why. Anyway, is she still having it?"

"Yeah. I'll come and get you later," Shaquanna said, walking away with images of Mike on her mind.

Mike and Naheema both headed for the bathroom at the same time.

"So who's having a sex party?" he asked. "And where is it going to be?"

"My girlfriend Dina. She's having it at her place in the next building."

"Really? And you're going?" Mike turned to face her, his penis hard in his hand.

"Yes, I am," she said, looking at him.

"I don't think you should be going to that type of party."

"Mike, don't start. It's called a sex party, but it's only going to be a bunch of women at this party."

Mike was horny as hell. He stepped closer to her, grabbed her waist, bent her over, and forced himself deep into her.

It hurt at first, because she wasn't wet, but after a few deep thrusts in and out of her, she was hot, wet, and matching him thrust for thrust.

He grabbed her hair and pulled her head back to him as he pounded away at her walls.

"Aagh! Yes, Mike, like that."

"Like that?" he asked, pounding away. He pushed her over until she was holding on to the faucet. He stepped on the sides of the tub, and pushed down on her clit.

Naheema yelled at the top of her lungs, "Oh shit! Oh shit! I'm coming! Aah! Don't stop!"

Mike continued to slow-grind in and out until he released. "Aah! Yes! Yes!" he screamed as her pounded his semen in her vagina.

His legs began to shake, so he stepped off the sides of the tub and almost fell, but he caught himself by grabbing on to Naheema's waist, and she cracked up laughing at him.

"That shit is not funny," he said, laughing.

They washed up again, rinsed off, dried up, and left the bathroom.

As Mike was getting dressed, he voiced his concerns again, but Naheema assured him that it wasn't that type of party, and he said okay.

After he got dressed, he gave her a kiss and left the apartment.

Naheema slipped into one of Mike's white T-shirts and went to make herself some breakfast.

After she ate, she cleaned up her kitchen, went into her living room, and turned on her television. An episode of *Maury* was on. Naheema loved watching the show because she couldn't understand how these women never knew who their children's fathers were. This particular show was about "abusive men and the women who stay with them." She settled in to watch the show, and ended up dozing off.

Later on that evening, while Naheema was getting dressed, Mike called her.

"Hello."

"Hey, baby. What are you doing?"

"I'm getting dressed for Dina's party."

"So you're going then?"

"Yes, Mike, I am." Naheema could hear a lot of commotion in the background. "Where are you?"

"I'm in the neighborhood. Why?

"Just asking. But let me finish getting dressed, and I'll call you back."

"All right."

Mike leaned back into his seat, allowing Shaquanna to go down on him. He began moaning as she deep throated him, causing him to say, "Damn, I can't wait to hit that."

"I can't either," Shaquanna said, removing his swollen penis from her mouth.

Naheema heard it all and began screaming through the phone.

"What the fuck is this? Mike! Mike!"

Naheema was screaming his name so loud that Shaquanna noticed it. She stopped short, making Mike lift his head up.

"Don't stop. You're not finished."

"Your phone is still on," she said, sitting up.

"What?" he asked, realizing his mistake. "Oh shit!"

Just as he was about to put the phone to his ear, Shaquanna grabbed it and ended the call.

"You're right. We're busy," she said, bending over to finish. "Oh yeah, I think she heard me."

"I doubt it," he said, unsure.

"I bet you that if she doesn't get in contact with you, she's going to call me."

"Whatever. Just finish what you were doing. I'll deal with your sister later," he said, pushing her mouth onto his penis.

Naheema was beside herself. She didn't want to believe that Mike was cheating on her, but in her mind, she knew better. She heard the entire conversation, and the voice of her sister in the background. As tears streamed down her face, she started screaming all types of obscenities in her room. She picked up the phone and dialed Mike's number, but it went to voicemail. She dialed his number two more times and got the same results, so she decided to call Shaquanna.

"Hello," Naheema said, angry.

"Hey, Nah. What's up?"

"Nothing. Where you at?"

"I'm around the way. Why?"

"Don't lie to me. Shaquanna, are you with Mike?"

"No, but I just saw him. He was parked on the Ave. I stopped and said what's up to him," Shaquanna said, as Mike fingered her. "Why? What's up?"

"Nothing," Naheema said, trying to listen for any background noise.

"Why you sound like that? What happened?"

"Don't worry about it. I'll see you at Dina's house."

"I thought I was going to come and get you?"

"Yeah. I forgot about that. All right then. Later."

Shaquanna hung up and began laughing. Mike asked her what she was laughing for and she said, "I told you she heard me, and I knew she was going to call me."

Mike parked the car in front of the pier on Van Brunt Street. He put the car in park and leaned his seat back. He took a deep breath and started to say something, but he quickly lost his train of thought when Shaquanna leaned over, unzipped his pants, pulled out his dick, and put her wet warm mouth on it, instantly causing him to swell.

"Oh yeah," he moaned. "Just like that."

Mike was in heaven as Shaquanna sucked him like a Charms lollipop. He knew what he was doing was wrong, but he couldn't help himself. Shaquanna was like a drug to him. Every time he said he was going to end it with her, she did this to him, and he would forget about ending it. He just prayed that Naheema would never find out.

He grabbed Shaquanna's hair and pushed her head up and down, faster and faster, until he felt like he was ready to explode. "Oh, yeah, do that shit."

Shaquanna was horny as hell, and was ready to fuck. Mike was ready to explode, and Shaquanna knew it. She stopped, released the Ben Wa balls from her vagina and quickly climbed on top of him.

"Chill. Get up," he said, attempting to push her off him. "Chill. Put the condom on."

But Shaquanna ignored him and began tightening the muscles in her vagina, driving Mike crazy. He loved when she did that.

As her muscles tightened around his manhood, she began sliding up and down on his penis, releasing and squeezing her vagina walls along the way.

"Oh shit! Damn! Oh shit! I'm about to come."

Shaquanna began bouncing up and down, harder and harder, screaming, "Yes! Yes! Yes!" until they released together. "Aah! Aah!"

Shaquanna lay on top of him, panting and out of breath. "Damn! That felt so fucking good. I want some more."

Mike looked at her like she was crazy. He pushed her off and smacked the shit out of her. "What the fuck is your problem?" he spat, fixing his self. "Are you trying to get pregnant? Bitch!"

She screamed, "What the fuck you hit me for? I ain't see you pulling out. Don't ever put your fucking hands on me." She removed her thong and used it to wipe between her legs.

Mike pulled his seat upright, reached over, and squeezed her neck. "Bitch, who the fuck do you think you're talking to?"

She tried to remove his hands from her throat, but it was useless. His vise-like grip was hard to break.

Squeezing her throat with his left hand, Mike smacked her with his right hand then balled up his fist and punched her in the stomach.

"Bitch, you better pray your ass don't get pregnant." He unlocked his car door and pushed her out.

She was shocked that Mike kicked her out of his car. She was still in shock that he even hit her. She had never seen that side of him before. She got up and started yelling at the top of her lungs.

Mike attempted to pull off, but a NYPD car with flashing lights pulled up and blocked his path. The officers jumped out of their car. The officer in the passenger's seat stood in front of Mike's car, his hand on the butt of his gun, and shouted for him to turn off the ignition. Meanwhile, the other officer walked over to Shaquanna and began questioning her.

Mike shut the engine off, rolled down his window, and placed his hands on top of the steering wheel.

The first officer went over to driver's side window and asked Mike for his license and registration.

While Mike was handing his information over, Shaquanna was making a statement to the second officer. She told him that she and Mike got into an argument, and that he broke up with her. She told the officer that was the reason she was yelling.

The officer didn't believe her because the right side of her face was beginning to redden. When the officer questioned her about it, she told him she was having an allergic reaction to her makeup.

After calling Mike's information in, the officer asked him to step out of the car with his hands over his head, and Mike complied. The officer had him face up against the door as he searched him. He asked Mike if he had any weapons or drugs on him or in his car, and Mike told him no.

As the officer searched him, the radio cackled that there was a warrant for his arrest. Mike was pissed. His lawyer was supposed to take care of that.

The officer read Mike his rights.

Seeing Mike in handcuffs caused Shaquanna to start yelling for them to let him go, but the first officer explained to her that there was a warrant for his arrest. She calmed down and then asked them where were they taking him, and the officer said, "To the Seventy-Sixth Precinct on Union Street."

As the officer put Mike in the backseat of the cruiser, Mike told Shaquanna to take his car to the avenue. She knew that meant to get Randy. The officer backed up and drove away, leaving Shaquanna standing there alone. She knew she had messed up bad. When she got in Mike's car, she looked down and saw her Ben Wa balls. She opened the glove compartment, took out a napkin, picked up the balls, and placed them inside the glove compartment.

She made her way to Columbia Street. When she got there, she didn't see Randy, so she parked the car, got out, and proceeded to walk to the building where Mike did his business. She checked her watch and noticed that it was now seven p.m. She had to hurry up and get to Naheema.

She entered the building, taking the steps up to the top floor. As she climbed to the third floor, she overheard voices. As she got closer, she overhead Randy two other people talking with two men.

"We finally got your boy locked up," Detective Davies said.

"Yeah, but not for long," Detective House said.

"What do you mean by that, House?" Randy asked.

"We got him on a technicality. He had an old arrest warrant out for him for failing to pay a traffic summons," Detective House answered.

"Funny thing is, the summons was dismissed, but someone forgot to remove it from the system," Detective Davies said, laughing.

"All right, so how long can you hold him for before somebody notices the mistake?" Randy asked.

"Two or three hours maximum if he don't start making a fuss," Detective Davies answered. "Why?"

"Because that would give me some time to get over to the spot and bug it, but I won't have enough time to get to his apartment in the city and bug that," Randy said, becoming frustrated. "Davies, you think you can push his release time back by an hour or two extra?"

"I can give you an extra hour. I'll just make sure his paperwork gets lost," Detective Davies answered, smiling and slapping Detective House a five.

Shaquanna was shocked. She couldn't believe what she was hearing. *Randy is an undercover cop.* She was sick to her stomach. Feeling the bile rise up in the back of her throat, she began taking deep breaths, forcing herself not to throw up. Feeling her nerves beginning to settle, she realized that she could no longer hear their voices clearly. She knew that she would have to get a little closer in order to hear them, but just as she was about to take a step up, an elderly woman opened her apartment door, screaming, "Hey, you! What are you doing listening to my door? Shoo, get away from here." Then the lady proceeded to swing her broom at her.

Shaquanna jumped and took off running back down the steps and out of the building.

Randy ran to the hallway window to see what was going on, as the two detectives peeked over the railing. He saw Shaquanna running out of the building and knew that his cover was blown. "Shit! Shit!" he screamed.

One of the detectives asked, "What the fuck just happened?"

"I just got noticed. I have to take care of this shit." Then he left the building in pursuit of Shaquanna.

Shaquanna practically ran around the block, but she wasn't fast enough. Randy caught up to her just as she tried to run through Housing's parking lot.

She started screaming, "Please, let me go. I won't say anything. I didn't hear anything."

Randy held her from behind. "Walk and shut up!" he said, releasing her neck. "If you try to run, I will shoot you."

Shaquanna did as she was told.

Randy led her to a dark blue Saturn with tinted windows, and they got in. "Put your seat belt on," he said.

"Please," she pleaded as she locked the seat belt, "I won't say anything."

"I said shut up. I'm not going to hurt you. We're just going to have a nice long talk." Randy started the car and backed out of the parking lot.

They drove in silence to the second pier on Columbia Street. Randy was thinking about how he was going to approach the subject, while Shaquanna was thinking about how she was going to get out of this situation.

Randy removed his seat belt and turned to face Shaquanna. "Look, we have a serious situation here, and I think you know what the right thing to do is. However, I'm going to give you two options. I can arrest you on some bogus charges and keep you locked up for the next two months, or I can give you the chance to get back at a man who killed your best friend's cousin. Which one is it going to be?"

Shaquanna couldn't believe what she was hearing. Mike had nothing to do with Dina's cousin dying. She refused to believe what Randy was saying, and he saw it on her face.

"Look, you don't have to believe me. I don't have to prove my case to you, but you can sure believe that I won't allow you to fuck up a case I've been working on for the last four years. So you better think real hard about what you're planning to do."

Shaquanna already knew. She wasn't going to go to jail over no man. She licked her lips and said, "Then I guess I will be taking door number two."

Randy watched her and thought to himself, *Damn! This bitch is sexy as hell.*

Then an idea came to him. He was going to use her as his snitch. He knew she was fucking Mike behind her sister's back and decided to use that to keep her in line, but first he wanted to fuck her. He reached over, moved his hand up and down her leg.

She knew what he wanted, so she played along. She lay back in her seat and allowed him to finger-fuck her. "Ooh, that feels so good."

"You like that?" he asked, using his right hand to fuck her while he pulled out his dick and began to jerk off.

"Yeah, daddy. Umm . . . just like that."

Randy liked that she didn't have on any underwear. He removed his hands from her and pulled out a condom.

Shaquanna snatched the condom from his hand, ripped it opened with her teeth, slipped the condom onto her mouth, and rolled it onto his dick.

Randy was whipped. He'd seen it done in the porno flicks, but he'd never had a woman do that to him.

Shaquanna sucked him through the condom then jumped on top of him and blew his mind. She had him releasing within two minutes.

Randy was embarrassed. That had never happened to him. She was definitely going to be fucking him again.

After they cleaned off, he drove her to Naheema's building.

Just as Shaquanna was about to get out of the car, her cell phone rang. It was Naheema. "Hello."

Naheema screamed, "Where the hell are you? Do you see what time it is?"

"Naheema, calm down. I'm coming into the building now."

"Hurry up, with your slow ass."

"Bye." Shaquanna tried to open up the door.

Randy grabbed her left arm to stop her. "Don't forget what we agreed on. Oh, and from now on, I want to know every time Mike makes a move that I don't know about." He smiled.

"What? We didn't agree that I would be your snitch."

"You're right, we didn't, but we're agreeing now. Unless you want your sister to know that you've been fucking her man. Or how do you think Mike or your sister would take it when they hear that you got him arrested for raping you in the back at the pier on Pioneer Street?"

"You bastard!"

Randy smiled. "And you're a whore, so?"

"Fine. Whatever. Are we finished here?" she asked, her teeth clenched.

"Yes, we are. I'll call you later for some more of that sweet ass. Now get the fuck out of my car. You're stinking it up," he said, laughing.

Shaquanna stormed out of his car, slamming the door shut and speeding into the building. She'd never felt so cheap and disrespected before. She knew she was going to have a problem on her hands with Randy.

She got on the elevator and tried to calm herself before getting off. She knocked on the door, and Naheema let her in.

"You are a nasty bitch," Naheema teased. "I smell the sex all over you."

"Shut up. Are you ready?"

"Yes, I am."

"Well, give me a few minutes. I need to use the bathroom."

"Hurry up. Every time you come here, you need to use the bathroom. Stop fucking in the streets like a common whore." Naheema laughed.

Shaquanna didn't say anything. If Naheema only knew how close she was to the truth. She grabbed a rag and towel from the linen closet, went into the bathroom, turned on the shower, and jumped in.

While Shaquanna showered, Naheema called Mike for the seventh time. She couldn't believe he wasn't answering his phone or calling her. She wanted to kill him. In her heart, she felt that he was cheating on her again. She just couldn't prove it yet with hard evidence. Evidence that Mike couldn't deny or cause her to second guess herself.

Shaquanna exited the bathroom, went into Naheema's closet, pulled out a nice yellow linen pantsuit, and got dressed.

As Naheema was finishing her message, her sister walked into the living room. "I know, the fuck, you didn't," she said, hanging up the phone.

"Naheema, I promise I will bring it back. I had to change my clothes."

"And you used my makeup, Shaquanna?"

"Girl, stop tripping. What is really good with you?"

"Sorry about that. Mike is pissing me off. I called him and left several messages, and he hasn't called me back."

"Damn, girl. Sorry to hear that, but you know he may be tied up somewhere and can't call you."

"I bet he *is* tied up somewhere."

"Naheema, stop it. I don't mean like that."

"I know. I'm just so used to him calling me, no matter what."

"Look, I'm quite sure he'll call you later, when he can. Come on, we have a party to attend." Shaquanna grabbed Naheema by the arms and pulled her up from the couch.

"You're right," Naheema said, feeling a little better.

The girls left the apartment and headed over to 595 Clinton Street.

Everything was set up lovely, and everyone mingled around talking, getting to know one another. Naheema and Shaquanna were surprised to learn that Dina's sex party was primarily for couples. Luckily, there were a few good-looking single men standing around.

Naheema went searching for Dina and found her in the back room. "Hey, girl. How have you been?" Naheema asked.

"I'm good. How you been? I haven't seen you in a while." Dina stood up to hug her.

"I'm good. I've been relaxing. You know how that goes." Naheema sat down on the bed. "What are you doing hiding out back here?"

"I'm not hiding. I had to take a call from the strippers, and I had to get the catalogs in order." Dina handed Naheema a catalog. "I know you're going to buy some things, especially since you're always with your man."

"You know I am."

"All right, then. Let's get this started," Dina said, getting up from the bed.

As Naheema got up to leave, her cell phone rang. "Dina, give me a minute. Let me take this call."

Dina left Naheema alone in the room while she went out to start the party. Naheema looked at the number and didn't recognize it. She started to let it go to voicemail, but a nagging feeling that something was wrong made her answer it.

"Hello."

"Naheema, where are you?" Mike asked.

"No! Where the fuck are *you*? I've been calling you and leaving you messages."

"I'm locked up."

"What?" she asked in a panic. "Why? What happened?"

"An old traffic summons."

"You've got to be kidding me? They locked you up for an old summons?" "Yeah. Apparently, a bench warrant was issued for my arrest for failing to appear in court, but I spoke with my lawyer and while I was on the phone with him, he checked it out. Apparently the summons was dismissed, but it wasn't removed from the system."

"Damn! What do you need me to do?"

"Nothing. My lawyer is taking care of it. I'll be out of here in about an hour."

"Why didn't you call me? I was worried sick about you. Then I started thinking the worst about you," she said, calming down.

"When they gave me the one phone call, I used it to call my lawyer. When he got to the precinct, he gave me some change so I could make this call. Listen, I have to get off the phone now, but when I leave here, I'm going to go to your place and get in the shower."

"All right. Call me when you get there."

"I will. Naheema?"

"Yes, Mike."

"I love you."

"I love you too. Talk to you later."

"Later."

Naheema was able to breathe a sigh of relief. She'd been tormenting herself about what Mike may have been doing. Now that she knew that he was okay, she was able to go enjoy herself at the party.

She left the room and walked back into the living room. Dina was standing next to a table that held all different types of toys, gadgets, oils, and powders, and sending samples around the room for everyone to see.

Naheema looked around for her sister and found Shaquanna all hugged up with some guy on the couch. She shook her head, smiled, and went to find a place to sit.

The only space available was next to this tall, light-skinned male. She stepped over to him and sat down. He had his arm around the back of the chair. Naheema started to ask him to move it but decided against it. Next thing she knew, everyone was looking at them like they were coupled up.

Dina's presentation ended, and she began handing out the catalogs. By this time everyone had drinks in their hands and was chatting and laughing while viewing the books.

After everyone put their orders in, the activities began.

Naheema and the guy sitting next to her won a couple of gifts. She was enjoying herself. She looked at her watch and realized that it was almost midnight and Mike hadn't called her yet.

Dina told everyone it was time to separate. She told the ladies to go into the bedroom, while the men sat in the living room. Everyone did as they were told.

After five minutes in the back room, the ladies started becoming anxious.

Just as Shaquanna was about to leave the room, a guy burst in wearing a policeman's uniform and started stripping to some Ginuwine.

The women starting chanting, "Take it off!"

Naheema was embarrassed, yet she was enjoying the sight of the male before her. The guy made his money that night. Those women damn near attacked him.

After a half an hour, everybody was back with their significant other.

While Naheema was partying, Shaquanna was calling Mike. He answered on the first ring, and Shaquanna started apologizing.

Mike cursed her out and was about to hang up on her when she said, "I didn't know that you and my sister broke up."

When he asked her what she was talking about, she went on to say that Naheema was at Dina's house hugged up with the next man.

Mike hung up and called Naheema. When she didn't answer, he got up, got dressed, and headed over to Dina's place.

With all of the commotion going on, Naheema didn't hear her cell phone ringing. She had two missed calls from Mike.

Mike walked into the apartment and surveyed the room. He was pissed, because Naheema lied to him and said that the party was for women only. From his perspective, everyone in the place looked like they were coupled up.

He continued his search for Naheema. As he pushed his way through the crowd of people, he noticed her in the corner with a big-ass smile on her face. Naheema and the guy were so deep in conversation, she never noticed him walking toward her.

He stormed over to them when he saw a man's arm wrapped around the chair. Before Naheema could do or say anything, Mike had already smacked her, busting her lip.

The guy sitting next to her jumped up and stepped into Mike's face.

Mike looked at the dude like he was crazy.

"What the fuck is your—?"

*Wham!* Mike pistol-whipped him.

Everyone noticed the commotion and started running out of Dina's apartment, yelling and screaming that somebody had a gun.

Shaquanna and Dina came running out of the room in time to see Mike choking and punching Naheema in the face, and Naheema attempting to fight him back.

Dina was first to run and attack him. She jumped up on his back and started raining blows on his head. "Get the fuck off of her!" she yelled, pounding on Mike.

Dina noticed Shaquanna's hesitation. She screamed at her, "Help, bitch!"

Only then Shaquanna ran to the aid of her sister and friend.

Mike shook them off as if they were lightweights. Dina fell and banged her head on the wall, and Shaquanna fell but got back up and went back to fighting Mike. "Get off of her!" she screamed, punching him in the face.

That got Mike's attention. He released Naheema, and she crumpled to the floor. Then he turned to Shaquanna. "Bitch, you ain't get enough yet?" he said, approaching her.

Dina got up and pulled a 9-millimeter handgun from under the couch, removed the safety, cocked the hammer back, and pointed it at Mike. "Get the fuck out of my place! Now!"

Mike stopped in his tracks. He looked at Dina and smiled. "All right. You got that for now, Dina."

Dina stood there calm, although she was shocked that he remembered who she was. "I'm glad you remember me. Now get the fuck out of my apartment!"

Mike just smiled. He looked from her to Shaquanna and then at Naheema before leaving the apartment.

Shaquanna ran to the door and put the locks on it. She was scared shitless.

Dina put the safety back on the gun and walked over to Naheema, whose right eye was swollen to the size of a lemon. And her mouth was swollen and bleeding. Dina helped her up and sat her on the rocking chair. "Shaquanna!"

Shaquanna didn't answer. She just sat on the floor, balled up like a baby, crying.

"Shaquanna! Get the fuck over here!"

Shaquanna jumped up and ran over to her sister.

Dina told her they needed to call the cops and report this, but Naheema told them no, to leave it alone. Dina looked at Naheema like she was crazy. But Naheema was adamant about not calling the cops.

Dina and Shaquanna helped Naheema get cleaned up. Shaquanna cleaned up the apartment, while Dina made up the bed in her mother's room.

Dina gave Naheema two Vicodin pills and made her lay down, and Shaquanna and Dina sat down on the couch and passed out. It was after four in the morning.

While Naheema slept, Mike was blowing up her cell phone, leaving her ten messages.

When Naheema got up the next morning, she was a little disoriented. She forgot where she was until visions of what happened the previous night played in her head. She was in serious pain. Her entire body hurt.

As she struggled getting out of the bed, Dina walked into the room in time to help her up, and they headed into the bathroom.

Naheema started complaining about severe cramping in her stomach.

Dina told her to stay put and left her to go get two more pills.

Being hardheaded, Naheema attempted to stand up, but a sharp pain knocked her back down, and she felt something warm run down her legs. When she looked down and saw blood, she started screaming, "Dina! Oh my God!"

Dina came running into the bathroom to see the puddle of blood on the floor. She ran out of the bathroom, grabbed the phone, and dialed 9-1-1.

While they waited for the ambulance to arrive, she washed Naheema up as best as she could. She opened up a fresh pack of panties, placed a maxi pad in a pair, and put them on Naheema. Then she dressed her in a black sweat suit and laid her on the bed.

Naheema, in severe pain, began sweating and shaking uncontrollably.

Dina was so scared, she ran back into the living room to call 9-1-1 again. Just as soon as she picked up the phone, there was banging at the door. She dropped the phone and ran to the door. She checked the peephole and saw two EMTs. She let them in and took them to Naheema.

They checked her, questioned her, hooked her up to an oxygen machine, and escorted her out the door.

Dina locked up and followed them on the elevator, out the building, and into the ambulance.

They took Naheema to Long Island College Hospital, located on Henry Street.

While Naheema was being rushed into surgery, Dina called Shaquanna and informed her about what happened, and Shaquanna said she would be there as soon as she could.

# Chapter 10

Shaquanna left Dina's apartment at seven in the morning. She was scared to death. She didn't want to be there in case Mike returned. She did have some questions about the comment Mike made to Dina about remembering who she was.

As she was about to jump into the shower, her house phone rang. "Hello," she answered, out of breath.

"What the fuck did you think you were doing yesterday?" Mike yelled.

"Look, you ain't have no business hurting my sister like that!" Shaquanna yelled.

"Like you give a damn about your sister! I'm on my way to see you."

"No, you're not. Don't come here. I have to leave," she said, not sounding too convincing. "My sister's in the hospital thanks to you."

"Bitch, stop lying!" he yelled.

"Fuck you! You ain't nobody for me to have to lie to."

"Shut the fuck up and open the door!"

Shaquanna was shocked. She dropped the phone and slowly walked to the door. She peeked through her peephole and saw Mike standing there, holding a bouquet of white roses.

She backed away from the door, as quietly as possible, and moved farther into her living room. She picked the phone off the floor to talk.

"Look, Mike, I think you should leave. I don't think this is a good idea."

"Look, I just came to talk and apologize. I'm not going to hurt you, I promise."

"Mike . . ."

"Shaquanna, come on. I'm not going to hurt you."

"Okay."

She clicked the off button on the phone and walked back to the door, phone in hand. She unlocked the door and let Mike in.

Mike handed her the flowers and grabbed her to kiss her.

All of her fears suddenly went out of the window. She knew she should stop him and make him leave, but after he kissed her, she couldn't think straight. He began touching between her legs, which caused her hormones to sing.

They made it as far as the living room floor.

Mike had Shaquanna in every position.

After an hour and a half, he still hadn't released. She tried to push him off, but he was having none of it. He enjoyed every moment of it. Finally, he pulled out of her.

Shaquanna was exhausted. She assumed he was finished with her, so she attempted to get up.

She rolled over to climb onto her knees, but Mike grabbed her from behind and forced himself into her asshole.

Shaquanna screamed as Mike pounded away, tearing her open. She pushed back to get him off, but he held on tight to her waist and pounded and pounded, pulling in and out of her, until he finally released inside of her ass.

Mike got up, walked to the bathroom, and jumped into the shower, leaving her balled up and bleeding on the living room floor.

When he was done, he walked back into the living room, dug into his pocket, pulled out a roll of hundreds, peeled off ten, and threw them on top of her.

"Go get yourself cleaned up. Then go and buy your sister some flowers and take them to the hospital. Tell her they're from me, since we know you don't give a damn about her. Make up a story how I ended up giving them to you." Then he walked to the door, stopped, turned around, and said, "Don't forget to tell her that I love her." Then he left, slamming the door shut.

Shaquanna was pissed at herself for being so stupid. She pulled herself up from the floor, walked to her bathroom, and jumped into the shower.

Back at the hospital, Dina found out through one of the nurses that Naheema had a miscarriage. The nurse also told her that they were going to keep her for a couple of days because of the bruises, and that she could visit with Naheema for a little while.

Dina thanked the young nurse and headed toward the recovery room. Naheema's bed was at the end of the room. As she approached the bed, she had to stop herself from crying. Naheema looked horrible. Her right eye was swollen shut, the bridge from her eyes to her nose down to her mouth had turned purple, and her mouth was swollen. Dina had to pull herself together. She approached the bed and began rubbing Naheema's hand.

Naheema opened her left eye, and saw Dina standing there. Tears fell out of her eyes.

Dina wasn't sure if the doctors told Naheema about the baby, so she kept quiet.

Naheema tried to talk, but because her throat was dry, she couldn't pronounce her sister's name. "Where . . . is . . . Sha?"

"I called her. She's on her way," Dina said, trying to hide the fact that she'd called Shaquanna almost two hours earlier and she still hadn't come yet.

Naheema struggled to say, "I'm sorry."

"Shh. Just rest. We'll talk when you get better." Dina handed Naheema a cup of water and let her sip it.

At first the water hurt going down, but after a few more sips, it began to feel better.

Naheema looked at Dina and started to say something more, but two detectives came in and walked over to her bed. They asked Dina to leave so they could ask Naheema some questions.

Dina started to protest, but Naheema squeezed her hand and shook her head from left to right, letting her know it was okay for her to leave.

"Are you sure?" Dina asked.

"Yes, I'm sure," Naheema said, a little clearer.

"Okay. I'll be back."

The black detective began questioning Naheema about the bruises. He asked who attacked her. She lied and said she didn't know the guy. He then asked her where the assault took place, and she lied again, telling him that she was on her way into the building when a guy came from behind her, choked her, and dragged her into the stairwell. She said that he tried to rob her and she fought him. She told them she thought he was going to rape her too.

The white detective looked at her like he knew she was lying, but he stayed quiet. He then asked her why it took so long for her to report it, and she told him she was scared.

They took her statement, she signed the end of the form, and the black detective gave her a copy of the form. Then they left.

When they were out of earshot, the white detective said, "You know damn well she knows who did that shit to her."

The black detective nodded. "Uh-huh."

Dina was in the cafeteria ordering something to eat when her phone rang. "Hello."

"Dina, where is she at? What floor is she on?" Shaquanna asked, rushing through the lobby.

"Where the fuck are you? I called you two hours ago. You are so selfish."

"Look, I'm here now. Where are you at?"

"Come to the second floor. I'm in the cafeteria." Dina hung up.

Shaquanna made her way to the cafeteria and found Dina sitting at a table by the window. She walked over to the table and sat down. "What's up?"

"What the fuck do you mean, what's up? Your sister is in the hospital because she had a miscarriage after her muthafuckin' punk-ass man beat the shit out of her in my apartment while you stood there trying to decide who to help first."

"Look, I didn't come for all of this. I came to check on my sister."

Shaquanna attempted to stand up, but Dina grabbed her wrist and forced her to sit back down.

"Sit the fuck down!"

"Dina, get your damn hands off of me!"

Dina stared into Shaquanna's face for a minute before Shaquanna looked away. "Oh, shit! Don't tell me you fucking your sister's man."

"What? What are you talking about?"

"Don't lie, Shaquanna. That's why you didn't want to jump in and help her yesterday. I saw it on your face."

"Please . . . I don't know what you're talking about," Shaquanna said, looking all around the place.

"Damn, Quanna! I knew you get down and dirty like the rest of them chickens, but to do it to your own sister? That's some foul shit."

"Dina, please don't act like you're an angel. So, tell me what the fuck did Mike mean when he said, 'I remember you'?"

"He *should* remember me. That muthafucka was the reason for my cousin's death. I made it my business to let him know who I was. I was the reason why his barbershop was closed down last year. What the fuck did you think he meant? I'm not like you."

"Whatever." Shaquanna got up to leave. "What room is my sister in?"

"She in the recovery room on the third floor, but before you leave, let me ask you one question."

Shaquanna turned to face Dina. "What?"

"Are you so jealous of your sister that you're willing to destroy your relationship over a piece of dick that she had first? You know what? Don't answer that. I just hope you have enough sense to tell her after she gets released from the hospital." Then Dina got up and walked off.

Shaquanna stood there feeling stupid. Everything Dina said about her and to her concerning her sister was true. She didn't know why she did the things that she did, but she knew for sure that now wasn't the time to tell Naheema. She would wait until Naheema got better to tell her the truth about her and Mike, and that she was the reason Mike showed up at Dina's house last night.

She left the cafeteria and went to visit with her sister. The visit was short, because Naheema was fast asleep. Shaquanna walked over to her, kissed her on the forehead, and whispered in her ear that she loved her. Then she left.

Shaquanna got into her car and pulled off. She had to see a man about a plan. As she stopped at the red light on Columbia Street, she dialed Randy's cell phone number. He picked up on the second ring, and she explained to him that she needed to see him and fast. He gave her the directions to his shop in Flatbush and told her to meet him there, and she said she'd be there in forty-five minutes.

She made a U-turn at the corner and headed back the way she came, jumping on the BQE headed to Coney Island.

Dina went back up to see Naheema before she left, but Naheema was sleeping. She kissed her on the forehead, told her that she loved her, and left. She exited the hospital, made a left, and walked up to the corner of Hicks and Atlantic Street. She crossed the street and stood in front of a bar called Montero's Bar and Grill to wait for the B61 going to Red Hook.

While she patiently waited for the bus, she was trying to decide what to do with the information she had about Shaquanna and Mike. She had been friends with Naheema first, way before the Naheema and Shaquanna found out that they were half-sisters. Though her loyalty was to Naheema, she and Shaquanna had both done some things behind Naheema's back that Naheema had no idea about, like sleeping with each other when they both were in between men.

As she climbed on the bus and paid her fare, she decided she would give Shaquanna a chance to tell Naheema herself.

# Chapter 11

Mike pulled up to the hospital's garage and pulled inside to park. He couldn't believe that he'd lost his temper again. It was all Shaquanna's doing. If she hadn't called him and told him that Naheema was hugged up and flirting with some guy, he wouldn't have come there and done what he'd done. At first, he started to curse Shaquanna out for even calling him, but something inside him urged him to go. So when he stepped into the apartment and saw some guy touching Naheema's leg, and she was smiling at him, he lost his mind. He should have known it was a setup. That Shaquanna wanted him to see her sister in another light. But he let his pride and guilt from what he was doing get the best of him.

He grabbed the flowers with the balloons and exited his car. He locked the door and walked to the elevator. He took it up the main floor, walked to the information desk, and asked for Naheema's room number. The guard gave him the floor, made him sign in, and handed him a visitor's pass.

Mike made his way over to the elevator and rode it up to the second floor. When he got off the elevator he froze. He started sweating and getting dizzy. The smell on the floor made him deathly sick. He had to go to the side visitor's room to have a seat and collect himself. He hated the smell of hospitals ever since the murder of his little brother.

He was nine and his brother was seven. Their father was fighting with their mother because she was high. Mike Senior was supposed to be taking them for the weekend, but his mother wouldn't let them leave unless their father gave her some money. When he refused, she spit in his face and they fought. Disgusted and frustrated, their father left without them.

Later that night, while their mother was passed out from drinking and smoking crack, Mike snuck out of the apartment. He found the drugs his mother had hidden in the house for another dealer and decided he was going to make some money for him and his brother.

While he was out hustling his little heart away, the young dealer was inside his apartment looking for his missing work. He flipped out when he realized it was gone. The young dealer assumed that Mike's mother had smoked his work, so he began beating her unmercifully. When she couldn't tell him what happened to his drugs, he ran into the kids' room and dragged Mike's little brother out of his bed. He punched, kicked, and slammed the little boy all around the living-room. When he still didn't get the answer he wanted, he pulled out his gun and pointed it at the little boy's head.

After selling all of the drugs, and satisfied with the amount of money he made, Mike ran back to his building. He couldn't wait to get upstairs, wake his brother up, and show him how much money he'd made.

As he made it to the top step, he heard two loud gunshots, then he saw the young dealer running out of his apartment. He almost knocked young Mike down the steps.

With money in hand, Mike ran to his front door, opened it, and screamed. His mother lay in a pool of her own blood, with one shot between her eyes. He walked farther into the living-room and saw his baby brother on the floor with blood coming from his stomach. He rushed over to him, yelling and screaming for him to hold on.

Hearing the screaming coming from next door caused the neighbor to call the police. Mike's family was rushed to Long Island College hospital. His mother was pronounced dead on arrival, while his little brother died during surgery.

From that day forward, the smell of hospitals made him sick.

That memory caused him to shake out of it. He had to pull himself together, if he wanted to visit with Naheema. He sat there for five minutes, taking in deep breaths, inhaling through his nose and exhaling through his mouth, until he calmed down.

The sight of Naheema lying in that bed tugged at his heart. He made a promise to himself at that moment that he would never beat her again. He placed the flowers, card, and balloons on the table beside her bed. Then he pulled a chair up and sat down and just stared at her. She looked so peaceful, the way she was laying there. Although her face was badly bruised, he still thought she was beautiful.

While he sat watching her, her doctor came over to check her vitals and read her chart. He asked Mike who was he to her, and Mike said, "Fiancé."

Mike asked the doctor how Naheema was doing, and the doctor asked Mike to follow him out of the area.

"Okay. How is she?" Mike asked.

"Can I see some identification first, sir?" the doctor asked, a little skeptical about Mike.

"Sure." Mike pulled his identification out of his wallet and handed it to the doctor.

"Well, as you can see, Ms. Morgan was assaulted, and because of the assault, she had a miscarriage. I am so sorry for your loss."

Mike's face said it all. He had no idea Naheema was even pregnant, but the fact that he was responsible for the death of his child hit him hard.

"Doctor, how pregnant was she?" he asked.

"She was three months," the doctor answered.

Mike looked like he wanted to faint. He held onto the desk for support. Seeing that look before, the doctor asked him if he was okay, and Mike told him he was fine. The doctor informed Mike that they were going to keep her for a couple of days before releasing her. He also told Mike that Naheema would be transported to her room within the hour. He asked him if she had any health insurance, and Mike said he would find out and bring it back.

Mike thanked the doctor and went back in the room and sat down.

"Naheema, I am so sorry. I didn't know about our baby. Please forgive me." He kissed her on the forehead then left the hospital and went to Naheema's place to rest.

Naheema was awake, but she pretended to be asleep. She didn't want to see him.

The day that Naheema was supposed to be discharged, she had a high fever, which caused the doctor to draw some more blood and run various tests. After patiently waiting for two hours, she was informed that she had an infection, so she ended up staying two extra days in the hospital. Mike made it his business to visit with her every day she was there.

Dina and Shaquanna came too, but at different times. It seemed like they were trying to avoid each other. When she asked Dina about it, Dina brushed it off as Shaquanna being Shaquanna, and said that it was nothing. But when she questioned Shaquanna about it, she noticed that her sister ignored the question.

As a matter of fact, Shaquanna started acting differently toward her after that. Shaquanna was acting as if she had something to tell Naheema, but didn't know how.

Meanwhile, Mike was trying his hardest to get her to talk to him. After spending one week in the hospital, Naheema was discharged, and Mike was there to pick her up. He drove her home and tended to her every need. He even called her supervisor the day after she was admitted to let them know what happened. He took the hospital notes to her job, and Naheema was able to take a paid leave of absence until she was well enough to return to work.

Mike moved in with Naheema. He'd lied and told her that he had to sell his condo because it had been robbed, when in fact the FBI had raided it, and he was ordered to sell it. He was pissed off because, little by little, his world was falling apart, but he played it off in front of Naheema.

The first month of Mike living with Naheema was great. Their relationship was blossoming, and it was working out well for them. He was home every day, and if he went out, he made sure to call to let her know if he was going to be running late.

Little by little, she allowed him back into her heart. When he was home, he always turned off his cell phone. Naheema loved that about him. He was the man that she'd first met, and she was falling in love with him all over again.

Now that Mike was always home, Naheema was seeing less and less of her sister, and she couldn't understand why. Dina, on the other hand, refused to come to Naheema's apartment as long as Mike was living there. At first, that pissed Naheema off, but the more she thought about, the less it bothered her. That became her excuse to leave the apartment—going to visit Dina.

A week after Naheema returned to work, things between her and Mike started to change and their relationship began to suffer. Mike started hanging out more and more. He was drinking more and began smoking weed. His attitude was starting to change as well. Now, when he came home, he would leave his cell phone on, and it would ring all times of the night, which led them to argue more and more.

The arguments would lead to Mike choking Naheema until she blacked out, or him slapping the taste out of her mouth. Then he would leave and not come home for one or two nights.

Naheema was becoming tired of his shit. She would come home from work and Mike would have some of his boys over at her apartment, smoking weed and drinking Hennessy. She would get off the elevator and smell the weed floating through her apartment. She would walk in and have a serious attitude, and Mike would look at her and just laugh, causing her to flip out. And after his boys left, a fight would ensue.

More and more, Naheema was going to work covering a black eye or busted lip. Her supervisor was starting to notice, and she sent Naheema to a domestic violence retreat. That weekend, Naheema packed up and left for a peaceful weekend away from the drama that was her life.

Mike pitched a fit like he really cared, but deep down inside, he didn't. While Naheema was away trying to get herself together, he was at home having the time of his life. The last shipment of drugs was now being sold throughout the community, and his shop was open again, and was run by a woman he'd been messing with before he met Naheema.

Chyna was operating his shop like it was her own. She loved every minute of it. She got to see more of Mike and was able to fuck him whenever she wanted. She knew he had a woman, but she didn't give a damn.

Chyna had something she knew Naheema didn't have, and that was his baby growing inside of her. She was thrilled when Mike told her he was going to be free this weekend, because that meant she could spend the weekend with him and share the good news.

While Chyna was at the salon making plans about spending the weekend with Mike, Shaquanna was in Flatbush getting her back blown out by Randy. She'd started having sex with him on a regular basis after she went to visit him at his shop. She was really starting to catch feelings for Randy, although she was still sleeping with Mike whenever Naheema wasn't around.

She was ready to end it with Mike and tried to tell him on two different occasions, but she always chickened out.

She and Randy finally planned how they were going to set Mike up. She didn't like the idea of being the bait, but there was nothing she could do about it.

Randy told her that she was going to use her pregnancy to bait Mike in. He told her that all she had to do was tell him that he had to break it off with Naheema, because she was pregnant with his baby. Randy knew Mike wouldn't go for it, so Shaquanna was supposed to threaten him, saying she was going to tell Naheema herself, if he didn't break up with her.

Shaquanna cried as she listened to Randy go over his plan. Mike would kill her if she called herself threatening him with that shit. She really didn't want Mike to know that she was pregnant. She wasn't sure if Mike was really the father, especially since she and Randy where having unprotected sex damn near every day. But that wasn't the problem. She wasn't sure if she was going to even keep the baby.

She tried her hardest to get Randy to change his mind about the plan, but he was adamant, saying they had to do it because it was the only way to make a case stick to him. Randy assured Shaquanna she would be fine, because they would be listening to her through the device she would be wearing. He told her all she had to do was say the safe word, *bananas*, and they would bust in and arrest him.

Shaquanna agreed to do it. They then planned to do it the following weekend.

She and Randy left the shop and went to dinner at Red Lobster on Forty-Second Street in the city. Shaquanna thought over the plan the entire ride into the city. She knew she was going to have to improvise, because she knew in her heart that Randy was just using her as a means to get Mike.

She decided then and there that she was going to cover her ass as well. Before she allowed Mike or Randy to get over on her, she was going to get them first.

After dinner that night, Randy dropped her off in the front of the projects on Clinton Street in Red Hook. She made her way to the back. She really missed seeing her sister, so she headed to Naheema's building.

Mike opened the door to let Chyna into Naheema's apartment. Chyna was impressed with the way the apartment looked. Although it was a step down from the way Mike was living, it would work for what she had planned for them.

Mike was very aggressive with Chyna and wasted no time with foreplay. She attempted to kiss him, but he wouldn't allow it. He pulled her pocketbook away from her and threw it onto the couch. Then he pulled her into the living room and pushed her onto the couch, and she fell back.

As he removed his belt from his waist and unbuckled his pants, she started to protest, but he forced his manhood into her mouth. Chyna knew the game Mike wanted to play, so she went along with him, playing the part of the female servant.

While Chyna was giving Mike a blowjob, Shaquanna was entering Naheema's building. She got on the elevator and rode it up to the eighth floor. She got off the elevator and walked to Naheema's door, where she stood for a while contemplating how she was going to approach her sister. Shaquanna heard a voice coming from the other side of Naheema's door, but it didn't sound like Naheema's. She listened a little longer but didn't hear it again, so she assumed it was coming from another apartment.

Mike felt ready to release, so he pushed Chyna away from him. He told her to get up, strip, and bend over on the couch.

She knew what was coming next and was ready for it.

Mike spit into his hands, rubbed his hand on his dick, then he pushed deep into Chyna's cave.

"Oh yeah!" she screamed.

Mike continued to pound in and out of Chyna, who moaned in pleasure and satisfaction, matching him pump for pump.

As they were about to release, Shaquanna stuck her copy of the key into the door, unlocked it, turned the knob, opened the door, and walked in.

"Oh, God! I'm coming. Oh, God! Yes! Yes!" Chyna screamed.

Shaquanna was shocked. There was Mike and some woman fucking like rabbits on her sister's couch.

Mike looked up and saw Shaquanna standing there, and he smiled before he released inside of Chyna.

"Oh, no! The fuck, you ain't!" Shaquanna yelled, running to them and attacking Chyna first.

She punched Mike in the face, which dazed him for a spell, before she grabbed Chyna's weave and dragged her over the couch. She proceeded to stomp Chyna out.

Chyna attempted to cover her stomach, while Mike sat there laughing at the whole scene.

Chyna was able to get a hold of Shaquanna's foot and flipped her. She climbed on top of Shaquanna and started raining blows on her face.

Mike let them fight for two more minutes before grabbing Chyna off Shaquanna.

"Bitch, you're gonna get yours!" Shaquanna got up. "And, you, you're a good-for-nothing bastard. Where is my sister?"

"Shaquanna, you better get the fuck out of here."

"Yeah, bitch, if you know what's good for you," Chyna echoed.

"Yo, shut the fuck up!" Mike told Chyna. "I don't need a sound piece."

"Or what? You gonna tell my sister that I fucked your sorry ass and got pregnant by you? That shit don't scare me anymore. I'm telling her myself."

"What?" Mike and Chyna asked simultaneously.

"You heard me. Just wait." Shaquanna backed up to the door. "I'm telling her everything."

"I know that bitch did not just say she's pregnant by you, Mike. How the fuck is that possible? I'm fucking pregnant too," Chyna screamed, as she started getting dressed.

Mike looked at the both of them as if they'd lost their minds. He started laughing. He couldn't believe that both of these tricks were trying to trap him. He was even surprised at Shaquanna. She knew better than to talk to him like that.

"You two bitches done lost your fucking minds. Y'all both know I'm not the father of either one of y'all babies. Y'all both"—He pointed his finger at both girls—"can kiss my ass. As a matter of fact, get the fuck out! Chyna, grab your shit and follow Shaquanna out the door to find y'all baby daddies."

Mike grabbed all of Chyna's stuff, grabbed her arm, and pushed her and Shaquanna through the door and slammed it in their faces.

Shaquanna took the stairs down, while Chyna waited for the elevator.

Mike was raging. He threw a glass vase through Naheema's window. He couldn't believe that he'd played himself that way. He knew there was a chance that he was the father. He had to make some changes and fast. He wasn't sure how he was going to do it, but he had to calm both of them down before Naheema found out about it.

After he cleaned up, showered, and dressed, he left the apartment in search of Randy.

Chyna hopped in her car and drove home. She couldn't believe Mike would do that to her and wanted payback.

As soon as she got home, she jumped into the shower and cried. Mike had broken her heart for the last time. She got out, dried off, oiled up, and lay across her bed plotting her next move.

She grabbed her cordless phone and dialed a number she was familiar with. When Mike's lawyer answered the phone, she put her plan in motion.

Within the hour, Mike's lawyer was at Chyna's house lying butt naked on her bed and handcuffed to the post, with the video camera hidden in the closet recording.

Naheema was enjoying herself at the retreat. It was very informative, and she was sad that she would be leaving in the morning. She had no idea what was waiting for her when she returned home.

Sunday morning came, and Naheema boarded the Greyhound bus with a new attitude and plan for her life. Unfortunately, that plan and attitude wouldn't prepare her for the hell she was stepping into.

Naheema came home to a mess. The window in the living room was busted and had gray duct tape all over it. As she walked farther into her apartment, she noticed her end table had been flipped over, and one of the lamps was busted. There were Dutch fillings all over the floor, and two empty bottles of Hennessy lay on the floor next to the couch.

She dropped her bags and started flipping out. "Oh, hell no! What the fuck happened in here?" she screamed, as she began lifting the table up. "Mike! Mike!"

Mike got up with a severe headache, and hearing Naheema in the living room was making his head pound even more. He got up and walked into the living room.

"Naheema, what the fuck are you in here screaming about?" he said, looking at the mess inside of the living room.

"What the fuck happened in here? What did you do?"

Mike held his head, trying to come up with an excuse. "Can you stop fucking yelling?"

"You better tell me what happened in here, and now!" She stepped closer to him.

"Look, I'm sorry about the mess. I had a few friends over last night, and they got a little drunk, and a fight broke out."

"A *little* drunk," she said, sarcastically, her hands on her hips.

"I'll take care of it, I promise. Randy is coming to fix the window for me, so don't worry about that. Let me just get myself together, and I'll clean up in here."

"You better. I don't believe this shit." Naheema grabbed her bags and headed for the bedroom. "I go away for two days, and this is what I come home to."

Mike walked behind her and went into the bathroom to wash up. He turned on the shower and jumped in.

Naheema entered her room and was knocked back by the smell of stale sex and alcohol. She dropped her bags and began searching her bed for signs of another woman being there.

Mike screamed for her to bring him a towel, but she ignored him.

She frantically searched her bed, pulling the covers and sheets off. When she didn't see anything, she dropped to her knees and checked under her bed. Right in her face laid an open condom wrapper. Her heart began to race, and her hands began to shake, as tears spilled out of her eyes. She used Mike's sock to pick up the condom and placed the sock and condom on the nightstand as she stood up.

She looked on her mattress and noticed a small amount of blood on the sheets. She picked up the sheet and inspected it, as Mike came out of the bathroom dripping wet.

Mike stepped into the room. "You didn't hear me calling you to bring me my towel?"

"You no-good, dirty bastard! How could you?" Naheema threw the sheet at him.

"What the fuck are you talking about?" he yelled, grabbing his towel to dry off.

She picked up the sock with the used condom inside and threw it in his face. "You fucked another bitch in my bed?"

"Naheema, you're bugging. Throw something else in my face, and I'm going to hurt you up in here."

"Do it then! Do it! You can't hurt me any more than you already have. I hate you! You are one sorry bastard!"

Naheema swung with all of her might and hit Mike square in the face.

As blood began to pour out of his nose, he looked like he was ready to kill her. He wiped the blood from his nose, balled up his fist, and knocked Naheema into the closet. Then he jumped on her and started banging her head against the closet.

Mike grabbed her by the neck, picked her up, and threw her on the bed like a rag doll. He blacked out and began choking the life out of Naheema, who was yelling and fighting him back, clawing at his hands and pulling skin.

When his cell phone rang, he finally came to. He looked down and realized that he almost caught a body. He released Naheema and slid off the bed.

"I'm sorry, baby. I'm sorry," Mike said over and over again.

"Get out! It's over!"

"Baby, I'm sorry." Mike tried to touch her face, now swollen with welts and bruises from his abuse.

Naheema finally caught her breath and sat up completely. "That's it. I can't do this anymore. I want you to leave."

"I'm sorry. Listen, I'm going to give you some space."

"No, I want you to leave! Get the fuck out of my house! I hate you, you sorry bastard! Just leave! It's over!"

Mike knew he couldn't leave Naheema like this. He knew he was wrong for putting his hands on her, but he couldn't believe she'd hit him. He knew she needed to calm down, so he got dressed.

He looked at Naheema again. He walked over to her and started kissing her.

Naheema tried to pull away, but he grabbed her hands and turned her around. Then he bent her over with her back facing him and her hands on the bed.

Naheema tried to stop him, but Mike grabbed both of her arms and pulled them behind her. With his left hand, he held both of her wrists together, and with his right, he lifted her skirt and ripped her panties. Then he positioned himself directly behind her and pushed in with all his might, forcing himself straight into her.

Naheema shrieked from the pain, but soon the pain turned into unadulterated pleasure as Mike slowly moved around in circles, pushing in and out of her, while massaging her nipples and playing with her clit. She started to feel a hot sensation overcome her.

Slowly Mike slid back inside her, making sure his dick reached her G-spot. He grabbed her left leg and put her foot up on the bed.

Naheema moaned again. "Ooh, yeah, right there."

"Right there, baby?"

"Ooh, yeah, right there."

Mike was ready to come, so he let Naheema's left hand fall to the bed as he grabbed her ass and squeezed her ass cheeks together, causing friction. The feeling caused him to dig deeper and deeper into her abyss. He felt her walls tighten around his head. He knew he had to make her come now, or he would explode, so he continued to grind deeper into her.

"Ooh, daddy! Ooh, daddy!"

Mike started slapping her ass again and again, each hit harder than the first, while he grinded his hips in a circular motion.

Naheema was ready to explode. Mike had never made love to her like this before. It felt so good, the way he was grinding in and out of her spot. It was like he was performing a dance inside her. She touched her wetness and licked her fingers. She knew it was time.

Mike felt her walls tighten around his dick, so he went in for the kill. He started to fuck her harder, and with each push, he made Naheema come with an explosion. Mike felt her walls tighten even more, and he exploded into her with his own orgasm.

"Ahh! Ahh! Ahh!" he moaned.

After they made love, Mike continued to apologize to Naheema, stressing how sorry he was, and asking her to forgive him, but Naheema refused to answer. Mike got up, went into the bathroom, and cleaned himself up. He went into the living room and began to clean up.

Naheema lay on her bed crying and in pain. She was tired of Mike and his ways. He changed so much. She was ready to walk away from the relationship. She got up, looked around her room, and cried. She left the room, walked into the bathroom, turned on the shower, stripped off the rest of her clothes, and got in.

Mike's cell phone rang again, and he answered. It was Randy informing him that the block and spot were raided and that they were in jail. Mike told Randy not to worry, and that he was calling the lawyer to inform him of the situation.

Randy explained that he would be seeing the judge in the morning, so Mike needed to make sure the lawyer came to see him today, so he could get a bail set.

Mike said that he would and he hung up. He looked around the living room and saw it was clean, so he walked to the back to let Naheema know he had to make a run. He stepped into the bathroom and saw the bruises on Naheema's back.

When she turned to face him, he saw that her face was beginning to swell around her right eye and lips. He felt like shit.

"Baby, I'm so sorry. Why did you swing at me?"

"What?"

"You know how I am. All you had to do was talk to me."

"You had another woman in my apartment, in my bed, and you want me to be calm about that?"

"You're wrong, Naheema."

"Really? So that wasn't a used condom in that sock, and there isn't blood on my sheets? Are you saying that I'm making this up?"

"No, you're not, but that condom isn't mine. That's why the house looked the way it looked. My boy snuck some bitch in our room and fucked her. I caught them and dragged his ass out of the room. We fought, and then I kicked him out."

"Whatever."

"Naheema, I'm not lying to you. I promise I would never disrespect you or us like that. I know I've done some foul things in the past, but I thought we got over that."

"All right, Mike."

"Baby, I have to make a run. Randy got knocked this morning, so I have to go to the shop to get some money to give to the lawyer. I should be back in an hour or two."

"Okay."

"Maybe we can go and do something today. I really missed you. Don't go away again. I don't think I can deal with that." Mike kissed her and left the bathroom.

"Yeah, I'll try," she said, wishing he would just leave already.

Naheema wrapped herself in her towel and left the bathroom. She went into her room, oiled up, and threw on some sweat pants and a T-shirt. She looked at the sheets again and shook her head. In her mind, she knew Mike was lying, but her heart was telling her to give him a chance.

As she began to clean up her room, Mike made a call to the lawyer. He got the lawyer's voicemail, so he left him a message telling him about Randy. Then he hung up and left the apartment.

# Chapter 12

Randy phoned Shaquanna and told her that he'd made the call to Mike about being locked up. He told her that he was going to see the judge on Monday and that he needed her to come to court for him. He didn't tell her that Mike was going to be there as well. He wanted things to heat up.

Everything was now coming to a close with his investigation. They had over four witnesses who were willing to turn state's evidence.

Dina's cousin was happy to turn state's evidence against Mike, after finding out that Mike wanted him dead. Dina was happy as well. Her family had been put through hell when they assumed her cousin was dead. Then, when the detectives came to them and told them the story of the hit on their family member's life, they were ecstatic to know he was still alive. But, for the sake of their case, they were asked to keep up the pretense of him being dead. Dina's family gladly agreed, so she couldn't wait for the day when she would witness Mike's end.

Shaquanna was thrilled as well. She was getting an abortion on Tuesday, thanks to Randy, who gave her the money to get it done. She was also happy because she knew that by Wednesday Mike would be locked up, which meant she wouldn't have to tell Naheema that she'd been sleeping with him or that she'd gotten pregnant by him. But she did plan to tell Naheema about the girl who was at her house. She just had to figure out a way to switch the truth a little.

Meanwhile, Chyna had her own little thing going to get back at Mike. She was planning to hit him where it hurt—in his pockets. She was sleeping with his lawyer, and had begun taping her sessions with him.

Mike's lawyer was a married white man living high off drug dealers. He lived in the suburbs in a nice mini-mansion overlooking the city, with the white picket fence, two children, and a dog.

Chyna knew his wife would destroy him if she found out about him and his secret sex life, so she made it her business to tape him every time he came over.

A freak of nature, Mike's lawyer liked to be manhandled and dominated by Chyna and for her to strap on her ten-inch Mandingo dildo and rape him.

Chyna used that to get what she wanted, and since Mike's lawyer knew all about his finances, she made it her business to know it too. Mike's lawyer talked a lot and told more than he should have. With the information at her fingertips, it was time for Chyna to put her plan in motion.

She made a compilation of the tapes, showing the lawyer in very compromising positions, and mailed it to his law firm. She knew that by Monday she would be a very rich bitch, all thanks to Mike and his lawyer. She laughed to herself every time she thought about how rich she was going to be. She was going to make Mike pay for taking her heart and breaking it into a million tiny pieces.

When Mike pulled up to the corner of Lorraine and Columbia Streets, he smelled smoke and assumed that somebody's apartment was on fire. As he drove down the block, he noticed the fire trucks, police, and ambulance on the corner of West 9th and Columbia. He parked in front of the building where his drug spot was and got out to walk the rest of the way to his shop.

As he got closer, he noticed a small crowd of people standing around looking at the buildings on the left side of his shop, which were badly burnt from the fire. He began to walk a little faster until he made it to his shop, and was in shock at the destruction. His shop was burnt to the ground. He wanted to die. Everything was gone, which meant that all of his money and drugs burned in the fire. He stood there feeling like his world was finally crumbling.

He pushed his way through the crowd to get a better look. He overheard a cop and fireman talking. The cop asked the fire inspector if it was an accident, and the fire inspector said no. The fire inspector told the cop that this was arson; that someone had deliberately poured gasoline all over the place and lit a match.

The cop asked the fire inspector where the fire started, and the fire inspector told him that the fire started in the shop.

The cop looked around. "I'd hate to be the owner of this shop."

The fire inspector looked at the cop and said, "Who are you telling?"

Mike put his head down. He waited with the rest of the crowd to see if anything else was going to happen, and sure enough, two detectives walked out of the burnt shop, called over their captain, and began to talk.

Mike heard a little of what they were saying. Apparently, they'd found a safe inside. The safe had been cracked opened, and stashed inside were twenty pounds of cocaine and eight pounds of weed. Mike was stunned. The detectives had never mentioned the money. He knew there was over a hundred thousand dollars in that safe. Someone had stolen the money from the safe before setting the shop on fire. And only two people had the combination and a copy of the key to the safe. One was Randy, who was in jail, and the other was the lawyer.

He turned around and pushed back through the crowd and made a hasty departure to his car, where he pulled out his cell phone to call his lawyer again. He got the voicemail and left a threatening message to the lawyer. He jumped into his car and began yelling and banging on the steering wheel.

After he calmed down, he picked up his phone again and dialed Chyna's number. She answered on the second ring. Mike told her that he needed to see her, that it was urgent.

He backed out of the parking spot, made a right turn, and drove straight down past his shop. He jumped onto the BQE heading towards the Prospect expressway. He was headed for some extra relief.

Mike parked in the driveway of Chyna's house. He turned off his engine and sat in his car. He looked at the time. It was going on twelve in the afternoon. He'd promised Naheema he would call her if he was running late. He figured he still had an hour left, so he jumped out of the car, slammed the door shut, and walked up the steps to Chyna's house.

Since Chyna was expecting him, he let himself into the house. He closed and locked the house door. He walked through the foyer, pushing the door open to enter into her living room.

Chyna's house was exceptional. Her parents had passed away some years ago and left it for her. It was paid for, so all she had to do was pay the taxes on the property, pay the gas, light, and water bills, and keep the grounds up.

Mike loved walking through Chyna's house. As he passed the living room, he looked to his left and saw that the dining room furniture was covered with a tarp. *She must be having repairs done.* As he walked up the steps, he stopped to look into her kitchen, which was also covered with a plastic tarp. He walked up a second flight of steps and made a left.

Her house was really huge for only one person. On the first floor of the house, she had a living room, den, dining room, bathroom, and kitchen. Before her parents had passed, they'd turned their basement into an apartment for Chyna to move into, but that never happened.

Chyna had two ways to get into her room without her parents seeing her. She and Mike used to enter through the backyard door and take the back stairs up to her room. On her floor were three bedrooms. Her father had turned one of those rooms into a gym for her, and the other room was an entertainment room for her and her company. The biggest room on that floor was her bedroom. Her father had made a full bathroom inside her room, and for her guest, there was a separate bathroom on the outside of her room.

The third floor was where her parents slept, and there was a full bathroom on that floor as well.

Chyna was living large and Mike loved it, but he couldn't see himself living there. He entered Chyna's bedroom to find her laid out across her bed butt naked. He knew that he didn't have time to play with her. He only came there to get some information from her and to tell her about the fire, but as he stood there watching her finger herself and licking those juicy lips, he instantly caught a hard-on.

Chyna stared at him watching her. She kept licking her lips, sensing that she had his full attention. She slipped her hands down her neck and onto her breasts, rubbing and caressing her nipples. Then she slid her right hand down to her pussy and resumed fingering herself.

Mike walked over to the bed as he unbuckled his belt. Just watching her made him want to explode. He grabbed her by her ankles and pulled her to the end of the bed and stood her up so that her clit was facing him. Mike pulled her sex to his face and had dessert. He teased her by licking the opening of her wetness, gliding his tongue up and down the walls of her kitty-cat, and listening to her purr as he sucked and nibbled on her clit.

Chyna grabbed the back of Mike's head and pushed his face deep into her forest "Yes, baby, yes!" she screamed.

"Like that?"

"Shush! Don't talk. Just finish," Chyna moaned.

Mike continued to nibble on her fat, juicy clit.

"Agh, baby, yeah, right there," Chyna said in short breaths. "Ahh! Ooh! I'm-I'm coming! Um! Um!" And she came all over Mike's face.

Mike softly pushed Chyna off the bed and grabbed her by her hair. He whispered in her ear, "Pull the pillows to the end of the bed and stack them up."

Chyna did as she was told.

Mike spread her ass cheeks apart and pushed himself deep into her asshole. Chyna gave a little moan and, being the champ she was, gave him all of her.

Mike continued to ride Chyna like a bat out of hell, and after several minutes, he released his nut in her ass. He smeared the rest of his sweet come on her ass as he pulled out.

Chyna stood and started to whistle. "That was fun," she said, sitting up on the bed and facing him. "Now what was so important that you had to rush over here?"

Mike sat up on the bed, after propping the pillows up behind him. "So it's like that now?"

"Don't get me wrong. I'm glad you came. As you can see, I was about to have my own little party, but I'm glad I wasn't alone."

"Well, listen. Some serious shit went down with the shop. It was set on fire."

"What? Mike, stop fucking playing with me."

"I'm serious, but that's not the problem."

"What? What is it?"

"The cops found the safe with the drugs in it. Now I have a serious question for you. What happened to my money?"

"Why the fuck are you asking me? I don't know."

Mike sensed her nervousness. "Chyna, be honest with me. That's a lot of money that's not accounted for, and I want it back."

"Mike, I'm telling you the truth. I don't have the combination to that safe. Remember, I never had a use for it. All of the money for shop went deposited into the bank to cover the taxes for the property, the bills, and the salaries. That's all I dealt with."

"Well, I'm going to need a copy of the books. I need to check the balance."

"Okay, but I will have to get it for you. I don't have them here with me." Chyna got off the bed.

"What the fuck you mean, you don't have them here?" Mike grabbed her wrist and pulled her back on the bed.

"Mike, please . . . You're hurting me," she said, trying to remove his hand from her wrist.

"This ain't nothing if you're playing with me." Mike applied pressure, bending her wrist.

"Ouch! I'm not playing. I purchased a safety deposit box from the bank and placed all of the important papers in there, so nothing would happen to them. Please, Mike . . . You're going to break my wrist."

Mike held on to her wrist a little while longer before releasing it. "I'm sorry. I'm stressed right now. Everything is going to hell, and I—look, I'm sorry." He got up. "Listen, can I take a shower here before I leave?"

"Sure. I'll turn it on for you," she said, rubbing her wrist.

Chyna left the bedroom and entered her bathroom. She closed the door and took a few deep breaths. She looked inside of the vanity mirror dresser drawer to make sure her plane ticket was there. She pulled her notebook over it, just in case Mike decided to go snooping. She turned on the shower and walked back into the bedroom.

"It's ready. I'll be in with you in one minute."

Mike walked past her and went into the bathroom. She waited another minute to make sure he was in the shower, and after seeing that the coast was clear, she went into her dresser drawer, retrieved a small package, and walked over to where Mike's jacket lay. She opened the jacket, placed the small package in the inside pocket, and put it back on the chair the way he had it.

Then she opened his phone, went through the numbers, found Naheema's home number, wrote it down on a piece of paper, and placed the paper under her pillow. She then walked to the bathroom and climbed into the shower with Mike.

Chyna grabbed the soap and started soaping Mike's back. She turned him around to face her and continued to wash his body, starting with his chest, rubbing down his stomach, and ending at his dick.

Mike was hard and ready to fuck again, so Chyna got on her knees and let the water rinse the soap off his dick while she licked his balls. Mike leaned his head back and let the water flow over his body.

Chyna stood, licked his neck, and traveled down his chest, slowly making circles with her tongue as she reached his navel. She sucked on his navel and slid down until she was back on her knees. She licked the vein protruding from his balls to the head of his dick, slowly teasing the head, placing her tongue around the head.

"Mmm! Mmm!" Mike moaned. "I'm about to come."

Chyna deep-throated him and swallowed all of his little soldiers.

"Damn, girl! You're trying to kill me?"

"No, I'm not. I just missed you. I wanted to let you know that I want to be with you. I think you should come home to me and our child. I want you to myself. I'm tired of sharing you with Naheema. I was here first, Mike, and I'm tired of playing second fiddle to all of these other bitches."

Mike didn't respond. He finished washing up and got out of the shower. Chyna got out right after him, and they both got dressed.

"Mike, look. We need to talk," she said, standing with her hands on her hips.

"Talk about what, Chyna?"

"I'm pregnant; you know that."

"By who?"

"By you! Who else would I be pregnant by?"

Mike looked up at her for the first time, and laughed. "You really want me to answer that?"

"Oh, hell fucking no! I know you're not trying to play me," she said, moving her head from left to right, while talking with her hands.

Mike didn't say anything. He leaned over to finish tying his boots when his cell phone went off. He went to grab the phone, but Chyna got to it first and answered.

"Mike?" Naheema asked, surprised at the female's voice.

"This ain't Mike, bitch! Who the fuck is this?"

Before Naheema could answer, Mike grabbed Chyna by the hair and punched her in the face.

Naheema heard a female screaming wildly in the background, and then the line went dead.

"Bitch, what the fuck is wrong with you?" Mike yelled. "Didn't I tell yo' stupid ass not to play no fuckin' games with me? I put this on my gangster. If that was wifey on my jack, I'ma beat you like a fucking runaway slave."

"Fuck you, muthafucka! Don't no nigga put their fucking hands on me!" As she was yelling, she started running toward Mike, ready to fight.

Mike took a step back, threw a hard jab, and busted her bottom lip.

Chyna reached for her mouth and felt the warm blood pouring out of her mouth. "Fuck you, Mike! I don't need you, nigga. And, oh yeah, it was that sorry-ass bitch Naheema. By the time I get finished telling her how we fucked and sucked each other to sleep, your bitch ass going to be looking for a new place to live, nigga." Chyna gave him a sadistic smile, wiping the blood from her mouth.

Mike leaped forward and grabbed her by the throat.

By the time she realized he had her by the throat and was going to choke the life out of her, it was too late. She had to do something quick before this nigga killed her.

Mike saw the fear in her eyes and sensed her death was near, so he loosened his grip. Killing this hood rat wasn't even an option. He wasn't going to do twenty-five years in prison for killing this gangbang groupie. He let go, got up, grabbed his jacket, and headed for the front door.

As he was opening the door, Chyna threw a glass vase at his head. She would have knocked his ass the fuck out, had he been two inches to the left.

Mike turned around to look at her. She wasn't worth his time. He laughed. "You're a dumb-ass bitch, and a real easy fuck," he said before slamming her door.

Mike knew he had fucked up bad this time. He should've gone straight home after checking out his shop, but his dick wouldn't let him. Now he had to try to explain the situation to Naheema. But first he had to get to his car and call her to see if it was safe to go home.

After Mike left her place, Chyna had to make a hasty escape. Between the missing money, burning down the shop, and the doctored books, she knew she was in a lot of trouble. Not only did she steal the money, thanks to the help of Mike's drunken lawyer giving her the combination and his copy of the key, but once Mike made it home, she was going to rock his world. She was going to call Naheema and let her know what she thought about her, and drop a bombshell on her world as well.

She cleaned herself up, got dressed, and pulled her suitcase from under her bed. She began packing very lightly, knowing that with the money she had already, she could shop once she made it to the Caribbean. She laughed out loud because she would have the last laugh. This time, she would make Mike regret the day he broke her heart for the last time.

As she sat on her bed and waited for the cab to come, she decided to give Mike a call and apologize to him for what she did—just another part of her game plan. She dialed his number and waited for him to pick up.

He answered on the second ring. "What the fuck do you want?"

"Look, Mike, I was only calling because I wanted to apologize. I am truly sorry for everything. I hope you can forgive me."

"Don't be. You can't help it 'cause you're a sorry bitch. It's over. Lose my number, bitch." *Click.*

Chyna knew that what she was about to do was the right thing for her. Mike was going to suffer the wrath of a woman scorned.

# Chapter 13

Mike knew he'd fucked up with Naheema for the last time. She was going to kill him. He was already an hour late, and he didn't call her to let her know it. He'd lost track of time. He was flying on the Prospect Expressway back to Red Hook. The speed he was driving at, he expected to be pulled over, but he was grateful that didn't happen.

He parked in front of South Brooklyn Health Clinic and sat there for a minute, trying to figure out what to do next. He knew he could lie about the call and say it was one of the workers at the salon, or his boy's girlfriend, but he didn't know if those excuses were going to be good enough. But the worst part was that Chyna was still claiming to be pregnant with his child. He knew that she was going to be a problem if he didn't take care of this situation.

"Damn. Damn. If I force this bitch to get an abortion, she's going to cause drama, and if she keeps it, I know damn well she's going to want me to be in their life." He said to himself.

He looked up at Naheema's building, thinking about all of the hurt he'd caused her and knew that if he told her the real truth about this situation, there was no way he would ever get her back.

"Fuck!" he screamed, banging on his steering wheel. "Fuck it. I'm going to get rid of this bitch, once and for all."

As Mike sat downstairs in his car, Naheema was upstairs fuming. She went into her room and began pulling Mike's clothes from the closet and throwing them in a pile on the floor in the hallway. She already knew he was going to come home and try to give her some type of bullshit excuse why some bitch had answered his cell phone, but she wasn't going to fall for it this time. She knew Mike was fucking around, but she never thought he would be stupid enough to let his bitch answer his cell phone.

Mike walked into the apartment at the same time Naheema's house phone rang. Naheema ran into the living room to answer it, but he got to the phone first.

"Hello?" he answered.

"Can I speak to Naheema?" Dina asked.

"Who is this?"

"It's Dina. Is she there?"

"Yeah, but she'll call you back." Mike hung up the phone in Dina's ear.

The look on Naheema's face told Mike that he might as well save his lies for another day, but he didn't let that look affect him.

Naheema took her house phone off the base and carried it with her into her bedroom.

Mike followed her and saw all of his clothes piled into a corner on the floor in front of the bedroom. "Naheema, what the fuck are you doing?" he asked, forgetting he'd just messed up.

"Spring muthafuckin' cleaning. I'm getting rid of shit I don't need, don't use, and damn sure no longer want in my closet," she said, hands on her hips.

"Naheema, stop playing with me. Why is my clothes on the floor?"

Mike closed the bedroom door.

"Ask the bitch who answered your phone. Ask her why is your shit on the floor." Naheema was moving her head from left to right, rolling her eyes and pointing at him. "Better yet, ask that bitch to come and get your shit out of my apartment before Goodwill come and get it!"

"There you go again accusing me of something. What is wrong with you? Are you that insecure that every time I have to make a move, you think I'm with a bitch?" he said, looking at her, and stepping closer to her. "Naheema, I thought you were smarter than that."

"Oh, no! The fuck, you didn't! You have a lot of muthafuckin' nerve to come at me like that. You know what? Fuck you, Mike! It's over. I want you to get this shit out of my place. Now!"

Naheema went back into the closet, pulled more clothes from the hangers, and threw them on the floor.

"Naheema, I swear, if I didn't love you, I would kill you in here." Mike grabbed her from behind. "Stop tripping. Listen, you need to calm down and let me tell you what's going on."

She screamed at the top of her lungs, "Get the fuck off of me!"

"I will, but first calm down."

"What, Mike? You have two minutes to lie about why another bitch answered your phone, and then I want you to get the fuck out of my place and my life forever." She sat down on the bed.

Mike took a deep breath. He told Naheema about everything—about Randy getting locked up, about his shop being burnt down, about the money stolen from the shop. He explained to her that he went to see the young lady who ran the shop for him to get a copy of the books, but she claimed that she had them in a safe. He explained that he almost broke her arm because he felt she was lying, but when the young lady explained to him that because it was a weekend and she wouldn't be able to get into the bank's safe until Monday, he had to apologize to the girl.

He told Naheema that before he left to come home, he'd asked to use her bathroom, and when he was in the bathroom, the young lady picked up his phone. That's why Naheema heard him arguing with her. Mike explained that he told the young girl she had until tomorrow morning to get his books and bring them to her.

Naheema didn't know whether to believe him or not, although the story sounded plausible. She sat there for a while contemplating if she should believe it.

Mike watched Naheema go through the motions. He knew he had her going with that story. "How about we go and get something to eat?"

"I'm not hungry," she said.

"Well, let's go to the movies. I need to clear my mind."

"Fine. Whatever."

"Cool. Let me jump in the shower first. I can smell the smoke from the fire on my clothes. I'll be ready in ten minutes."

"Whatever."

"Go put on something sexy for me, so I can show you off to the world." He laughed, opening the bedroom door to walk out. "Naheema, I really do love you." Then he left the bedroom to go into the bathroom.

Naheema rolled her eyes. "Yeah. I bet you do."

While Mike was in the shower, the house phone rang. Naheema answered it on the second ring, "Hello?"

"Hello. Can I speak to Naheema?"

"This is her. Who's this?"

"My name is Chyna."

"Okay." Naheema was becoming impatient. "How do I know you?"

"Look . . . you don't know me, but I know all about you."

"Really? And how is that?" Naheema asked with a serious attitude.

"I'm calling to tell you about Mike."

"What about Mike?"

"Look, I didn't call to pick a fight with you. I just thought you might want to know what your man has been up to behind your back."

"Well, here is your chance," Naheema said, walking into her bedroom.

"Listen, Mike and I have been fucking around with each other off and on since public school, and I just wanted you to know this," Chyna said as calmly as she possibly could.

"Really? So you're calling me out of the kindness of your heart?"

"Look, Naheema, it's no need for you to cop an attitude with me. You need to check your man because, like I said, I was with him first."

"Really? I should check him off of your word? Bitch, I don't even know who the fuck you are, and you expect me to believe you? Show me some proof."

"I'll let that slide, but if it's proof you want, then it's proof you shall receive. By the way, you have a lovely little apartment over there in Red Hook. I especially like the black leather sofa that Mike and I have sex on. Oh, and that picture of you on the wall is fabulous. Red is definitely your color. Oh yeah, did Mike tell you we were rudely interrupted by a female you know very well walking into your apartment?" Chyna smiled to herself.

"You know what," Naheema yelled, "fuck you!"

"No, thank you, but I really enjoyed fucking my man. And, apparently, your sister likes fucking him too. I don't know if she or Mike told you, but he's expecting from both of us." Chyna laughed. "I knew that would get you. Like I said, I didn't call to fuck with you, but since you want to be a bitch about it, I figured I'd be the one to bust your bubble with the news."

"What?" Naheema was floored. She couldn't believe what this chick was telling her, and didn't know what to say.

"What part don't you understand? I'm pregnant, and your sister is pregnant by Mike."

"You're lying!" Naheema's hands were shaking.

"Lying? Lying for what? You don't have to believe a word I say, so I will give you another piece of proof. Look in the inside pocket of his coat for the proof. I left a little present for you. As a matter of fact, it will be the present of a lifetime, bitch. Oh yeah, make sure to tell Mike I said thanks for the money and that I'm sorry he wasn't 'sleep inside of the shop when I torched that bitch." Chyna hung up the phone.

Mike got out of the shower and entered the bedroom just as Naheema was hanging up the phone.

She jumped up in his face and yelled, "You hateful black bastard! That's it! I want you out of this fucking house now!"

"Calm the fuck down, and tell me what the fuck happened first. What are you screaming about now?"

"Like you don't fucking know already. Get the fuck out! Better yet, give me your jacket."

"Naheema, you need to calm the fuck down . . . seriously."

"I'm not going to ask you again, muthafucka. Where is your fucking jacket?"

"Yo, who the fuck are you talking to like that? You need to calm yo' ass down before I fuck yo' ass up in here." Mike took a fresh pair of boxers from the dresser and put them on.

Naheema noticed Mike's jacket on the floor. Mike saw what she was looking at, but she was closer to it than he was. She ran for the jacket as Mike tried to jump across the bed and get it first. But he landed the wrong way and twisted his ankle.

As Naheema picked up the jacket, her hands shook from nervousness. She prayed that Chyna's nasty words weren't true.

All Mike could do was wince in pain and wait. He didn't think her looking in his jacket would cause any harm, because he didn't have any numbers or condoms in his pockets. But he still couldn't help but wonder why she wanted it.

After looking through all of his pockets on the outside of the jacket, Naheema went to check the inside pocket. She felt something there. She took the package out of his pocket and looked at Mike for a while before opening it.

Mike was getting nervous. He didn't remember putting anything inside that pocket. Then it hit him. *That bitch Chyna.* He had to find a way to get Naheema to give him the package.

Naheema unfolded the letter attached to the package and started reading it out loud.

*My dearest Mike,*

*From the time we first met, I knew we would be lovers. I never expected our relationship to last so long without some kind of commitment. I surely didn't expect that we would be ending this way either, but that's life. Right, baby? We've been through a lot of ups and downs in our relationship, but I never thought in my wildest dreams that you would make me your sideline ho for that chick. I know you told me about her, but you also said that y'all were having a lot of problems, so I figured eventually you would leave her alone. I knew in my heart that if I stuck it out with you, you would come to your senses and leave her.*

*I was hurt when you took her on that trip to the Bahamas, because you promised it would be us there, but I forgave you when you came home with that diamond necklace and ring set. You blew me away when you got on your knees to put that ring on my finger. I just knew we would be fine then, but a week later, we were back to the way things were. You stopped calling me and returning my calls. You stopped coming around as much as you did in the beginning. I was seeing less and less of you. Then months later, you pop up out of nowhere, and we picked up right where we left off, as if you never left. When you* surprised me with the lease to the shop, I thought you were teasing me, until you showed me that the shop was now in my name. I just knew that this was finally it. I was so happy.

You stole my heart that night when you decided to stop using condoms because you said you were ready to start our family. Mike, at that moment, there wasn't anything you could do wrong in my eyes.

But then, you started changing again. You went back to your old ways, pulling the disappearing acts again, even though I would see you at the shop. But it wasn't the same. It was like you only came to the shop when you wanted to get a nut off. I was becoming tired of that shit.

Then you decided to invite me to Naheema's house for the weekend. I had it all planned out. I wanted to celebrate with you that weekend the fact that we did it. Baby, my sweet, sexy, chocolate baby, we have created a child who will look exactly like us, but then that chick's sister opened the door and walked in. I knew then that it was over. I couldn't believe my ears. You were fucking that girl's sister and got her pregnant as well. How could you be so fucking stupid?

I trusted you. I believed in you. I believed when you said that you were leaving Naheema, but after that night, I knew it was all lies. I knew it was finally over, that I had to get away from you. When you put me out that night, you crushed my heart for the last time. So I decided to even out the odds.

I finally took your lawyer up on his offer and went out on a date with him. You know that your lawyer is a real freak behind closed doors. I really enjoyed getting to know him. But he was only a means to an end.

Apparently, your lawyer can't hold his liquor either. After getting him nice and drunk, he gave up the combination to your safe and the copy of the key to me. Unfortunately, he won't remember doing it. So, after he left Friday night, I went to the shop, took what

*I could, and burnt the rest. Oh yeah, don't worry about the rest of the money. I have that too. You know, for support for our child. He or she may want to go to college in the future, or private school.*

*So I am thanking you now in advance for all of your support. Oh yeah, I also left a nice little present for the missus. I figured that after I called her and told her about me, our baby, and the fact that you've been fucking her sister, who by the way is also pregnant with your child, that she wouldn't believe me. So I made sure I put some proof inside of your pocket, while you were in the shower earlier. Let's see you lie your way out of this one.*

*Smooches,*

*xoxoxo*

*Chyna Doll*

*P.S.*

*By the time you call yourself coming to get me, I will be long gone. Oh yeah, Mike, you better be careful, because the cops will want to question you about the drugs stashed inside of the safe, seeing that the lease is back in your name. Your lawyer helped me with that also. Tell him that I said thank you. Naheema, I am sorry that you had to find out this way, but I knew that lying bastard wouldn't be man enough to tell you the truth. Your best bet is to get him out of your apartment. I pray that you weren't stupid enough to put him on your lease, 'cause if you did, then you'll be living with that sister of yours and your nephew/stepson. Good luck.*

Mike could only stare in shock when Naheema finished reading the letter.

Naheema placed the letter on the bed and reached for the pregnancy test. She slowly took apart the packaging to find a pregnancy test with two pink lines. She already knew what that meant—*positive*—because she'd taken the same test last month and gotten the same results.

She calmly got up and walked over to Mike, who'd started to pull himself together getting dressed. He didn't know what to expect from her.

"How could you? You sorry son of a bitch! I tried to trust and believe in you, and this is my reward? You not only fucked another bitch and got her pregnant, but you was fucking my sister and she's pregnant too? Get the fuck out, you dirty, good-for-nothing, sorry black muthafucka. Get out before I cut off your dick, feed it to you, and mail you your balls while you're in the hospital," Naheema said through clenched teeth. "And you gave that bitch the lease to the shop? You lied. You fucked that bitch in my house. In my house! How could you? I hate you!"

Mike grabbed the letter and Chyna's pregnancy test. He knew it wouldn't be wise to say anything right now. He had to go to Chyna's place to see if she was bluffing about leaving. He was going to murder her.

He turned around to see Naheema with tears streaming down her face. "I'm sorry," he said.

But from the look in Naheema's eyes, he knew it was too little, too late, so he walked out the door.

# Chapter 14

Naheema packed all of Mike's clothing into garbage bags. She'd had enough of the bullshit. Normally she would have given him a chance to explain, but there was no explanation to change the fact that this lying, two-faced, grimy motherfucker cheated on her with her sister and some bitch, and then was stupid enough to get them pregnant. She felt so stupid for trusting him and for believing he could change and want a family.

There she was, pregnant again, and this bitch Chyna was talking about she was pregnant too. She was going to kill her sister. How could her own flesh and blood do that to her, after everything she did for her when that no-good father of theirs put her out? Then she worked overtime to help Shaquanna pay for her apartment.

Naheema was beyond hurt. She really didn't care about Chyna, because that female had no loyalty to her. She was more concerned with Shaquanna, her own flesh and blood.

Naheema felt like shit, because her own mother told her to stay away from Shaquanna, telling her that just because they were half-sisters and had the same daddy didn't mean they had to be friends. Her mother had warned her that Shaquanna was just like her mother and that she would eventually hurt Naheema.

But Naheema didn't want to believe it. She'd argued with her mother about it, and now look.

She felt nasty and disgusted. She was going to have to take an AIDS test—along with every other test known to man—to make sure his stupid ass didn't transmit anything to her. She started screaming in her apartment. "Why? How could you do this to me?"

She picked up her house phone and dialed her sister's number, but the phone went straight to voicemail.

"You dirty, lying fucking whore. How could you fuck my man and get pregnant by him? Are you that desperate for a man that you're willing to sleep with my man, or are you just that jealous of me? I hate you, Shaquanna. You better pray I don't catch up with your simple ass. It's on." Then she hung up.

Naheema cried her eyes out. She sat there wondering who else knew about Mike and Shaquanna. The longer she sat there, the madder she became.

Just as she got up to go back to her bedroom, there was a knock at her door.

"One minute!" she yelled.

Quickly she headed to the bathroom, washed her face, and then she walked over to the front door.

"Who is it?" she asked, before looking through the peephole.

"Dina."

She unlocked the door and let Dina in. "I was just getting ready to call you."

Dina stepped into the apartment and walked straight toward the living room.

Naheema locked the door and followed her.

"What's up? I called you earlier. How come you didn't call me back?" Dina sat down and looked at Naheema. "What's wrong?"

Naheema sat down next to her and broke down crying.

She told Dina everything that happened, and Dina was flabbergasted.

Dina put arms around Naheema. "Shh. It's going to be okay. Let it out."

Naheema cried her heart and soul out on the couch. After five minutes, she was able to calm down.

Dina walked to the kitchen and brought back a wet paper towel. She wiped Naheema's tears away.

Naheema looked at her. "Dina, can I ask you something?"

Dina knew what the question was. "Sure."

"Did you know that Shaquanna was sleeping with Mike?"

"Naheema, I love you and your sister, so you have to believe me when I say what I'm about to say. Can you do that for me?"

"Say it. I need to know."

"Yes—"

Naheema started crying again. "Why didn't you tell me? You're supposed to be my friend. How could you not say something?"

"I didn't know how to tell you. You are both my friends. I love you both, you have to believe that. I would never do anything to hurt you, Naheema. I didn't know how to tell you, but I did tell Shaquanna that she had better tell you, or I would." Tears began to drop down Dina's face. "I am so sorry."

"How long did you know about this?"

"I found out when you were in the hospital."

"That long? Damn, Dina! Why?" Naheema asked, as the tears poured out of her eyes. At that moment, it felt like her entire soul had left her body.

"I-I don't know what to say. I am so sorry you had to find out that way."

"Did you know that she was pregnant by him?"

"What? Hell no! Naheema, I swear to you. I didn't know all of that.

I found out that she had fucked him, and from what I understood, I assumed it only happened once . That's why I told her I was giving her the chance to tell you."

Naheema started crying. "I'm pregnant too."

"Damn! I'm sorry. What do you want to do? Where is Mike now? What did he have to say about all of this?"

"What can he say? The other chick Chyna blew it up in a letter she stuffed inside his jacket pocket. She also put her pregnancy test inside, as proof to me."

"Naheema, look at me." Dina lifted Naheema's face to look her in the eyes. "What are you going to do?"

"I'm getting rid of it."

"Okay. When you make the appointment, let me know when you're going to get it done, and I will come with you."

"Okay. My head hurts." Naheema started crying again.

"Do you have any Motrin in the medicine cabinet?"

"No, but I have some Vicodin left that I got from the hospital."

"Okay."

Dina went to get one of the pills out of the medicine cabinet and a cup of water, which she brought and gave to Naheema. She watched her take it then helped her into her bedroom and stayed with her until she went to sleep. Then she pulled the quilt over Naheema, and she lay down next to her and fell asleep.

Mike was disgusted. He drove over to Chyna's house and banged on the door but got no answer. He got back into his car and drove back to Red Hook. He knew that by the end of the week the cops would have a warrant out for his arrest. Chyna played him, with the help of his punk-ass lawyer, who wasn't returning his calls.

He now needed a place to rest. He couldn't go to his shop, thanks to Chyna, and now he couldn't go back home to Naheema.

He started yelling, "Fucking bitch! Chyna, when I find you, I'm going to kill you! Fuck! Fuck! Fuck!"

He made it into Red Hook a little after eleven. He drove to the spot where his boys hung out. He parked the car, got out, and walked into the building.

He walked into the apartment and was grateful that nobody was there. Everything had gone to hell in a matter of seconds. His workers were locked up, his main man was locked up, and he hadn't heard from his lawyer.

He searched the refrigerator for food. The only thing he saw was some baking powder, a jar of jelly, some butter, and a pint of Hennessy. He grabbed the Hennessy and walked back into the living room, where he sat on the couch. He reached for the remote and turned on the television.

As he watched music videos, he sipped on the Hennessy.

By one in the morning, he had a plan. He went to his car, grabbed the extra pair of clothes, soap, towel, and deodorant out of his trunk, and went back to the apartment.

He had to go to court in the morning to see about Randy. He prayed that the lawyer got his message and would be there despite the shit Chyna said. He hoped she was bluffing on that.

After showering, he put on a clean pair of boxers and a white T-shirt and went back into the living room. He grabbed the sheet that was already on the couch, covered himself, and went to sleep.

# Chapter 15

Mike was up and dressed by a quarter to eight. He ran to the store on Lorraine and Columbia to get him some breakfast.

Walking back to his car, he noticed a gray Taurus slowly driving behind him. He knew it was detectives, but he kept walking. As he approached his car, the Taurus pulled up and stopped. The driver rolled down his window as Mike turned to face them.

"What's up, my nigga?" the white detective laughed.

"You tell me," Mike said, taking a bite from his breakfast sandwich.

"Where's everybody at?" the white detective asked, still laughing. "Oh, my bad. They're all down at Central Booking, where your ass should be."

Mike didn't respond. He knew the detective was trying to bait him.

When the detective noticed his antics wasn't working, he said, "Don't worry. Your time is coming, homeboy." Then he rolled his window up and pulled off.

Though Mike stayed calm and smiled, he wanted to blow a hole in that detective's head. He threw his sandwich wrapper on the ground, jumped in his ride, and headed to the BQE.

Shaquanna was standing on line at the courthouse, waiting to go through security screening, when her cell phone beeped, letting her know she had voicemail. She entered her PIN and listened to her message.

*"You dirty, lying fucking whore. How could you fuck my man and get pregnant by him? Are you that desperate for a man that you're willing to sleep with my man, or are you just that jealous of me? I hate you, Shaquanna. You better pray I don't catch up with your simple ass. It's on."*

Shaquanna looked at her phone and then started looking around. She couldn't believe Naheema had found out about her and Mike. She deleted the message. She didn't know what she was going to do, but she would figure it out. She turned her phone off and put it back into her pocketbook.

After she made it through security, she asked the court officer where the information desk was, and he told her to go straight down the corridor and make a left.

On the wall by the information desk was a list of inmate names, last name first. She checked the first three papers and still didn't see Randy's name on the docket. After checking every paper on the wall, she went to the desk and asked the lady where she could find him.

The clerk informed her to go to the second floor, knock twice on the first brown door facing the elevator, and ask to speak to a Sergeant Hernandez. The clerk told her that they were expecting her.

Shaquanna headed to the elevators and rode to the second floor. She walked to the brown door and knocked twice, and a Hispanic woman opened the door. She assumed this was Sergeant Hernandez, so she introduced herself.

Sergeant Hernandez asked her for identification, and Shaquanna pulled out her license and handed it to her, and she was allowed in.

She walked into the room and was speechless. Inside of the room were Randy, three of Mike's workers, and Dina's cousin, who was supposed to be dead, all sitting down chatting at the table. Also in attendance was another white guy she didn't know, but later learned was Mike's lawyer.

As Shaquanna walked farther into the room, she noticed a female standing off to the back with her back turned. She walked over to Randy to have a seat.

Chyna turned to face her, and Shaquanna's mouth hit the floor.

"Surprised to see me? You can close your mouth now." Chyna sat down at the table.

"What the fuck is going on here?" Shaquanna asked, standing up.

"First, sit down and I'll tell you what's going on," Sergeant Hernandez said.

Shaquanna sat back down, and the sergeant began explaining the set up.

Dina got up from Naheema's bed and jumped in the shower. After she got out and threw on some of Naheema's sweats and a T-shirt, she went to the kitchen and made them some breakfast.

Naheema got up and jumped in the shower also. When she was done, she called her job to let them know that she wasn't coming in. Then she went into the kitchen and ate breakfast.

Dina cleaned up their mess, grabbed Naheema's house keys, and left. She told Naheema that she would be back later to check on her.

Naheema felt empty inside. Her heart was numb.

All night she'd tossed and turned. She had dreams of killing her sister and cutting Mike up into little pieces.

Then she dreamed that she'd poisoned him after walking in on him, her sister, and Chyna having a threesome in her bed.

She woke up with revenge on her mind, but first she had an important call to make. She got up from the couch and grabbed the Yellow Pages from the kitchen closet. She looked through the pages until she came to Planned Parenthood. She called them and made an appointment for an abortion.

Since there was a Planned Parenthood on Court Street, she asked for an appointment for some time today and was told to be at the clinic before three p.m. She was told to bring her health benefit card with identification, and not to eat anything six hours before the procedure was to be performed. The receptionist also told her to bring someone with her, if she planned on being put to sleep.

Naheema agreed and hung up. She looked at the clock. It was only nine in the morning. There was no way she was keeping Mike's seed now. She sat back down on the couch, turned on the television, and nodded off to sleep.

Dina came back to Naheema's apartment at eleven a.m. and let herself in and found Naheema knocked out and snoring on the couch. She went into Naheema's bedroom, pulled the quilt from the bed, and took it into the living room. She placed it on Naheema, causing her to wake up.

"Hey, thank you." Naheema pulled the cover up to her chin.

"No problem. Did you call and make the appointment?"

"Yeah. I have to be there today before three."

"Okay. Well, I'm going to make us some lunch."

"No. I can't eat anything six hours before the procedure."

"Okay. You go back to sleep, and I'll wake you up at one." Dina headed to the kitchen.

# Chapter 16

Mike was trying to find a parking space, but since there wasn't anywhere he could park, he drove to Macy's parking garage and parked in there. Before leaving his car, he checked his pockets to see how much he had on him. He had a little under a thousand dollars. He took three hundred and put the rest of the money inside of the glove compartment.

Mike did have over ten thousand dollars stashed away in Naheema's closet. He figured once she calmed down, he would be able to at least talk her into letting him get some of his things out of her apartment, so he could grab the money.

Running a little late, he wanted to get there before Randy went before the judge. He got out and headed over to the courthouse on Smith Street.

As Mike entered the courthouse, he checked his back pocket to make sure he had his driver's license on him. He stood in line for a minute before approaching the security checkpoint.

The court officer walked over to him, gave him a plastic bucket, and told him to empty his pockets and put everything in the bucket Mike did as he was told. The court officer took the bucket to his superior officer.

As the female officer passed the magnetic wand across Mike's body, her partner radioed to the second floor that their suspect had just arrived in the building. He was told to delay him for five minutes.

The male officer called his partner over and pretended he had something to tell her.

Mike became impatient. "What's going on?"

"Give us one minute," the male court officer responded.

Just as Mike was about to start flipping out, the female court officer walked over to him and allowed him to walk through the scan machine. She handed him his bucket and apologized for the delay.

Mike took it and went to the side of the table. He began putting his stuff away. He handed the bucket back to the female court officer. "Can you tell me where the information desk is?"

"Walk straight through the corridor, to the end, and make a left turn right before you get to the steps."

"Thanks."

The male court officer radioed that Mike was on his way to the information desk.

As Mike made the left turn, the clerk was putting up a new list of names on the wall. He walked over to the wall and checked to see if he knew anybody's name. He saw the names of eight of his workers on the list. He looked over to the next page and saw Randy's name on the wall. They were all to appear in front of Judge Silverman on the third floor. That wasn't a good look for the guys. Mike remembered the judge from his first stint in jail. Mike thought about what Chyna wrote in her letter and he prayed that she was lying about his lawyer because he really needed his lawyer to come through for him. He knew this judge didn't play any games.

If Mike had been paying attention, he would have noticed that the third floor was eerily quiet when he exited the elevator, but he was too preoccupied with his thoughts.

He pushed the heavy oak doors open and walked through them. He looked around the courtroom and saw his entire crew all handcuffed to one another, sitting on a bench at the front of the room over to the left. He found a seat in the front of the courtroom and sat down. He listened to the assistant district attorney call convict after convict up to the table to stand before the judge as each defense attorney tried to work out some type of plea agreement for their clients' crimes.

After about two hours, the courtroom started clearing out with the families of the men and women who were either released or remanded back to Rikers Island. Mike was getting agitated. His patience was wearing thin because they hadn't called any of the young men from his crew.

Mike got up to use the bathroom. He didn't notice that the court officer had locked the doors behind him when he'd entered the courtroom. He went to sit back down. He looked around the room and noticed it was almost empty. A feeling of sickness hit him. Something didn't feel right. He put his head down, took a few deep breaths, and tried his best to ignore the feeling that was growing in his stomach.

Mike heard the judge ask who was next, and the court officer read off a docket number and the name of one of Mike's workers. Mike looked up and saw the fear in the young man's eyes and just shook his head from left to right.

Then, out of the corner of his eye, Mike noticed Shaquanna sitting in the corner of the courtroom.

She must have felt him staring at her because she turned around in time to catch the look of rage on his face. She smiled at him and pretended that seeing him didn't have an effect on her, but that was a lie. Knowing what was about to take place, Shaquanna was scared for her life. She didn't know what Mike might do if he realized he had been set up to come to court for his own case.

Mike wanted so badly to walk over to Shaquanna and beat the daylight out of her, but he knew that would be a straight death sentence, so he sat there fuming, barely listening to his worker being remanded back to Rikers Island.

After another half an hour, Randy was led to the table to see the judge. Mike noticed his lawyer for the first time. The lawyer got up and stood beside Randy.

Mike's lawyer was nervous as well. His livelihood was on the line because of his affiliations with Mike. He knew he screwed up when he got up the next morning after seeing Chyna. The money Mike owed him was in the safe at the shop, so when Sunday morning came, he got up, got dressed, and headed out the door for the shop. When he got in his car, he checked to see if he had the key to the safe. He couldn't find it and went searching in his pants to see if it was there. That's when he found the note from Chyna inside his pocket.

As he sniffed the note, everything that had happened the night before came rushing back to him, and he began to panic. He had screwed up royally. If Mike found out that he had given Chyna the combination and key to the safe while he was getting his back blown out, he knew he was just as good as dead. Then when he drove out to Red Hook that morning to check on the shop, he saw flames shooting from the roof. He'd called 9-1-1 and got the hell out of Dodge.

So when Mike started calling him, he assumed it was about the money and shop, so he didn't answer. But later that evening, two detectives knocked on his door and gave him the shock of his life, but they also gave him a way out, which he took. He was informed that they had Mike at the courthouse and they wanted him to go and see him. They needed him to continue to be Mike's lawyer.

The ADA got up and started spouting off all of these charges, saying something about Randy being a co-conspirator to selling drugs, assisting in murder, and other crimes, which Mike tuned out.

After the ADA finished with his list, Mike's lawyer got up, pushing past his nervousness, and started doing his thing, and they went back and forth for a minute.

The judge then reprimanded both of them to be quiet. Then he said he was giving the ADA a chance to get their stuff together, and he got up and left the courtroom.

The court officer got up and said that court was in recess for ten minutes, and Randy was taken back to the holding cells.

Mike was relieved a little. He was ready to get out of the place, but he stopped when he noticed that his lawyer was now looking at him. The lawyer got up and walked over to him.

"Yo, what's up with you? Why the fuck you haven't returned my calls?" he asked, whispering. "We got a problem. You fuck up and you're going to fix it."

"I know. But we really have a situation right now," the lawyer whispered back.

"What the fuck are you talking about?" Mike asked, in a threatening voice.

The lawyer was scared. He began to stutter. "You-you don't—"

"Muthafucka, spit it out before you have me catch a case in here."

"Apparently, three guys from your crew made statements to the DA about their criminal activities. They implicated Randy, you, and your girlfriend, Chyna Fuller."

Mike got scared. "What? What the fuck you mean?"

Before the lawyer could answer, the ADA came over to the lawyer to talk, and the lawyer got up, leaving Mike to ponder his next move.

# Chapter 17

Dina woke Naheema up so she could go and get ready for the appointment. While she waited for Naheema, she made a phone call to her aunt and found out that Mike was at the courthouse and would be arrested by the end of the day. Dina was happy. She wanted to tell Naheema about it but decided that her friend had already been put through enough, so she decided to wait before telling her.

Thirty minutes later, Naheema walked out of the bedroom, dressed and ready to go.

Dina grabbed their pocketbooks, while Naheema turned off the television. Dina held the door open for her, and Naheema followed her out of the apartment. Dina locked the door, stuffed Naheema's keys into her pocket, and handed the pocketbook to her.

As they exited the building and headed up the block to catch the B61 bus on Van Brunt Street, Naheema felt so empty inside. Her heart felt like it had a black hole in it. At that moment she felt heartless, like her life no longer had meaning. She couldn't understand how she didn't see all the things Mike was doing.

As the bus slowly drove down the block, the girls took out their MetroCards. They boarded the bus, walked to the back, and sat down. The ride was a smooth one. They made it to Court Street by two-twenty. They got off, crossed the street, and walked three blocks back, passing the movie theatre, McDonald's, and Popeyes Chicken. They walked to the corner of Smith and Court Streets and found Planned Parenthood. They walked into the building, showed their identification, signed in, walked to the elevator, and rode it to the sixth floor.

Naheema walked over to the desk while Dina took a seat. The receptionist asked Naheema for her health insurance and ID cards and took both of them. Then she gave her a clipboard with a questionnaire to fill out. After making a copy of Naheema's information, the receptionist gave her back her cards and told her to have a seat.

Naheema then went to sit down next to Dina.

"How are you holding up?"

"I'm nervous and scared, but I'll be fine."

"Don't be. I'm here with you. I have your back." Dina smiled.

"Thank you."

Naheema started filling out the questionnaire, answering the questions as truthfully as she could. When she got to the bottom of the page, there was a question that caused her to break down and cry. It asked if there was a possibility that she could have contracted HIV and wanted to be tested for it.

Dina looked at her friend, read what Naheema was reading, and tears began to fall from her eyes as well. "You're going to be fine. Don't worry about that."

Naheema didn't say anything. She took a piece of tissue out of her pocketbook and wiped her eyes.

After she answered all the questions, a nurse came from behind the door and began calling names. Naheema was the fifth person to be called. She hugged Dina and followed the nurse into the back room.

# Chapter 18

The night before, while Mike was making his game plan and Naheema was bagging up his shit, Chyna was attempting to make a hasty escape from New York. After going through the screening process at the airport, which was fairly crowded for a Sunday, Chyna made it to the terminal with ten minutes to spare. She sat down and attempted to read the newspapers.

As she waited for the call to board the plane, she noticed two white guys in suits walking toward her. At first she paid them no attention, but when the guy pulled a picture out of his jacket and pointed in her direction, she knew something was up.

She calmly got up, grabbed her bag, and began to walk the other way, but they caught up with her. She stopped and asked what was wrong. The first detective politely asked her to come with them, but when she refused, the second detective pulled out a pair of handcuffs and arrested her on the spot.

The first detective grabbed her bag from the floor and opened it up. Inside he found the stacks of money they were looking for, and they took her to a room behind the ticket counter.

She asked them why they arrested her, and the first detective explained that they were watching Mike, not her. Not until they noticed her going into the salon earlier that morning. They watched her leave with a big duffel bag, but before they could apprehend her, the shop went up in smoke.

"You're under arrest for arson and theft."

Chyna broke down in tears. She claimed the money belonged to her, but when they told her that the money she took out of the salon belonged to the task force, she knew she was through.

The detectives told her that she had a choice. They needed her to testify against Mike to make the charge of theft disappear, and they would talk to the ADA on her behalf about setting the fire, and Chyna instantly agreed. And that's why she ended up in Brooklyn Criminal Court.

Before Chyna stepped fully into the courtroom, Mike had already smelled her White Diamonds perfume. When he looked up and saw her, he blacked out. He ran across the room to her and began choking her.

The court officer was too slow. Before he knew what was happening, Mike had Chyna on the floor, choking her and punching her in the face.

It took four court officers to grab Mike off her, but the deed was already done. In all of five seconds, Mike had crushed her windpipe, and she died on the floor of the courtroom. Mike was arrested, removed from the courtroom, and taken to Central Booking on Atlantic Avenue for processing. The judge cancelled court for the rest of the day.

Shaquanna sat in the corner, crying her eyes out as the ambulance took Chyna's body away. She knew that could have easily been her dead on the floor.

Shaquanna left the courtroom and the courthouse. She sat out front for over three hours waiting for Randy to come out. Realizing she was played for a fool, she left, pissed off. She walked to the parking lot across from the courthouse and produced her ticket for her car.

She knew she couldn't go running to her sister's apartment. She drove out of the lot and drove home feeling like her world had ended.

# Chapter 19

Naheema lay on a bed in the recovery room in tears, holding her stomach, feeling a great sense of loss. She knew she and Mike would never be, just as she knew she would never see her baby grow up. She cried and cried.

One of the counselors came over to her and tried to console her, but it was no use. Naheema was inconsolable. The counselor went out and asked Dina to come to the back.

Dina went over to Naheema and held her in her arms. Naheema cried for a good twenty minutes as Dina continued to whisper in her ear, "It will be fine."

After Naheema finally calmed down enough, a nurse gave her a pill to take then told her she could get dressed. The nurse asked Dina to follow her to the desk and gave her some prescriptions for Naheema to have filled. Then she led Dina back out to the waiting area.

When Naheema got dressed, the nurse took her over to the other side of the room for some refreshments. Naheema ate some snacks, drank some juice, and waited for half an hour before having to using the bathroom. She was able to move her bowels without complication.

The nurse gave Naheema a white business card with a phone number, and another three-digit number, explaining to her that she needed to call that number in a week to get the results of her HIV test, and that when she dialed the number, an automated service would ask her to enter her three-digit PIN, and the system would tell her whether the test was negative or positive. She told Naheema that she shouldn't take it as a death sentence if the test came back positive. She should go to her primary physician, and they would take it from there.

"Do not lose this card," the nurse told her, "because there would be no other way for you to get the results, and you would have to take the test all over again."

"Thanks." Naheema put the card inside her wallet, put the wallet into her pocketbook, and left.

Naheema started feeling a little dizzy, so Dina called them a cab, and five minutes later, the cab pulled up and took them to Naheema's building.

At the apartment Dina locked the door and told Naheema to go lie down.

Naheema went into her bedroom, kicked off her shoes, and climbed on her bed.

Dina came in behind her. "Hey, I need your insurance card. I'm going to go and get your prescription filled."

"It's in my wallet."

"Okay." Dina left the room and closed the bedroom door behind her. She unplugged the house phone, grabbed Naheema's insurance card from her pocketbook, and left.

Naheema began to cry. The thought of her sister being pregnant by Mike was driving her crazy. She desperately wanted to call her sister and ask, "How could you do that?" But she knew Shaquanna wouldn't answer her call.

Dina made it back to the apartment with bags in her hand. She placed the bags on the kitchen table and took the juice and medicine to the room. She gave Naheema two pills.

"Thank you."

"Girl, please. What are you thanking me for?" Dina put the bottle of apple juice on the end table.

"For being there, for being a real friend, and for being a real sister to me." Naheema started crying again. "For being everything my blood sister couldn't be to me."

Dina sat on the bed beside her. "Naheema, stop crying. Girl, you're going to be fine. You'll get through this."

"I don't know. I feel so stupid. I trusted them, and look what they did to me. I swear on everything I love, Shaquanna is going to get hers."

"Girl, don't waste your time getting revenge. Shaquanna is going to get everything that she got coming to her."

"Would you be saying that if it was your sister doing it to you?" Naheema asked, sounding groggy.

"Hell no! I would have murdered the bitch." Dina laughed. "That's why God made me an only child."

Naheema smiled. "You're crazy. That's why I love you."

"Girl, get yourself some rest, and when you wake up, I'll have some dinner ready for you. But, first, I have to go home and get me some clothes."

"Okay."

Dina kissed Naheema on the forehead, left the bedroom, and went into the kitchen to put the food away. She placed the chopped meat inside of the refrigerator and the rest in the freezer.

When Dina got home, she walked into her living room to check her messages. She had three urgent messages—one from her mother, the other two from her cousin. They all said that Mike had been arrested and that he'd murdered a girl inside the courtroom.

Dina starting laughing. Then she suddenly stopped when she realized she was going to be the one to tell Naheema about it.

She erased the messages and began cleaning up her apartment and gathering her clothes to take back to Naheema's place.

Naheema woke up in pain. Her stomach was cramping something terrible. She popped open the pill bottle, downed two pills, and drank some water. She sat back on her bed, pulling her knees to her stomach.

After twenty grueling minutes, the effects of the pills kicked in. She went to the bathroom and washed her face. Then she checked her voicemail. She had two messages, both from Mike. As soon as she heard his voice, her eyes watered up, and her pulse began to race. She was in no mood to hear his voice, so she deleted the messages without listening to them.

She then picked up her notebook and pen and headed to the kitchen, where she sat down at her table and looked out the window to watch the sun go down for the evening. She started writing.

*When I met you, I felt like I was hit with an African love potion; like my world wasn't my own, but filled with a roller coaster of joyful emotions, spinning around and around on this thing called life. Later, it turned out to be a Ferris wheel of sickening commotion, leaving me in a heartless state of mind, not just in a state of strung-out emotions, causing me to be afraid to look deep within myself. But you know what? I would have to take responsibility for this drowning, sinking feeling of being left out in the open for the world to see me, as I fight for right to be called, "The woman with no heart who loves with devotion."*

*I created this monster, because I wanted love to wrap itself around me and provide me with a reward no bigger than a token. But, you see, when I got what I thought I wanted, I realized I was worth more than the idea of having those three little words spoken to me. Especially when it was by the wrong man. A man who feels he needs to be the one controlling all of my feelings placed inside of a jar filled with my heart, a jar for only him to open.*

*Now here I sit, with a broken heart, feeling left out and hopeless, praying to God that He gives me enough strength to move forward in my life so I can stay focused.*

*Never again will I allow a man to feel like he's the one in control. Never again will I allow a man to make me feel like he owns my emotions. Never again will I be called, "A woman with no heart who loves with devotion."*

*Today I end my misery and start my rhythm with a new motion called, "I love myself, and to-hell-with-everyone-else devotion." I will no longer be heartless. When I love myself in the open, I will have the heart to tell every man that he must earn my devotion.*

*I, Naheema Morgan, will no longer allow you, Mike, or any man to cause me to become heartless.*

Naheema put her pen down when she was finished, got up, and prepared an egg salad sandwich. She poured herself some apple juice and walked into the living room, where she sat down to eat. She turned on the television to see what was on.

As she bit into her sandwich, the Lifetime network was about to premiere a movie, *Betrayal. Ironic,* she thought.

# Chapter 20

Shaquanna was home, throwing up, replaying the events of that morning in her head. She was still shaken by seeing a dead body.

Later on, she sat down on her couch, turned on her television, and began watching *Betrayal* on the Lifetime network. She cracked opened her Dutch and poured some weed from her dime bag. Then she began breaking the weed up. After rolling her blunt, she lit it and took a deep pull, holding in the smoke for a good five seconds. She started coughing. She looked at the blunt and said to herself, "This is some good-ass weed." She smoked half of the blunt before putting it out.

After watching the movie, she felt compelled to call Naheema. She knew she had some explaining to do. She wasn't sure how Naheema found out, but she assumed Mike was the one to tell her. If that was the case, then Naheema only knew half of the story, so she planned to try and appeal to Naheema's soft side. Hopefully, Naheema still had a soft spot for her.

She picked up her phone and dialed Naheema's number, but her voicemail answered, so she left her a message.

"Hi, Nah. I know you're mad with me, but you have to give me a chance to explain. You have to hear me out first. There is always two sides to a story, so whatever Mike told you, you need to hear the truth from me. Please, if you can find it in your heart to at least hear me out, then call me. No matter what you believe, I do love you and I am really sorry for what happened. Also, I don't know if anyone told you, but Mike is in jail. When you call me, I'll tell you what happened."

Shaquanna hung up the phone and went back to the couch, where she ended up dozing off.

Two hours later there was a knock at her door. She jumped up from the couch and looked around, forgetting she was in her own place. The banging on her door got louder.

"One fucking minute!" she screamed, walking to the door. "Who the fuck is it?" She looked through the peephole and saw Randy. Shaquanna was pissed with him for leaving her at the courthouse and was undecided about opening the door for him. "What the fuck do you want?"

"Shaquanna, open up the door. We have to talk."

"Well, then talk, nigga."

"Stop fucking playing with me and open up the fucking door."

Shaquanna noticed the anger in his tone and cracked her door open, keeping the chain on the door. "What? Talk."

"Stop playing. I can't talk to you like this. This is important. It's concerning your sister."

Shaquanna removed the chain from the door, opened it, and walked back into her living room. "Lock the door behind you. Now what's wrong with my sister?" She sat on the couch.

"Listen, I could get fired for telling you this, but I have to warn you. Your sister is in really deep shit. The DA is looking to charge her with conspiracy."

"What? For what? Conspiracy for what?"

"It's complicated," he said, sitting down.

"Fuck that! You better tell me what the fuck is going on."

"Look, the DA's star witness is lying in the morgue, and he feels that because Naheema is Mike's girlfriend, she knows all about his dealings. He's planning to charge her if she doesn't take the stand to testify about what she knows. So I'm asking, do you think that she knows something that may save her?"

"How the fuck do I know? We didn't talk about her relationship with Mike like that."

"Well, you better find out because the DA is coming after you as well. Apparently, before Chyna was murdered, she wrote out a statement about you sleeping with Mike and knowing about his business deals."

"What? That bitch did what? I don't know anything."

"That's not going to fly with this DA."

"I don't give a fuck! You better take care of this, Randy. You promised me if I helped you, I wouldn't have to be involved. Now you're telling me I might go to jail because of some lying slut?" Shaquanna stood up. "I don't think so."

Randy stood up and stepped to her. "Shaquanna, calm down. I didn't say I wouldn't try to help you."

"Then what the fuck are you saying?"

"Give me a day or two to try and take care of this. But you need to talk to your sister and find out what she knows." He pulled her into his arms.

"Gee, I wish I could, but that dumb muthafucka, Mike, told Naheema about us sleeping together. So she's not talking to me right now."

"Unfortunately, Mike wasn't the one who told."

"Really? Well, who told her then?"

"Chyna."

"How the fuck did that happen?" Shaquanna pushed Randy away. "And how do you know that?"

"I told you Chyna wrote a statement and everything was in it. So I suggest you make it your business to talk to your sister and fast."

Randy's cell phone beeped. He looked at the number and realized the code was from his sergeant. He closed the phone and looked at Shaquanna. "Look, I have to go, but you need to talk to your sister."

# Chapter 21

Dina walked into Naheema's apartment and found her sitting in the kitchen. She walked over to her and gave her a hug.

"What was that for?" Naheema asked.

"We have to talk. Give me one minute. I just remembered that I turned your ringer off." Dina walked into the living room, grabbed the phone and turned the ringer up. Just as she was about to walk back to the kitchen, the house phone rang.

"Hello," Dina answered.

*"This is the New York State Department of Corrections with a collect call from Mike Williams. To accept the call press one, to disconnect the call press two, to hear the charges for this call, press five."*

While the operator was talking, Dina walked into the kitchen to let Naheema know she had a collect call from Mike.

Naheema was shocked. She didn't know why Mike was calling her from jail.

Dina told her not to accept the calls, but Naheema felt like she needed to know what the hell was going on.

Dina pressed one and accepted the charges. Then she handed the phone to Naheema.

Naheema took the phone and left the kitchen for a little privacy. "Hello."

"Hey, baby. How are you doing?"

"What, Mike? What are you calling me for?"

"Listen, Naheema, I need your help. Please. I'm in a real bind."

"So, what's that got to do with me?"

"It has everything to do with you. I need you to come and see me. I'll be on Rikers Island by tonight. I'll be able to have a visit tomorrow."

"You must be out of your fucking mind if you think that I'm coming to visit your sorry, no-good, lying, cheating ass. You better call Shaquanna and tell that shit to her. That's your baby mama. You got me twisted with somebody who gives a damn."

"Look, I know I fucked up, and yeah, your sister is pregnant, but she's not pregnant by me. All that bitch did was give me a couple of blowjobs. I never stuck my dick in that bitch or that bitch Chyna. They both lied to you, but you rather believe them than to believe me."

"You're good. Wow! I never knew you were really a fucked-up individual."

The operator let them know they had two minutes left.

"Look, Naheema, I know you don't believe me, but I can promise you that your life will be forever destroyed if you don't come and see me tomorrow. I promise this is not a lie. You will go to jail if you don't come up here."

Naheema was about to start cursing him out, but the call was disconnected. She stared at the phone for a couple of minutes. She couldn't believe Mike had the balls to threaten her.

Could what he was saying be true? Could her sister be pregnant by someone else? But why would Chyna lie about that? She didn't know her from a hole in the wall.

She got up from her bed and went back into the kitchen to talk to Dina. She sat down at the table and took a deep breath.

"Are you all right?" Dina asked.

"No, I'm not."

"What did he say?"

"A lot of shit. I need some advice, Dina, but first tell me what you were going to tell me."

"I was going to tell you that Mike was in jail, but since you know that, I don't have to tell you. Did he tell you why he was arrested?"

"No, he didn't tell me. I didn't even ask him. I was so pissed that I forgot to ask him why he got locked up."

"Okay, well then I still have something to tell you, but first, I think we need to have a drink."

"No, I'm good. Tell me."

"Well, the girl that wrote you that letter was in court today, and Mike broke her neck."

"What? How? How the fuck did that happen?"

"I don't know the whole story, but from what I was told, Mike broke her neck before the court officers could get to him."

"What? Who told you that? How did you find this out?"

"Girl, don't trip about the *who*. Worry about the *why*. That's what I'm trying to find out."

"Look, I really need some advice. Mike said I needed to make it my business to visit him tomorrow on Rikers Island. He said something about me going to jail."

"Naheema, that's just him trying to get you to come and see him."

"No, Dina. I'm worried. I think I need to go and see him.

"I don't think you should worry about it. He's just conning you. Trust me, Mike is a con artist."

"Really? And how do you know that? You're talking like you know him."

"I did know him, years ago. My cousin was selling drugs for him."

"Are you serious? Why didn't you tell me this before I started messing around with him?"

"Yes, I'm serious. I didn't tell you because I didn't know who you were talking about until he came to my house and hurt you. I started to tell you then to be careful, but there was so much going on and you had just lost your child, so I didn't want to burden you with it."

"I appreciate that, but I still would have preferred that you told me. Damn, Dina, why have you been keeping all this stuff from me? First the Shaquanna thing, and now this!"

"Naheema, don't tell me you didn't know Mike was one of the biggest dealers in Red Hook."

"I knew he was dealing, but I didn't know how much. I just assumed that the majority of his money came from the salon."

"Damn! I mean, yeah, his salon was doing extremely well, but there is no way for him to have all that he has from the salon alone. You never questioned that?"

"There was no need to, because he never did his business in front of me."

"Well, I suggest you search your apartment to make sure he doesn't have anything in there." Dina raised a brow. "Just to be on the safe side."

"Believe me, I will check. I just feel like a fool right now. He's telling me to trust him, and in the same breath telling me that I'm being played."

"How so?"

"He claimed that Shaquanna only sucked his dick. He said he never had sex with her."

"Well, what do you believe?"

"I don't know."

"Did you call Shaquanna and ask her? I know you're pissed, but there are two sides to a story, Naheema."

"I know that, but I'm afraid of what I might do to her if I find out she's carrying Mike's baby."

"Well, there is only one way to do that, and that's to get on the phone and ask her."

"I know, but what if she lies and says that it's his, just to hurt me?"

"Okay, and what if she's not lying? Naheema, look at it this way. He has something to lose if he's lying, but what does Shaquanna have to lose by lying? If she did fuck him and got pregnant, what can she lose that she didn't already lose?" Dina looked at Naheema like she was crazy for seriously thinking about believing Mike.

"I don't know. I'm just stressed behind all of this. I want to believe he's telling the truth. I want to believe that this never happened, but I just don't know anymore."

"Just think about it before you do anything," Dina said, getting up.

"I will."

"Like I said earlier, she didn't say that they were fucking, but she also didn't deny that it happened."

"If it were you, what would you do?" Naheema asked, standing with her.

"To be honest, I would have kicked that baby out of her, and pulled a 'waiting to exhale' with his shit, but that's just me." Dina smiled.

"I hear you."

"Well, let me get out of here. I was planning on staying another couple of days with you, but you look like you could use some time alone."

"Thanks, Dina."

"For what?"

"For being a good friend and for having my back, and not judging me. For everything."

"Girl, please. Who am I to judge you? I've done some fucked-up shit in my life, so I don't have a right to judge you. Naheema, you're going to have to do what's right for you in the end. Being in love with someone and finding out that they're not what they claimed to be is hard enough." Dina took her bag and walked to the door.

"That is so true," Naheema said, following her.

The girls hugged before Dina left.

Dina thought to herself while she waited on the elevator, *I hope she's smart enough to leave his no-good ass alone.*

The cramping in her stomach stopped, thanks to the pills, so she decided that she should take advantage of it. Naheema went back into her living room, grabbed her cordless phone, and walked back into the bedroom to finish packing up Mike's belongings.

After she bagged everything, she set the bags in front of her bedroom door. She went back into her closet and noticed two black gym bags stuck in the corner of the closet. She pulled on the bags. They were really heavy, so she dragged them, one at a time, out of the closet.

She sat Indian-style on the floor with the bags in front of her. She unzipped the first and received the shock of her life. She started screaming, "Oh, my God! No! Oh, my God!"

Inside the bag was ten kilos of what looked like cocaine in blocks, six pounds of weed, two silver Smith & Wesson handguns, two marble notebooks, and four boxes of bullets.

She quickly got on the phone and called Dina. Dina wasn't home yet, so she left her a message telling her to hurry back to her apartment and to bring a book bag with her. She hung up the phone, ran into her kitchen for some black bags, and rushed back into her bedroom.

She sat down on the floor and slid the second bag between her legs and unzipped it. It was filled with hundreds, fifties, twenties, tens, and singles stacked together with rubber bands. She screamed and cried. She couldn't believe Mike had all of this stuff in her house. She knew at that moment, she was going on a visit.

She closed the bag with the drugs and dragged it over to Mike's clothes. She opened it, removed the marble notebooks, then started placing some of Mike's clothes on top of the drugs. Then she stuffed the black gym bag up under the garbage bags.

She went back into her room and removed ten stacks of hundreds from out of the bag and placed them with the two marble notebooks on top of her bed. She zipped the money bag closed, dragged it over to his pile of clothes, and stuffed it under the clothes, next to the other bag.

She went back into her room and began to look around for a place to hide the money and the notebooks but there wasn't anywhere she could hide it without somebody finding it, so she placed the money safely under her mattress. She walked back to her room and cleaned it up. She sat down on her bed and opened up the first notebook. She couldn't believe her eyes. Mike had dates and times of when and where he picked up the drugs, the name of the person he got the drugs from, and the amount of each transaction. He also had bank statements stapled to the paper.

She closed that notebook and opened the second one. Yet again, she was in disbelief. This book had all of the hits he had contracted out, who he contracted the hits out to, the name of each person murdered, and date, time, and the transaction amount for every hit.

She put both books on her bookshelf, next to her class books from when she went to college. She grabbed a T-shirt, some underwear, her robe, and towel then headed into the bathroom to take a shower. She promised herself that tonight she was going to rest. Tomorrow, she would take care of the rest.

She was just about to go to bed when Dina entered her apartment.

"What happened? I got your message." Dina locked the door behind her.

Naheema told Dina to follow her to the room. When Dina stepped into the room, Naheema began opening up bag after bag, showing her everything she found.

Dina was in shock. She quickly pulled herself together and began grabbing the bags with the guns and drugs toward the living room. Naheema followed her.

Dina took all of the bags into the hallway and began dumping the drugs and guns down the incinerator chute. She walked back into the apartment, locked the door, and sat down.

"Dina, I need you to do me a favor."

"Sure, name it."

"Come back to my room."

Dina followed her. They entered the room and Naheema walked over to her bed, lifted her mattress, and grabbed the black sack with the money in it. Naheema opened the bag and showed it to Dina.

"Oh my God! How much is in there?"

"I don't know, and I don't want to count it here. Can you take this and these books to your house for me?" she said, walking over to her bookshelf.

She grabbed the black and white marble notebooks and handed them to Dina.

"I need you to hold these too."

"Sure. What do you want me to do with this?"

"Take whatever you need, open up a safe deposit for me, and put the money in it along with the books."

"No problem." Dina removed the money from the bag and placed the stacks in her backpack. Holding the books, she looked up at Naheema. "Are these what I think they are?"

"Yes. Those are his death sentences," Naheema said.

Dina placed the notebooks inside of the backpack, hugged Naheema, took the empty black bags, and headed for the door. She dropped the bags into the incinerator and walked to the exit door. She turned around and smiled at Naheema. "You're going to be fine."

Naheema locked her door, turned off the lights inside of her apartment, and said a prayer before going to bed.

# Chapter 22

Shaquanna sat at home and cried her eyes out. She wanted to go to her sister's house to warn her about what was going on, but she knew that Naheema wouldn't believe her. She had already fucked up big time, but she had to do something. She picked up the phone and dialed Naheema's home number. The phone rang twice before the answering machine picked up.

*Hi. You've reached Mike and Naheema. We're not available at the moment, but leave us a message and we'll get back to you. Bye.*

"Naheema, it's me. We really need to talk. It's urgent. I know I fucked up, and I'm really sorry. I have no excuse for what I did, but believe me, I'm not the only one to blame. Look, please call me back. It's important. The—"

Naheema picked up the phone. "How could you? Of all the people in the world that you could have fucked over, why would you do that to me?"

"Naheema, I am so sorry."

"We know that already. But why? Why would you go after the man I was with?"

"I don't know. What can I do to make it right?"

"It ain't shit you can do. I never, in my wildest nightmare, would believe that you hated me so much, that you would fuck my boyfriend and get pregnant by him." Naheema began to cry.

"Naheema, please forgive me. I never meant to hurt you. I don't know why I did it."

"Bullshit! You know why you did it. You always go after somebody else's man. That's all you ever do. You're a miserable slut! Just like your mother!"

That hit Shaquanna hard. She screamed, "No! The fuck, you didn't! My mother don't have shit to do with the fact that you can't keep a man happy. How dare you talk shit about my mother? If that's the case, then I guess the apple don't fall too far from the tree concerning your mother, or did you forget? Your mother was the reason my mother slept with our father. So fuck you and your high horse! "

"No, bitch! Fuck you! Wait until I catch you."

"Really? And what the fuck are you going to do?" Shaquanna laughed.

"Keep talking, Shaquanna. I promise you, when I see you, I'm going to fuck you up. I'll make sure that bastard of a child don't see the light of day."

"I'd like to see you try, especially since you'll be doing a long-ass bid, bitch!" Shaquanna slammed down the phone.

Naheema slammed her phone down as well. She started yelling and screaming obscenities all around her apartment, calling Shaquanna every name in the book. By the time she was finished, her head felt like it had been slammed into a brick wall. She went into the bathroom, opened the medicine cabinet, and grabbed two Vicodin pills. She swallowed them and drank water from the faucet. She left the bathroom and went into her bedroom. She was steaming mad. She was ready to murder her own sister. Naheema sat on her bed for about a good twenty minutes before the pills began to take effect. She fixed her pillows, lay down, and went back to sleep.

Shaquanna was yelling and screaming as well. She was mad at herself more than at her sister. She let her emotions take over, and she neglected to really warn her sister about the DA. She picked up the phone and dialed Randy's number. His voicemail picked up. She left him a message telling him she needed to see him. She hung up, walked through her dining room, and went to her bedroom. She was hurt and mad. She knew that Naheema had every right to be mad at her, but she didn't expect her to take it there, concerning their mothers.

Naheema and Shaquanna knew the whole story concerning Shaquanna's mother getting pregnant. As a matter of fact, Naheema's mother was the reason for Shaquanna being here.

If Naheema's mother wasn't so desperate to have a man, they wouldn't have been in that situation. In order for their father to marry Naheema's mother, he wanted to have a threesome first. So, Naheema's mom set it up and asked Shaquanna's mother to join them. One thing led to another, and their father was sleeping with Shaquanna's mother every chance he got after their little threesome.

Naheema's mother started to assume that her husband was cheating, so she asked Shaquanna's mother to help her set up their father. Shaquanna's mother was supposed to try and push up on their father and see if he would take the bait. But little did Naheema's mother know, she was the one being played. Before long, Shaquanna's mother was pregnant, Naheema's mother found out by whom, and that was the end of their ten-year friendship.

As Shaquanna sat on her bed thinking about that, she got madder and madder. "Who the fuck do she think she is? She has a lot of nerve to talk about my mother like that. So she think I'm like my mother?

Fine. Fuck her. She wants to be like that then so be it." She decided she was going to really get even with Naheema, deciding then and there she was going to keep her and Randy's baby, but she was going to continue to let Naheema think it was Mike's child.

She got up from her bed, grabbed her robe, gels, and sponge and headed to her bathroom to take a nice hot bath. She was glad that she continued to fuck Randy. Although their last couple of encounters were brief, Randy did start to come around. With everybody going through their issues, Randy started coming over to her house more and more. He eventually began staying the night over, although he would only come during the late night hours, and would leave her place before the sun came up. However, she was still happy because she assumed it meant that they were becoming a couple, even though he never officially asked her to be his woman.

She assumed that it was only a matter of time before he asked. She just had to be patient. She had to hurry up and get herself ready before Randy got there. As she set up the tub, placing her vanilla-scented candles around the edges of the perimeter, she thought about how she was going to tell Randy he was the father, not Mike. She turned the water off and began to light her candles. She stripped down to her birthday suit and thought about how she was going to surprise him with the news.

She knew he wasn't going to believe her, but there was nothing she could do. When she went to the doctor and found out she was pregnant, she was shocked. When the doctor told her how many weeks she was, she assumed it was Mike's, until she went for the sonogram and found out she was only six weeks pregnant, not twelve weeks like the doctor first said. She knew in her heart that her baby belonged to Randy because she had stopped sleeping with Mike once she started catching feelings for Randy.

She got in her tub and soaked her body. Her house phone rang. It was Randy calling to let her know he would be at her place within the hour. She hung up the phone and went back to relaxing.

An hour later, she got out of the tub, dried off, oiled her body down, cleaned out the tub, and went into the kitchen to prepare a quick spaghetti dinner.

At ten, Randy knocked on Shaquanna's door. She finished setting the table, left the kitchen to go and open the door. Randy walked in, hugged her, and tongued her down before closing the door behind him. Shaquanna was hot from his kiss. She wanted more, but she wanted them to sit down and eat dinner first.

"Go clean up and come back to the kitchen. I made something for us to eat," she said, pushing him off.

"Don't worry. I'll eat dinner after I've had my dessert." Randy smiled wickedly.

"That's nice and all, but no, go and get cleaned."

He kissed her again before asking if she was sure.

Shaquanna was pulsating between her legs. She had to find strength to push him away. She didn't want their evening to start off like it always did, sex first, another kiss, and then he was out the door. She had plans for him, depending on how he would respond to her little surprise, so she pushed him away and told him to go and get clean.

He sighed before walking to the bathroom. He stepped in and was surprised. The bathroom smelled of cherries and vanilla, and the bathtub was filled with bubbles. He stripped down to his birthday suit and stepped into the tub.

Shaquanna heard him moan. She knew he was staying tonight. She thought to herself, *So far, so good.* She opened the bottle of Merlot and poured some in his wineglass. She lit the candles, made their plates, and placed them on the table.

Randy finished in the bathroom and headed into the kitchen. The aroma was delicious and was causing his stomach to do a belly dance. He walked into the kitchen and smiled.

"Damn, girl! You really did your thing."

"You like?" she asked, sweeping her hand across the table.

"I do." Randy pulled out her chair for her before sitting down at the table to eat.

Dinner was wonderful for Shaquanna. They talked about everything. She asked Randy how he felt about having kids, and he said he planned to have some one day. She asked him about marriage.

"If I find the right woman, I could see myself getting married."

Shaquanna felt a little hurt by that remark because she felt *she* was the right woman for him.

Randy sensed her attitude change, but he ignored it. He was having fun with Shaquanna, but he knew she wasn't the type of woman you brought home to Mother. Even though his mother was gone, he still had his grandmother. Shaquanna was good for a few rolls in the hay, but that would eventually grow tiresome.

They ate, and he helped her clean off the table.

As she washed the dishes, Randy walked up behind her and started kissing her on the back of her neck and shoulders. It felt so good to her. While she washed the dishes, he started exploring her body, rubbing his hands down her back as he kissed down her spine, licking his way down to her butt. He turned her to face him, spread her legs, and went deep-sea fishing. The plate she had in her hand crashed to the floor, sending pieces of the plate flying everywhere.

Using his thumb and index finger as a guide to spread her lips apart, he licked, nibbled and sucked on her clit, pushing his middle finger of his right hand in and out of her vagina, licking her juices off his finger as it slid out of her.

"Um, oh, Randy! Oh yes!" she moaned, at the verge of release.

Randy pulled his finger out of her and sucked her juices off his finger. He started kissing her as he pulled and squeezed her nipples between his fingers. He spun her around, bent her over, moistened his finger, and rubbed it up against her asshole.

"Oh yes! Yes, baby."

He gently pushed his pointer finger in her hole, while sticking his middle finger back into her vagina.

"Yes! Yes!" she begged.

He pushed his boxers down, pulled out his penis, and massaged himself. He finger-fucked her while he massaged himself. As his manhood got harder, he moved his finger out of her vagina and pushed his dick deep inside of her, holding it there, while playing in her asshole. Gently he pushed in and out of her, in and out, while finger fucking her in the ass.

She begged him for more, for him to fuck her harder, and he obliged. Little by little he pounded her walls as she screamed in pure pleasure.

After fucking her brains out for an hour in every position he could think of, he released.

They got into the shower, dried each other off, oiled up, and climbed into the bed.

Shaquanna was ecstatic, but her nerves were running wild. She knew she had to tell him. She just prayed that what she had to say wouldn't ruin their night.

Finally finding the courage at one-thirty in the morning, she sat up on the bed and told Randy her secret.

He sat up, and for a few minutes didn't speak. He couldn't believe she was trying to pin her pregnancy on him after she'd told him Mike was the father.

She sat there scared out of her mind. Randy still hadn't said a word after five minutes. Just as she was about to open her mouth, he got up out of the bed and started getting dressed.

"I don't believe this shit. I knew you were a conniving, ruthless bitch, but damn!" he said, tying the strings on his Air Max. "Do I look stupid to you, Shaquanna? Do I look like an asshole?"

"What are you talking about?" she screamed. "Randy, you are the father. I was wrong because my doctor said I was twelve weeks along, but after the sonogram, he said I was only six weeks. I knew it was yours. I stopped fucking Mike when I started fucking you." Tears started falling down her face.

"Look, you can save that shit for somebody who don't know you. I met and fucked you right after you fucked Mike. Remember? So don't try to kick game to me." Randy pulled his shirt over his head. "You took a perfectly good evening and fucked it up." He pulled a wad of money out of his pocket, peeled off ten hundred-dollar bills, and threw them in Shaquanna's face. "I did say I would help pay for the abortion, so here. That should cover it." Then he peeled off five more hundreds and threw them on the nightstand. "That's for a great fuck and dinner." Then he stormed out of her apartment.

Shaquanna cried herself to sleep.

The following morning, she decided she wasn't going to let Randy get off that easily. She was going to force him to take responsibility for his actions, or make him lose his job for fucking a witness.

# Chapter 23

All night Sunday, Naheema tossed and turned, thinking about Mike. She was so hurt and betrayed, but she had questions and she needed them to be answered. She knew the only way to get those answers would be to visit Mike. Naheema knew it would be a mistake going up there, but she had to go. She would not be able to put her mind at ease if she didn't try to get some answers. Knowing what she had to do, she fell asleep.

Her alarm went off at six in the morning. She climbed out of bed, dragging. She knew that she had a long ride ahead of her. She jumped in the shower, oiled up, and got dressed. She wore her blue jean Baby Phat dress with her open-toe sandals. Because she was going to the jail, she knew to leave her cell phone home, and she put her wallet with her information, keys, and money inside her purse. She checked herself in the mirror and headed for the door.

Right before she walked out, her house phone rang. She was tempted to leave and not answer it, but she changed her mind. After listening to the operator, she pressed the number *one*, and Mike started talking.

"Get a pen."

"Go ahead."

"These are my numbers, 97A4359. You're going to need that when you get up here. Love you. Later." Then he hung up.

Naheema looked at the phone, because she knew she was hearing things. She hung up the phone, left her apartment, and locked her door. She took the stairs down and exited the building.

She walked up to Sullivan Street, and crossed. She continued walking up the block, passing the Patrick F. Daly School. As she got to the playground, she noticed the bus coming. She took off running up the block, hoping her breasts didn't pop out of the top of the dress. She made it to the bus stop intact as the bus was pulling up to the stop. She got on, pulled out her city Metro card, paid her fare, and walked to the back of the bus to sit down.

She looked at the time. It was only seven-thirty a.m. It was too early to call out of work. She thought, *I'll be lucky if I still have a job when this shit is all over with.*

The bus pulled off, and she pulled out her book and began to read.

An hour into the ride, Naheema looked around. She checked her watch. It was eight-forty a.m. She knew that as soon as she got off the bus, she was going to have to call her job.

At nine-fifteen in the morning, the bus was pulling up to the last stop, Long Island City. As Naheema and two other young women exited the bus, she asked the bus driver where to catch the Rikers Island bus, and he told her to stand directly across the street and catch the R101. She crossed the street, found a pay phone, and called her job.

The receptionist, Ms. Gary, answered the phone and transferred Naheema to the manager. Naheema explained to her manager that she had a family emergency and that she needed to take off another day as well as today. Her manager told her to hurry back to work, or else she would have to write her up for taking off too many days. Naheema promised she would be back to work on Wednesday, and then they hung up.

She walked to the bus stop and waited for the bus. After standing there for more than ten minutes, Naheema started to feel like she was standing at the wrong stop, but then more and more women with children started coming to the stop. Then from listening to some of the conversations going on, she knew she was at the right stop.

Five minutes later the bus came. Everyone paid their fares, got on, and sat down. Naheema sat at the back of the bus. There was a lot of laughter and chatter on the bus.

Naheema overheard two women on the bus talking about two young girls who were apparently on their way to see the same dude. Only, they didn't know it. Naheema shook her head. She didn't want to be mixed up with any shit concerning those two once they got off the bus. She stopped listening to the women talk and looked out the window for the rest of the ride.

As they began driving over the bridge, the women and children on the bus began to stand. Naheema hurried and made her way to the front of the bus. The bus made a U-turn inside of the Rikers Island parking lot and parked in front of some clear side panels. Naheema's nerves were dancing in her stomach.

Everyone exited the bus and started running toward the glass panels to line up. Naheema just looked around in amazement as she stepped off the bus and walked to the end of the line.

Two corrections officer approached them, and the male officer spoke.

"All right, ladies. We all know the drill. I know this is not the first time that many of you have come to Rikers Island. However, there may be some first-timers. For those of you that don't know the rules, I am going to say it only once. The rules are: no cell phones, cameras, or contraband are allowed on the premises. Contraband items are: cameras, cell phones, recorders, knives, blades, box cutters, cigarettes, weed, alcohol, and drugs. If anyone has this on their persons, then they can drop them inside of the red box located to your left, without prejudice. Now if you are caught with any of these contraband items, you will be arrested and prosecuted to the fullest extent of the law. Please have your identifications out. Enjoy your visit."

After he was finished with his speech, the line began moving, and not a moment too soon. Naheema had to use the ladies' room really badly.

The female officer was checking everyone's identification. She looked over Naheema's then let her pass. Naheema walked up the steps and was stuck in yet another line. This one was for the body machines, like those in the airports. Naheema was pissed. At the rate these women with children were moving, she was liable to pee on herself. She put her head down and thought to herself, *What woman in her right mind would bring their child into a prison to see his or her father?*

When she looked up, she realized the young woman with the child was one of the women that the ladies on the bus were gossiping about. Homegirl was straight ghetto fabulous with the big gold nameplate earrings, hands full of jewelry, hair full of gel and spray, and "name-branded-out" like she was a billboard for the company.

The young woman turned around and looked Naheema in her eyes.

Naheema looked away. *I know she didn't hear what I was thinking. She better turn her head around and watch that dirty-ass child she got with her. She got enough to deal with when she sees that the other chick with the baby that she was smiling it up to is here to see the same dude too.*

She turned back around to see if the girl was still staring at her, but she wasn't. The girl and her child went through the machine. The line moved quickly after that.

Naheema went through the machine without a hitch. She asked where the restrooms were. A female officer told her to make a right turn, go all the way around the sign-in, and make another right turn. Naheema followed the directions and found the restroom. She ran inside and rushed into one of the stalls. She almost didn't make it.

As she walked out the stall, she caught a young woman pushing something up between her legs. "Oh my God! Excuse me," Naheema said, embarrassed.

The young woman told Naheema not to worry about it. The young woman had no shame in her game. She finished what she was doing and went to the sink at the same time as Naheema.

Naheema asked the woman where was she supposed be in order to sign up for C-78. Since the woman was going to the same place, she told Naheema to follow her. Naheema was a little apprehensive about walking with the woman because, if that woman got caught with whatever it was she stuffed up her kitty-cat, Naheema was sure to go down with her, so she walked two steps behind the woman.

They entered a little opening, where men, women, and children sat around holding papers in their hand. Naheema had to step up to the woman to ask her what she was supposed to do. The lady told her to stand on the line behind her and take out her identification number, along with the inmate number of the person she was going to see.

This line moved a little faster. As Naheema handed the corrections officer her information, he handed her an eight-by-ten cut-off piece of paper. He told her to write all her information on the paper, along with the inmate's name, date of birth, cell block number, and his ID number.

As she sat down to write the information on the paper, a white and blue, beat-up school bus pulled in to park behind the little stationhouse.

The driver walked into the building, said something to the correction officer, and then said, "Now leaving for C-78."

Everyone got up and, in single file, walked out of the door and boarded the bus. Naheema stepped on the bus and headed to the back, but the young woman she met in the bathroom grabbed her arm and told her to sit down next to her. She told Naheema she didn't want to be at the back of the bus when it was time for them to stop. Naheema thanked her and sat down.

The ride was short. They basically backed up, made a U-turn, and drove around the parking lot to another brown building. Naheema shook her head from side to side, thinking to herself, *This is un-fucking-believable. We could have walked across the fucking lot.*

The young woman sitting must have read the expression on Naheema's face. She started laughing. She told Naheema the reason why the visitors can't walk across is because inmates work on the grounds in plain clothes, and the correction officers didn't want to confuse them with the visitors.

Naheema just looked at the young woman. She asked her what made her tell her that, and the woman told Naheema the expression on her face gave it away. Naheema smiled, and they exited the bus.

Naheema looked at her watch and realized she'd spent an hour and a half just being processed from one building to another.

The doors to the correction facility opened, and groups of men, women, and children exited the building and boarded the bus. As the bus filled up, a corrections officer came out and repeated the same rules told to them on the way into the first building.

When the bus pulled off, the officer started stamping the backs of people's hands with some invisible ink as they filed into a second line into the building. After the last person was inside, the corrections officer locked the door and pushed his way through the crowd.

Everyone began stripping again, removing jewelry, rings, keys, and change from their pockets. The only difference this time was that they had to remove their footwear if they were wearing boots or sneakers. Since Naheema had on sandals, she went through without any problems.

She placed her bag on the scanner, handed the officer her papers, and walked through the machine. She was handed her papers, which were now stamped with the date and time of arrival to the building, and handed a key to a locker. She walked to her left and found the locker that the key belonged to. She placed her wallet inside of the locker, locked it, grabbed the key, placed it in her pocket, and grabbed the papers.

She had to go and stand on another line to be checked again before going on a visit. She hoped like hell that this would be the last checkpoint.

She looked at the paper and noticed the time. It was already eleven-thirty. She was hungry and pissed off. This would definitely be her first and last visit to Rikers Island. She was searched again and told to go upstairs. She reached the top of the steps and was buzzed into a visitors' waiting room. She thought to herself, *Oh hell motherfucking no. This is it.* She handed another corrections officer the papers and was told to have a seat. The whole process made Naheema feel like she was in prison.

She looked around the gated room and saw the two young ladies who were going to visit the same man. They were no longer speaking to each other, and from the looks of it, neither one of them wanted her child to play with the other's. Naheema shook her head again. *Ain't that a bitch? Apparently the officers need to get their daily dose of entertainment too.*

Outside of the visitors' waiting room, plastic chairs and tables of different colors were set up in another part of the room. In the back of that was another gated fence where the inmates came through. A bell rang, and inmates started appearing on the floor, making noise, catcalling, and slapping each other five. To Naheema, it looked like they were happy to be there.

While the inmates were on one side of the room, acting like children, the women waiting to see them were acting like high school teenagers, calling out their men's names like they were at a high school basketball game. Naheema continued to look around at the madness of it all.

The corrections officer who took her papers started calling out the visitors' and inmates' last names. One by one, the women stood with the children and followed the officer to their tables.

Naheema was praying her name would be called in the first batch, but it wasn't. The officer locked the gate back and walked away. He slipped some papers inside of a panel made of glass and covered by some type of black material. Naheema guessed that the other officers were behind it, looking out at the floor.

And she guessed right because, two minutes later, another officer came walking out of the door. He had some papers in his hand.

As he walked over to the door, he opened the gate and stood in front of it, blocking Naheema's view of the floor. He began calling names, "Morgan for Williams."

Naheema stood up and walked over to the officer. He closed and locked the gate and told her to follow him. He walked her across the visiting floor, to the back of the room, and told her to have a seat.

A few minutes later, Mike came on the floor, in shackles, smiling at her. The officer placed him in a glass-plated room, pushed him inside, locked the door, and told him to turn around. He did and put his hands through an opening where they unlocked the shackles from his hands and legs. He rubbed his wrists and sat down.

Naheema was staring at him like he had two heads. She had never seen Mike unkempt. He was always clean-shaven, with an immaculate haircut, so to see him looking like a homeless man threw her out of whack. She started to talk, but Mike picked up the phone and nodded his head for her to do the same. She was dumbfounded as she picked up the phone and put it to her ear.

"Hey, baby. I didn't think you were coming," he said, as if this was normal to him.

"What? What?"

"Aw, Naheema, it's all right." Mike mistook her stuttering as concern for his safety.

"What the fuck is wrong with you? You act like this is normal."

"Damn! I thought—"

"Thought what? That I was concerned about you? Well, you're wrong. Yes, I was thrown for a loop when I first saw you, but let's not pretend that I'm here out of concern for your well-being."

"All right then. Since it's all business with you, no problem."

"Yeah, no fucking problem. Now, what was so fucking important that I had to come up here to see your sorry, no-good, deceitful ass for?"

"First off, watch how you talk to me. Don't think that I can't get at you from behind this glass. Don't let the appearance fool your stupid ass. That's one."

"No! Fuck you! You're the stupid one. You fucked my sister and then had the audacity to get her pregnant. And you fucked some other dirty bitch too and got her pregnant. Oh, muthafucka, you've got it twisted. I don't give two fucks about what you think you can or can't do to me. So speak about why the fuck I'm here."

"You know what? I'm going to let you have that, but I'm not always going to be in here."

"Whatever, nigga. Tell me what the fuck is up, so I can be out of here. I got a real man waiting outside for me," she said, smiling.

"Oh word? It's like that? You fucking some dusty muthafucka already? Damn! I thought you were better than that. I guess you and your sister are more alike than you think." Mike laughed.

"Maybe so. But one thing is for sure. I'm out here with your money, and you're in there with nothing. So laugh. I'll be like my sister in your mind, but I know, and the man out there waiting for me knows, that I am the real muthafucking thing."

Mike didn't expect that. He wanted to bust through that glass and choke the shit out of her. He was going to have to take this one because he needed her right now. He needed for Randy to get his shit out of her place. If another nigga was living there, then he knew he had to hurry and get that shit out even quicker. He looked at her, calmed down, took a few deep breaths, and smiled.

"Look, Naheema, I know I was wrong, but on the real, you need to let Randy come and get that shit out of your crib. I don't know what is going to happen to me, but I do know that they're looking to try to indict me, which means they're going to have warrants to bust up inside of your house, looking for that stuff."

"Really? Like you even give a damn, Mike. I am no longer stupid for your ass. You don't have to worry about none of that stuff. I threw everything out. I had my man drive me to the landfill on Staten Island, and I dumped the drugs, guns, and everything in that black gym bag there."

"YOU DID WHAT?" he yelled. "What about my fucking money?"

"Oh that? Let me see," she said, fucking with him. "Since I am so much like my sister, I gave her the majority of the money inside of the bag, and the rest to my man to buy your shop." Naheema laughed.

"You dumb fucking bitch! I am going to kill your ass when I get out of here. Just wait."

"Really? Well, by the time you actually get out of here, I will have already died of old age 'cause when I get finish giving the feds your little journal highlighting all of the murders you committed, you won't see the light of day, unless they're opening your casket to let someone view your body. Oh shit. Nope, not even then, 'cause there isn't anybody out there who'll miss you or give a damn about you." She stood.

Mike started yelling, screaming, and cursing Naheema out, calling her all types of motherfucker, whore, tramp, and bitch, but Naheema just laughed as the officers came flying down to put the shackles on him.

After they calmed him down, he sat there looking like this was checkmate and his life was over. He held the phone to his ear as tears dropped from his eyes.

Naheema turned around one last time to face him and felt her heart break into tiny pieces until there was nothing left to feel. She picked up the phone and said to him, "Now you know what it feels like to be left heartless. You showed me how to do it. I learned from the best." Then she left.

She walked over to the officer, and he escorted her off the floor, back to the gate. She was buzzed through, and she walked down the steps feeling like a new woman. She walked over to her locker, grabbed her stuff, and stood at the back of the line. Salt-N-Pepa's "You Showed Me" kept replaying over and over in her mind while she waited for the bus.

When the bus came, she got on, made her journey back to the main building, and jumped on the R101, which was ready to leave.

As the bus pulled away from the island, she gave it one last look before erasing the visit and Mike from her memory. The bus ride back to the drop site was quicker coming back than going to the island. She got off the bus, ran up the block, crossed the street, and boarded the B61 going back to Red Hook. Not one time did she think about Mike as she rode the bus home. She decided then and there that she was turning over a new leaf. She made a vow to herself and God to be celibate until he found the right man to enter her life.

Naheema made it home a little after four p.m. She took off her clothes, turned on the shower as hot as she could stand it, and jumped in.

After taking her shower, she oiled up and put on a long white T-shirt. She started taking Mike's clothes out to the incinerator and dumping all of the bags.

She came back in, locked her door, and went into her kitchen to make herself a sandwich. She placed two pickles on her plate with some chips, grabbed her plate and a glass of orange juice, and went into the living room to eat.

After dinner, she cleaned up her mess, turned off her television, walked to her bedroom and got into the bed. She had two more things to take care of before she could start her life anew. One was to get back at her sister, and the other was to turn Mike's notebooks over to the feds. With that in her head, she went to sleep.

# Chapter 24

While Naheema was fighting to keep her sanity on Rikers Island, Shaquanna was going insane at the precinct where Randy worked. She spoke with Randy's sergeant concerning his movements. She lied and told Sergeant Hernandez that she was Randy's fiancée and that they were expecting a baby. She said she was afraid for his mental state because of the case he was working on. She also told the sergeant she'd caught him smoking marijuana and sniffing cocaine and was really worried about him and that they should pull him off the case he was working on so he could get the help he needed.

Randy's sergeant was shocked. She didn't think all of that was happening, but because Shaquanna was a good actress, she had to take what she was saying into consideration. To her, Randy was changing, but the sergeant assumed it was because they hadn't locked Mike up for good yet. Randy's sergeant thanked Shaquanna for the information.

Shaquanna explained to the sergeant that she didn't want Randy to know she told on him because he would hurt her. She asked her to keep it quiet about her showing up.

The sergeant started to become a little suspicious of what Shaquanna was asking, but when she explained how much she loved Randy and didn't want to see him lose his job because nobody reached out to help him, that did it. She agreed to keep Shaquanna's visit to the precinct a secret.

She left the precinct on cloud nine. She was going to take away everything Randy cared about. She wanted him to feel like he had no one to turn to, so he would come crawling back to her. She climbed into her car and pulled off.

Just then Randy was pulling into another parking spot two cars back. He'd just missed Shaquanna by two minutes. He got out of his car and entered the precinct. He punched his time card and walked around to his sergeant's office to let her know he was now on the clock.

His sergeant called him into the office and told him she was pulling him off the case. Randy flipped out, causing his sergeant to look at him in a different light, making her think that maybe Randy's fiancée was correct in coming to report him. She told Randy to hand in his badge and gun, and to report to One Police Plaza on Tuesday morning at nine a.m.

Randy was pissed off. He couldn't believe he was being pulled from the case without any explanation. He stormed out of the precinct without punching out. He jumped into his car, backed up, and peeled out of there.

Shaquanna wasn't through with Randy yet. While he was out blowing off steam, she was pulling up to his apartment's management office to report him. She got out of the car, carrying a folder full of fake documents.

She walked into the management office, stepped to the window, and asked the receptionist if she could speak with the manager. The receptionist asked who she was, and Shaquanna said, "The wife of Detective Randy Simms."

The receptionist asked what it was in reference to, and Shaquanna told about some man renting an apartment under her deceased husband's name. She said she was there to provide documents to the manager. The receptionist told her to have a seat, and five minutes later, Shaquanna was escorted to the manager's office.

Shaquanna sat down and handed the manager a folder of falsified documents with a picture of a white man as Detective Randy Simms. They talked for almost two hours. Shaquanna played the manager like a stringed instrument.

Before she left the management office, she had a conference call with the manager, the borough director, and assistant director of the housing authority, who all promised her the man assuming her husband's identity would be kicked off the premises by the end of the day. They went so far as to try to have him arrested, but Shaquanna talked them out of it, telling them the man was a close friend of her deceased husband, and when her husband was murdered, he took it really hard. She explained that the man was already mentally unstable, but when he found out her husband was murdered, and the way he was murdered, he snapped and started using her husband's identity.

They all understood and said as long as she would sign an agreement stating that she wouldn't sue them, they were willing to not press charges. But they were adamant about having the marshal remove his stuff from the property. Shaquanna took out her checkbook and wrote a check out to cover the cost of having the marshal come out and to put Randy's stuff in storage.

The manager thanked her and commended her for looking out for the unstable man, and then she escorted Shaquanna out of her office.

Shaquanna left the management office satisfied with herself. She jumped back into her car, pulled out, and headed back onto the BQE. She was ready to sit back and let Randy come crawling to her. She felt like she had it all set up; like nothing could break her plan.

Shaquanna made it home within the hour due to traffic on the Jackie Robinson. She smiled, noticing that is was only seven-thirty in the evening. She decided that she was going to treat herself to a movie and some food.

While Shaquanna was out enjoying herself, Randy received a call from the manager at his development. She informed him about Shaquanna coming to the office and told him everything that happened. Randy was pissed.

The manager knew Shaquanna was lying because she knew Randy when he was an officer working the Brownsville projects, where she was a housing assistant. When she was leaving work, she was attacked, and Randy was the arresting officer on her case. So when Shaquanna came in with her bullshit, she quickly put two and two together and set up her own thing.

Shaquanna had assumed she was on a conference call with the assistant director and borough director, but she was really on the phone with two other housing assistants. As soon as she'd left the management office, the manager had called Randy and informed him about the visit.

Randy left the bar on Atlantic Avenue and headed back to Union Street to the precinct. He barged inside of his sergeant's office, demanding to speak with her.

The sergeant looked up then told Randy to close the door. As soon as he closed the door, the sergeant began yelling at him, telling him she should write him up for insubordination.

Randy stood there and silently cursed his supervisor.

After the sergeant finished threatening Randy, she told him, "Have a seat."

Randy sat and began explaining his situation to her.

His sergeant sat quietly for a moment, thinking over Randy's story before telling him about the woman who claimed she was his fiancée.

When the sergeant finished telling Randy the story of why he had to turn in his gun and badge, Randy was floored. He didn't think Shaquanna could be so stupid. He asked his sergeant if this meant he could get his gun and badge returned to him.

The sergeant opened the desk drawer, pulled out Randy's gun and badge and placed them on his desk. When she reached for them, she pulled them back and asked him, "What are your plans?"

"I plan on arresting Shaquanna Morgan for impersonation, fraud, identity theft, and mishandling of fraudulent documentation to a city agency." *And get me some more of that good stuff before I arrest her ass for fucking with me.*

The sergeant handed Randy his gun and badge and told Randy to give her five minutes to call a judge and get a warrant issued for Shaquanna's arrest.

Randy was grateful. He left the sergeant's office and walked over to his desk.

Ten minutes later, the desk officer was handing him a warrant, signed, sealed, and faxed from Judge Silverman of the NYC Criminal Court. He folded the warrant, put it in his back pocket, and left the precinct.

It took him thirty minutes to get to 104-92 Street in the Ridgewood section of Queens. He parked his car five blocks away from Shaquanna's place. He reached over, opened his glove compartment, and pulled out his tool kit. He put it in his pants pocket and opened the car door. He pulled the lever to release the hood of his trunk, grabbed his keys, and got out of the car. He walked to the back of his car, lifted up the hood, and rummaged through his trunk. He had a small cardboard box in his trunk with his car cleaners inside of it. He dumped the box and started filling the box with junk from his car. He wanted to give Shaquanna the impression he was coming back to her place to stay with her.

He grabbed the box and closed the trunk then headed down the street to her house. He got to her door, put the box down, and rang the bell. He waited two minutes before he rang the bell again.

Seeing she wasn't there, he pulled his tool kit from his pocket, took out the necessary tools, and picked her lock. He let himself into the house.

He sat the box down on the side of the front door, walked to her kitchen, opened the cabinet, and poured himself a shot of Hennessy. He took the bottle and the shot glass with him into the living room and sat down in the chair facing the door. He was going to wait patiently for her to come in. He made two more drinks and started dozing off. He wanted her to think he was drunk and depressed.

Shaquanna finished her meal and waited for the waiter to bring her the bill. She looked at the time. It was almost ten p.m. She figured Randy should be on his way to her house to beg her to let him stay with her. She paid for her meal and left the restaurant. She jumped into her car and headed home.

Three blocks away from the house she was renting, she was on the lookout for Randy's car. When she didn't see it, she figured he hadn't gotten off work yet, so she pulled into the driveway and parked her car.

She shut the engine off and got out of her car. She looked around before walking to her porch. She hated her block because it was so dark, with only two streetlights, both at opposite ends of the block.

She hurried to her door, stuck her key into the lock, turned it, and opened her door. She locked the door and turned around to step and almost tripped over the box that Randy had left there.

"What the fuck is that?" she yelled, turning on the lights in the living room.

"Oh shit! What the fuck are you doing in my house?" she yelled, waking Randy from his sleep.

"What? What time is it? Where the fuck am I?" he asked, pretending to be drunk and confused.

"Randy, how did you get in my house?" She stepped closer to him. "And what the fuck is in that box?" she asked, smiling inside.

"I rang the bell and knocked, but you didn't answer, so I let myself in."

"You picked my lock? Are you out of your fucking mind?" She walked back over to the door and examined the lock.

"Girl, please, I didn't have to pick your lock. You left the window open." The Hennessy bottle dropped to the floor as he got up from the couch.

Shaquanna looked around ready to catch him in a lie, but noticed the window was indeed cracked. "Oh, sorry."

"Don't be. If you didn't, I would be still standing outside on your porch, waiting for you to come home. But, listen, I need to talk to you."

"About what?" She threw her purse on the couch. "The last time we talked, you stormed out of my place. Remember?"

"I know, and that's what I want to talk to you about. I was wrong for doing that. I freaked out. I was scared when you said I was the father. Can you forgive me?"

"Umm . . . I don't know if I can," she said, pouting. "You said some foul shit to me, and it hurt."

"I'm sorry. How can I make it up to you?" Randy pulled her into his arms and kissed her. "Huh? Tell me how I can make this right between us." He was getting sick to his stomach.

But Shaquanna was smiling inside, thinking her plan had worked. "Well, I don't know. It might take a while before I can forgive you."

"I know how to start." Randy held her hand and led her to the back of the house, toward her bedroom.

"That's a start."

Randy pulled her into the bedroom, closed the door behind him, and began stripping her clothes off. She was enjoying the moment. *Damn, I should have thought of this a long time ago.* She was ready for whatever he had planned for her.

He reached on top of her dresser and removed two baby wipes from the box. Then he got on his knees, spread opened her lips, and started wiping in a downward motion. He wiped her clean. He rolled her onto her stomach, pushed open her legs, and wiped upward from her vagina, up through the crack of her butt.

It felt so good to her. She wanted him to hurry up and fuck her already.

When he was finished, he excused himself to the bathroom, where he pulled out his cell phone and called his partner, informed him that he was going to make the arrest in an hour, so he needed him to bring the car to 104-92 Street in Queens.

He hung up the phone, pulled a condom out of his pocket, looked inside of her medicine cabinet, and grabbed the K-Y Jelly. He squeezed some into the condom before slipping it on. Then he squeezed some into his hand and rubbed his hand over the condom. He put the K-Y back into the medicine cabinet and left the bathroom.

He entered her bedroom and caught her pleasing herself. He climbed onto the bed, grabbed her by her hips, and pulled her ass up into the air. She continued to finger herself as he slipped his dick deep into her cave. She was so into grinding her hips, she didn't notice he was wearing a condom.

Randy pounded her insides something terrible. What used to be pleasure for her was now feeling like torture. She tried to move away from him, but his vise-like grip was too strong for her to slip away from.

She started screaming, "Get off of me! Get off!"

That made him slow it down a bit. He didn't want to finish with her just yet. He wanted to pop her cherry before he placed the handcuffs on her.

"You're hurting me!"

"Baby, I'm sorry. You just feel so damn good. I'll take it easy." He began to "slow-wine" and grind, pushing deep inside and "wining," then pulling all the way out, and grinding it back in.

"Oh yeah! Just like that! Aah! I'm going to come."

Randy continued with the same method.

"Oh, God! I'm coming! Stop! I'm coming! Aah!"

Randy pulled out as her juices squirted out of her. She came harder than she'd ever had in her life. She was drained and was about to lay down, but Randy wouldn't let her.

"No, no. I didn't come yet." He pulled her up gently and pushed his dick in her ass. "Ah! Yeah!" he moaned, slowly pumping in and out of her. With her head in between the pillows, ass high up in the air, Randy leaned over her in a squatting position and began pounding her a new hole.

She couldn't move or try to push him off because of the position she was in. One wrong move and she could pop her neck. She knew it and Randy knew it.

As he pounded in and out of her with so much force, she started to think he was mad at her. She attempted to scream, but her cries were muffled by the pillows.

Randy pounded and pounded, pulling all the way out and pushing in deeper and deeper with each thrust.

After pounding her for another ten minutes, he noticed blood on the condom as he pulled out of her. That turned him on even more.

Randy had pounded her insides so hard, the condom burst when he let loose. "Ah! Ah! Ah! Damn! Shit!" He collapsed on top of her, forcing her to collapse on the bed. Randy finally climbed off and went into the bathroom.

She was crying. It felt like she had just been raped. She got up to get a towel, and a wave of nausea hit her like a ton of bricks. She dropped to the floor in burning pain. "Ah! Help me!" she screamed, blood gushing from between her legs.

Randy heard her, but he continued to rinse the soap off of his body. Then he dried off, got dressed, and exited the bathroom.

Randy walked in and saw her on the floor. He grabbed his cell phone and called for an ambulance. He gave his code to the dispatch, so they could hurry the bus.

While they waited, he ran into the bathroom grabbed two hand towels, ran back into the bedroom, and stuffed the towels between her legs. He ran to the front of the house, unlocked the door, and ran back into the room. He searched through her dresser drawers and found a large pair of white underwear and a T-shirt. He put the panties on her with the towels stuffed in them. Then he placed the T-shirt over her head.

He opened her closet and took out a pair of black sweat pants from the shelf. He put those on her and a pair of socks. She was crying and screaming from the pain. He lifted her up from the floor and placed her on the bed.

Just as he grabbed his phone to call, there was a loud bang at the front door.

"It's open."

Two paramedics rushed to the bedroom. One ran over to her and began taking her vital signs and blood pressure, while the other one questioned Randy.

He informed them he was a detective from the 76th Precinct on his way to arrest her, that Shaquanna was pregnant and may be having a miscarriage.

The male EMT screamed to his partner that they had to hurry up and rush her to the hospital. He started an IV and placed the oxygen mask over her face. Then he lifted her up and laid her on the gurney. The female tech strapped her on the bed as her partner rolled her out of her bedroom, through her living room, and out of the door.

Randy found out they were taking her to Jamaica Hospital and told them he would follow them after he secured the premises and called his sergeant.

With sirens ringing in the night, the ambulance sped off.

Randy looked around the apartment before grabbing his box to leave out of her apartment. He walked to his car and threw the box in the passenger seat.

He looked at the time on the dashboard as he pulled out of the parking space. Two-thirty a.m. He placed a call to Jamaica Hospital to make sure that they handcuffed his prisoner to her bed.

# Chapter 25

Naheema was at home having a peaceful dream about her new life. She had no clue that her world was about to be rocked and turned into her worst nightmare.

At three a.m. Tuesday morning, a crashing sound exploded throughout her apartment. She thought she was dreaming.

"Police! Kitchen, clear! Living room, clear! Bathroom, clear! Bedroom—Police! Get on the floor! Get on the floor! Now!"

Naheema jumped up as the covers were being pulled off of her, and she was being dragged to the floor.

"Stay down! Hands out to the side! Let's go!"

She felt a boot kick her arm straight. "What's going on?" she screamed, but there was too much commotion going on for anyone to hear her.

Then she heard someone say, "Clear. It's all clear."

The lights were turned on in the bedroom as she was being handcuffed and lifted off the floor. The female officer who'd kicked her sat her on the bed.

"Don't move!" the female said, leaving the room.

Naheema was too afraid to move. She was too afraid to breathe. Her arm was killing her where she was kicked, and it felt like the handcuffs was cutting off the circulation in her wrists.

Then she heard a man say, "Well, look at who we have here," and she knew she was fucked.

A white man in a suit walked into the bedroom, followed by a bad-ass looking black female in a pantsuit. The female sat down on the bed beside her, while the white man stood up facing her.

"What is this all about? Can you please loosen these handcuffs? They're cutting me."

Agent Freeman, who the white man was facing her, looked to the officer at the door and nodded his head. The officer walked into the room and loosened the cuffs on her wrist. Then he left the room.

The agent sitting next to her pulled out her badge and showed it to her. "Are you Naheema Morgan?"

"Yes, I am. What is this about?"

"We got a tip that Mike Williams was selling drugs out of this apartment."

Naheema shook her head. "That's a lie. Whoever told you that is lying to you."

"Really?"

Naheema wasn't too worried because she'd thrown out everything.

"What are you looking for?"

"Drugs, guns, and money," Agent Brisbon, the black female, said.

"There's nothing here."

"We'll see," Agent Brisbon said. She nodded to the officers to continue searching the room.

Each officer came up empty-handed.

"You can make this easy on yourself, Ms. Morgan, by just telling us where everything is. If you cooperate we'll tell the DA and they will go easy on you," Agent Freeman said, smiling.

"How many times am I going to say it? There is nothing here," she said, getting angry.

An officer began pulling the drawers out of her dresser, while the other one searched inside of the dresser itself.

"Sir, there's something here," the male officer said as he pulled a Ziploc bag filled with marijuana in little baggies. The officer walked over to Agent Freeman and handed him the bag.

"Well, well, what do we have here?" Agent Freeman asked, swinging the bag in front of Naheema's face.

Naheema was shocked. She never would have thought to check her dresser.

"That's not mine. I don't know how that got there."

"That is your dresser, right?"

"Yes, but my ex's underwear used to be in that drawer."

"And where is your ex now?"

"He's on Rikers Island."

"Well that's a shame, because you're going to be held accountable for this now," Agent Freeman said. "All right, officers, you can take her and the stuff. Bag it and tag it."

The female officer stepped in front of Naheema and grabbed her arms to stand her up.

"What are you doing? Get your hands off of me. That's not mine," she stated, trying to pull away.

"Now, now, Ms. Morgan, I know you don't want to be charged with assaulting an officer as well as resisting arrest, so just do what the officer wants so we can get this over with," Agent Freeman said.

"You have to believe me. That's not mine," she begged.

Agent Freeman smirked. "I heard you the first couple of times, so in order for everything to get straightened out, we need to go to the precinct."

As the officer walked into the room to help take Naheema out, Agent Brisbon finally spoke.

"Wait a minute. Ms. Morgan, is there anyone I can call for you to come and watch your apartment until we can get somebody to fix the door?"

Naheema looked at her then at Agent Freeman before answering. For a quick minute her brain was blank. She couldn't think of anyone to call.

"Ms. Morgan, there's no one you can think of?" Agent Brisbon asked, feeling sorry for her.

"Yes. Can you call my friend Shadina Weaver?"

"Sure. What's her number?" Brisbon asked.

Naheema gave her the number.

Agent Brisbon picked up her phone and dialed.

Dina answered her phone on the first ring. "Hello," she answered, sleep in her voice.

"May I speak with Shadina Weaver?"

There was a pause.

"This is Special Agent Brisbon with the Federal Bureau of Investigation. I have a woman by the name of Naheema Morgan in my custody. She asked me to call you and ask you to come and sit in her apartment until we can get her door fixed."

There was another pause, but Naheema gathered that Dina had asked to talk to her.

"Unfortunately, she is unavailable at this time, but she will be at the Seventy-Sixth Precinct until this afternoon. You can come by there to speak with her."

Brisbon disconnected the call and the officer grabbed Naheema by the arm and began pulling her out the door.

Naheema turned to Agent Brisbon. "Is it possible for me to get some sweat pants to wear?"

She told her yes, and Naheema motioned her head to the gray

sweats on the chair, and the female officer helped her into them.

The cops finished searching her apartment as she was being escorted to the awaiting navy blue van. The officer opened the door, helped her inside, and closed and locked the door. She went around to the other side and got in.

Two minutes later, they pulled off, headed toward the 76th Precinct.

Naheema was scared. She didn't know what she was headed for, but she was very hopeful she would be able to bargain her way out of it.

She put her head down and said a quick prayer, asking for the Lord for guidance and forgiveness for being so stupid and trusting. She lifted her head up and noticed they were a block away from the precinct. Her heart began to race with fear. She only remembered, from watching the cop shows, that she was entitled to at least one phone call.

She sat there wondering if they were going to put her in a cell with a bunch of hardened criminals. As that thought played around in her head, she began to tear up. She looked out of the back window and noticed they were entering the precinct through an alley.

They drove down the ramp, and she heard a bell sound. Then a gate went up, and a minute later, they were driving through the gate, into the dark, under the precinct. They pulled up to a door, and the van stopped. Both officers got out of the car and walked around to the side of the van. The door slid back, and the male officer helped her out of the van. He waited for his partner to come to the other side of the van so they could walk her through the doors, up six small steps, and onto the main floor of the 76th Precinct.

Naheema had to readjust her eyes to register the lights. She was shocked to hear how quiet the precinct was at this time of morning. She'd always assumed that the cops caught the most criminals at this time of the day, when they assumed everyone was in their homes sleeping.

The male officer sat her down on a bench and secured her cuffed hands to a linked chain that was bolted to the floor, while the female officer walked over to a tall desk and handed her papers over to the officer behind the desk.

"Will I get a phone call?"

"After you've been processed," the female officer said with her back to Naheema.

Naheema sat there as quiet as a mouse, looking at the clock. It was four in the morning.

The female officer unlocked the chain and lifted her up by the arm. She walked Naheema over to the desk and patted her down in front of the desk sergeant. . Satisfied that she didn't have any weapons on her body, the female officer took her back to the cell and pushed her inside. She told Naheema to turn around, step back into the gate, and put her hands up. The female officer unlocked the handcuffs and told her to turn back around.

Naheema turned to face the officer.

The officer looked her in her eyes and said, "Good luck." She walked away.

Naheema was shocked. She didn't think the female officer liked her too much.

She looked around her new home for the night as the reality of her nightmare set in. There was a silver iron sink in the wall, a silver iron toilet sitting behind a white brick wall, flies buzzing around it, and a bench where she was supposed to either sleep or sit. She chose to sit. She walked over to the bench, sat down, and began rubbing her wrists.

As she sat there, she thought about everything she'd read in those journals and she realized she never really knew the type of man Mike really was—how vindictive and calculating he was.

The gruesome details of Mike's actions played in her head. It was as if she was standing there watching them herself as the image of that young girl being beaten within an inch of her life played like a bad movie in her head. She remembered reading that after Mike had beaten her, he'd burned the young woman to death. All because her brother threw away his drugs. Naheema didn't want to believe she was ever pregnant by—or even in a relationship with—such a man.

Another one of Mike's death stories played in her head—the one where Mike paid one of his soldiers to burn down a family's house on Columbia and Kent Streets and had the nerve to complain about the cost of killing those families.

Then in 1992, a well-respected principal was murdered in the Red Hook community by three young men who were warring in the community over drugs. She remembered reading that Mike was responsible for it.

She broke down crying. She felt like at fool. She allowed a murderer into her life—a man who could cause her to lose everything she worked so hard to have.

She walked over to the sink, turned on the water, and began throwing some on her face. When she was finished, she turned the water off and looked around for some tissue, but there was none. She pulled her T-shirt up from the neck and dried her face.

She sat back down on the bench and bent over to rest her head. When she looked up, she saw Dina entering the precinct. She was so happy to see a familiar face. She got up and held onto the bars. Another wave of tears spilled from her eyes, as she watched her best friend wave to her.

As Dina walked over to the bars, Naheema cried her heart out. "I need you to help me."

"Sure girl. What do you need me to do?"

"I need a lawyer, and fast. I am in so much trouble right now."

"Don't worry about it. I already hired one of the best defense attorneys at my mother's firm."

"Oh, thank you. Oh, God! Thank you."

"Don't cry, Naheema. I got your back. You're going to get out of this mess."

"What is the lawyer's name? And when am I going to meet with him or her? I want you to show them the journals we have. I tried to remember as much as I could, just in case I couldn't get in contact with you."

"The lawyer's name is Janet Lebowitz. She's a genius with these types of cases. Her office is on Court Street. Don't worry about the books. I'm taking them to her as soon as I leave here."

"Okay. How much is the retainer?"

"Girl, please. When my mother told her it was for her niece, that woman kicked it up into high gear. She told my mother it was on the house."

"I can't accept that. What's going to happen when she finds out I'm no relation to your mother?"

"Naheema, stop tripping. My mother helped save a high-profile case for this woman, and that helped her get a promotion, so she owes my mother big time. Besides, my mother always calls you her niece."

"Thank you, Dina. I don't know what I would do without you."

"Girl, don't worry about that. Now, when we got off the phone with the lawyer, she was making some calls to find out what they're trying to charge you with. She said once she was finished with that, she was going to come and see you."

"Okay."

"I told you not to worry. It will all work out. Housing fixed your door, and I have the copy of the new keys. I gave the officer at the desk a bag with your clothes, toothbrush, toothpaste, comb, brush, rag, and a scrunchy for your hair. He said they will give it to you before they take you down to the courthouse to see the judge."

"Thank you so much," Naheema said, tearing up.

"Now, is there anything else you need me to do?"

"Yes. I need you to call my boss," Naheema said, crying. "Her name is Mrs. Brown. Her home number is hanging up on my refrigerator door. Tell her what's going on with me."

"Baby girl, stop all of the tears. Everything is going to work itself out. I need you to stay strong for me. We're going to get you out of this. I promise."

She sniffled. "Okay."

"Now, I have to go, but I'll call your manager and tell her everything. Also, the lawyer said to tell you not to talk to anyone before she comes. Don't answer any questions or write any statements before she gets here." Dina held Naheema's hand through the bars.

"I won't. I just want this to be over with already."

"Have patience and pray." Dina hugged Naheema through the bars and left the precinct.

Naheema's tears continued to fall down her face as she watched her friend leave the precinct. She looked at the clock on the wall behind the desk officer. Seven-thirty a.m. She couldn't believe she'd been sitting behind bars for three and a half hours already.

The female officer who had put her in the cell walked over to her and handed her a brown bag.

Naheema took the bag and thanked her. She sat down, opened the bag, and was happy that it was real food inside of the bag.

The female officer walked back over to Naheema. "I hope you eat bacon."

Naheema smiled.

"There is some orange juice in there too."

Naheema looked at her, head tilted to the side. "Why are you doing this?"

"Because we all have to eat," the female officer said, smiling.

"No, seriously. Why?"

"Ms. Morgan, you are not this first woman locked up because of a man, and you won't be the last. But I will tell you not to give up. Fight to get your freedom back." Then the female officer smiled and walked away.

Naheema did a double take as she stood there dumbfounded. Officer Rivera was right. She had to fight. There was no way she was going to jail for crimes she didn't commit and didn't help to commit. Hell, she didn't even have any real knowledge of them until she'd found those bags.

She slowly walked back to the bench, where she sat down and ate the bacon, egg, and cheese sandwich and drank the juice. She then sat back and closed her eyes.

# Chapter 26

Two hours later, Naheema was being escorted into a room in the back of the precinct by the two agents who had talked to her inside her bedroom. The female officer sat her in a wooden chair and locked her cuffed hands to another chain bolted to the floor.

Agent Freeman placed a recorder on the table, along with a folder. He pressed the record button and spoke. He recited his name, badge number, the date and the time, along with her information. He then asked her if she wanted something to drink before they got started.

"No."

Agent Brisbon recited her information then sat in a chair in the corner.

"Good morning, Ms. Morgan. How are you feeling?"

"I'm fine."

"Okay. Right now, it's not looking too good for you. You're being charged with unlawful possession of marijuana which is a misdemeanor, but because you had more than an ounce of marijuana bagged up, you're also being charged with possession with intent to distribute. Before we start, is there anything you want to tell us?"

"No," she said, feeling the weight of the world on her shoulders, and praying that her lawyer walked through the door.

"No?" Agent Freeman asked, like he was dumbfounded.

"No. I was told by my attorney not to answer any questions."

"Okay. But that's not going to help you beat this case. We can help you."

"That's okay. I'll wait for my lawyer."

Agent Brisbon was growing tired of playing nice with her. "Ms. Morgan, do you know you can spend three years of your life in jail?"

"For what? I didn't do anything. That's not my stuff."

"Ms. Morgan, in order for us to help you, you're going to have to help us," Agent Freeman said, trying another tactic.

"Help you with what? I don't know anything."

"How did you come to know Mr. Williams?"

"I met him two years ago downtown, Brooklyn. Why?"

"Really? So you've known him for two years, and you don't know who he is or what he was doing?" Agent Freeman asked in disbelief.

Agent Brisbon looked at Naheema like she was an idiot. She thought to herself, *This girl cannot be that stupid.*

"No I didn't."

"Ms. Morgan, do you want us to believe that you were in a two-year relationship with one of the most wanted drug dealers in Red Hook, and you had no idea?" Agent Brisbon asked. She could no longer stay quiet.

"Yes. That's what I've being saying to the both of you."

"I see," Agent Freeman, said looking at his partner.

"So where did the marijuana come from?" Agent Freeman asked.

"My ex-boyfriend."

"Ok, so now he's your ex-boyfriend?" Agent Brisbon asked.

"I've been saying that since you busted into my apartment this morning. He is my ex-boyfriend."

"How long has he been your ex-boyfriend?"

"Since last Friday."

"Well, that doesn't sound too convincing."

As the agent was about to ask another question, the door opened, and in walked a short, red-haired white woman with glasses wearing a brown pin-striped pantsuit.

"Okay," she said, "you've had your fun. Now this interrogation is over. Ms. Morgan, I am your attorney."

Naheema was so happy to see her lawyer enter the room. She broke down crying.

The attorney pulled out her card and gave one to the Agent Freeman at the table. He took the card, looked at it, then hit the *stop* button on the recorder. He picked up the recorder and the folder and stormed over to the door.

"Whatever my client answered or didn't answer will be stricken from your records." Ms. Lebowitz smiled.

"I don't think so," Agent Freeman said.

"Oh, I know so. The agent in charge is waiting for a call from the both of you. Have a wonderful day." Ms. Lebowitz sat down in the chair.

The agents slammed the door on their way out of the room.

The lawyer sat down and started asking Naheema a whole bunch of questions concerning her relationship with Mike.

Naheema informed the lawyer that she had been abused by Mike during their two-year relationship, how Mike came to move into her apartment with her, and about how he lied to her about who he was and what he did for a living.

The lawyer explained to Naheema the charges pending against her. She also stressed that the two FBI agents and a special narcotics unit in the NYPD had been working together to lock Mike up for years, but never had any real proof to seal the deal. She went on to explain to Naheema that the only way she would be able to get the charges reduced or even dismissed was if she had hardcore evidence that they could use as leverage with the DA.

Naheema told her lawyer about the two composition notebooks she gave to Dina.

Ms. Lebowitz informed her that she did receive those books, and that she would see what she could do for her. She said, “If Mike has a good attorney, he could argue that you made the books up.”

“How? Most of the stuff inside of those books happened before I even met him.”

“Okay, but I just want you to be prepared. Naheema, this is the reality. They’ve been trying to lock Mike behind bars for years, but he’s always gotten off. So right now, even with the death of that young woman, the District Attorney’s office can’t afford a mess up. So yes, they can get him a life sentence for that young woman, but they want more than that. They want to put the needle in his arm, so they’re willing to sacrifice you if they have to.”

“Why? What more do they want from me?” she asked with tears in her eyes.

“Listen to me. I will take care of this. I just want you to understand how serious this is. They’ve spent too much of the taxpayers’ money on this case, so they’re not leaving until they are satisfied. From what I’ve researched about this case, Mr. Williams is a very deadly man who has left many families victims to his atrocities. However, that’s where I come in. It’s my job to make sure that you don’t become a victim after the fact.”

“Okay, so what’s the next step?”

“Well, I’m going to go see the judge and the DA to see what they are talking about. But, first, let me ask you this. Who else knows about these books?”

“Nobody, but Dina, you, and I. And Mike, of course.”

“How did you get the books?”

"The night before the FBI came to my home, I found all of this stuff as I was cleaning out his clothing to throw away."

"Since Mike has been in jail, have you gone on a visit to see him?"

Naheema was stuck. She couldn't understand why that was any concern of the lawyers.

"Naheema, I need to know."

"Yes. I went to see him. He called me and said he needed me to come up there because I was in danger."

"And that's all?"

"Yes. Get the tapes from Rikers. It will show you that it wasn't a pleasant or friendly visit. You can also ask the guards about it because Mike began threatening me on the visit. They had to come and subdue him."

"Okay, I'll put the motion in for the request. I'm quite sure the DA's office did the same thing to cover their asses. Okay, you're doing good."

"What are the chances that I'm going home today?"

"Look, I need to be as honest as possible. You may have to go to Brooklyn Detention Center for a couple of days until we can get all of this stuff sorted out."

"What? I can't. I won't survive there."

"Yes, you will."

"Please help me. I didn't do anything wrong. Please."

"I'll see what I can do. Do you have a change of clothes?"

"Yes. Dina brought some to the precinct."

"Okay. I'll ask them to let you get cleaned up before I leave. After you're done, they're going to transport you over to the courthouse. Don't panic or worry, and don't talk to anyone about this. I'll be at the courthouse to see you as soon as I'm done with this."

"Okay," Naheema said, afraid of the outcome.

Ms. Lebowitz knocked on the door twice to inform the officer that she was finished. She then asked the officer to let Naheema clean herself up before they took her over to the courthouse, and the female officer agreed to do it.

As the lawyer left, the female officer unlocked the chain from the chair and led Naheema out the door and back to the main floor. She sat Naheema on the bench, while she retrieved her bag from behind the desk. Then she escorted Naheema downstairs to the showers. She removed the handcuffs from Naheema's wrists, handed her the bag, and stepped outside of the bathroom door.

Naheema was beyond happy to take a shower and clean herself up. When she was done, the female officer handcuffed her wrists in front of her, instead of behind her back, and walked her back to the cell.

Naheema looked at the clock. It was now going on one in the afternoon. Lunch was served and she was given a bologna sandwich, one apple, and a container of apple juice. She finished everything.

A little after two, she was transported to the NYC Criminal Court on Jay Street, where she was placed in another holding cell with eight other females. She sat down on the bench at the far end of the cell, praying no fights broke out.

One by one, the women were escorted out of the cell and taken upstairs to see the judge. Out of all eight women, two were sent back to the holding cell to be transported to Rikers Island.

It was in that cell Naheema really understood what the female officer at the precinct was talking about. Both of the women brought back down to the holding cells were locked up on charges stemming from their men being drug dealers. Naheema wished she could introduce her lawyer to the women, but she had to worry about her case first.

At two-forty in the afternoon, Naheema was escorted upstairs to another room, where she was locked inside.

Two minutes later, her lawyer entered the room.

Naheema looked into her eyes to see if she could see if the lawyer had good or bad news, but the lawyer's face revealed nothing.

The lawyer sat down and took a deep breath before looking into Naheema's eyes.

Naheema's heart started racing, her palms started sweating, and her eyes filled with water. She said, "I'm ready. How many years am I serving?"

"They're looking to give you one year in jail, but after I made some calls, spoke to the DA, and handed over those journals, the DA will need some time to verify the facts in the books."

Naheema broke down crying. She was afraid to do one day in jail. She wouldn't make it in there for one year.

"This is not fair."

"I agree with you. It's not fair, but the Feds claim you had a little over two ounces of marijuana packed for sale that was taped inside of your dresser drawer. So we're going to have to deal with this. Like I said, I will make sure that you don't do what they're asking," Ms. Lebowitz said, handing her a napkin.

"What am I going to do? What happens next?" she asked, wiping her eyes.

"They're going to bring you upstairs to see the judge about bail first, and we'll take it from there," Ms. Lebowitz said, standing up to leave. "Just trust me." Then she left.

For the first time since her mother's death, Naheema felt alone.

She began thinking about her sister. She was still pissed off, but she knew she would eventually have to get over it. She just wasn't sure if she wanted to forgive her. One thing she knew for sure: she was going to make it her business to have a face-to-face with her sister, once she got out of this mess.

Five minutes into her thought process, a court officer entered the room to escort her upstairs to the courtroom.

She was nervous. She held her head up as high as she could, pushing through her fear, and entered the courtroom. She was placed inside of a clear box and told to have a seat. She looked around the courtroom and saw two friendly faces. Dina and her mother were sitting in the second pew behind the lawyer. Dina saw her and smiled. Naheema smiled back. She was feeling at little better, knowing she had people out there who actually cared for her.

She looked around again and saw Randy sitting in the pews as well. Her mouth hit the floor when she saw the gold badge hanging from his neck.

Dina registered the look on Naheema's face and turned her head around to face the back of the courtroom to see what she was staring at. She saw Randy with a gold badge hanging from his neck, sitting there like he was waiting for someone.

Randy saw the girls staring at him but refused to acknowledge them. After leaving Shaquanna with the paramedics, he'd called his precinct and found out that they were holding Naheema there. He found out from the female officer that Naheema was going to be taken to court for the afternoon session to see the judge. He thanked the officer, hung up, got into his car, and drove with his lights on to the courthouse in Brooklyn. He wanted to let her know that her sister was in the hospital. He also had to get to the courthouse because Mike was going to see the judge today too. He sat there waiting patiently to see the case he was working so hard on come to a close.

A docket number was called, and Naheema was escorted over to the defendant's table with her lawyer. Then he walked away.

The judge asked who was representing Naheema, and her lawyer stepped up. Then the prosecutor stepped up. The judge looked at both attorneys and Naheema. He said, "Ms. Morgan, you are being charged with one count of unlawful possession of marijuana, and one count of possession with the intent to distribute. How do you plea?"

"Not guilty, Your Honor," Ms. Lebowitz spoke.

"Counselor, what are you asking for?" the judge asked the DA.

"Your Honor, we're asking for one year in, followed up with six months probation."

"Ms. Lebowitz do you accept this?"

"No, Your Honor. May we approach the bench?"

Naheema was told to sit down, while the DA and her lawyer talked with the judge.

"Your Honor, the DA was presented with new information by my client on another case. He agreed to look it over before requesting a sentence," Ms. Lebowitz said, pissed at this new change from the DA.

"Is this true, counselor?"

"Yes and no," the DA answered.

"Please explain."

"Ms. Morgan is still accountable for the charges that are pending against her. However, Ms. Lebowitz did turn over some new evidence regarding another trial."

"That's right, Your Honor, and the DA neglected to tell you that if this new evidence turns out to be credible, than he is going to need my client to testify about how she came to posses that evidence."

"Is that true?"

"Yes, Your Honor. But that does not weigh on the fact that the defendant is going to be charged," the DA said, trying to hustle his reasoning to the judge.

"Okay. Go back to your sides."

Both counselors walked back to their respective tables. The court officer told Naheema to stand up again. She wanted desperately to ask her lawyer what happened, but Ms. Lebowitz refused to look at her.

"It has come to my attention that some new evidence was given to the DA concerning another case and because said evidence was retrieved from the defendant, the DA is going to need time to review the validity of the source. Is that correct?"

"Yes, Your Honor," the DA answered.

"Very well," the judge said, sitting back to weigh his decision. "Counselor, do you have anything to add to this?" he asked Ms. Lebowitz.

"No, Your Honor, we are willing to give the DA a chance to play catch up. He can verify the authenticity of the new evidence."

"That settles it," the judge said, looking at the DA. "Is the DA looking for bail on this?"

"No, Your Honor, we are asking that the defendant be remanded until verification has been provided."

"Your Honor, this is ridiculous. My client is a city employee who's never been in any trouble with the law. This is just a tactic on the behalf of the DA to ensure that my client helps them close a case that they couldn't close for the last ten years."

"Is this true?" the judge asked, pissed that the DA was trying to snowball him.

"No, Your Honor, it's not, but I do reserve the right to question the defendant concerning how she ended up with the evidence."

"Counselors approach."

The judge gave them both and earful. He did not like being played for a fool. He ordered them back to their tables.

"It's a sad day in law when the DA decides to play both judge and juror. However, I've made a decision. Ms. Morgan, please stand. You are remanded, but due to the nature of this case, I am granting the DA's office thirty days to examine this evidence."

*No. I can't be hearing this right. Did he say no bail?* Naheema thought to herself. She just knew she heard the judge wrong, but the look on the DA's face made the words a reality.

"Counselors, does July 15th work for you?"

"No, your honor, the fifteenth does not work for me," Ms. Lebowitz responded, looking through her calendar book.

"That's not good for me either, Your Honor," the DA answered.

"Ok. How about Wednesday July 28th, at nine a.m.?"

"That's fine," they agreed in unison.

"Ms. Morgan, your trial will be on Wednesday July 28th, 2004. This will give both sides a chance to work out a plea deal, if any, as well as give the DA a chance to examine this new evidence."

Ms. Lebowitz finally looked at Naheema. Naheema had tears falling down her eyes. Her life was over. She was too through. She trusted her lawyer would get her out on bail.

"Naheema, it's going to be okay."

"Bailiff, take Ms. Morgan to holding," the judge ordered.

Naheema just wanted to die. She looked back at her best friend, praying for a miracle as the bailiff escorted her back to the holding cell. She was strip-searched again before being pushed onto a NYCDOC bus, heading to Riker's Island. She was going to be housed at the Rose M. Singer Center.

Ms. Lebowitz packed up her briefcase and nodded to Dina and her mother to follow her out of the courtroom.

"What was that? I thought she would have at the very least gotten bail," Dina snapped.

"I thought so too, but right now we have to be patient. The judge gave the DA thirty days to look over the books. Until then there's nothing I can do."

"Mom, is she serious? Naheema will not survive in a jail for thirty days. There has to be something more than that to be done."

"Baby, unfortunately, Naheema is going to have to do this. She'll be fine. She's strong. Gina is doing everything that she possibly can right now. Don't worry," Ms. Weaver said, trying to calm her only child.

"That's not fair, Ma."

"Dina, I promise you that I am going to do all that I can to get a new bail hearing for Naheema. You have to trust me. I know what I'm doing," Ms. Lebowitz said.

"I don't like this. But all right, I'm going to trust you, but you have to get her out of there."

"I will," she said to Dina before facing Dina's mother. "Let me get out of here. I need to make some calls to see about the requesting a new bail hearing."

"Thanks Gina," Ms. Weaver said.

"For what?" Ms. Lebowitz asked.

"For everything."

The two ladies hugged, and Ms. Lebowitz left. Dina and her mother were standing in front of the door when Randy walked out.

"Excuse me, ladies. Can I have a word with the both of you?" he asked.

"Sure," they replied in unison.

"Do you mind if we go somewhere a little more private?"

"Fine. Lead the way," Dina answered.

They followed Randy into a small room on the side of the courtroom and he held the door open for them. He then locked the door.

Everyone took a seat.

" Dina, I'm sorry about Naheema's situation. I wish I could have said something to help her."

"You could have told us about you," Dina said.

"I wish I could have said something, but I was undercover, and I couldn't take the chance that you or Naheema would have told Mike about me. So I am sorry about all of this."

"It's understandable, but you know that charge is bullshit."

"It probably is, but that's not going to stop the DA. We've been after Mike for a very long time, and he's gotten away with too much already. The DA doesn't want to take any chances."

"That's fucked up. He killed a girl in court. Shouldn't that be enough to get a conviction?" Dina asked.

"Yes and no."

"What?" both mother and daughter asked, surprised.

"Listen, Mike's lawyer can easily plead insanity on that. Right now we don't want to give the jury a chance to have any doubts about him. They need to know all of the victims that he left behind."

"Damn," Dina said.

"Listen, not to give you more bad news, but Naheema's sister is in Jamaica Hospital."

"What? Why? What happened to her?"

"She had a miscarriage."

"Oh, my God! Is she okay?"

"She's stable. I gotta tell you, though, she's being charged with identity theft, impersonating the wife of an officer, and a couple of other things."

"Damn!" Dina said, not knowing what to do next. "Is that all?"

"No, it's not. I don't know if you want to know or not, but Mike is coming to see the judge today as well."

"Are you serious? Is he here now?"

"Yes, he is. They're bringing him up now. . ."

Both women decided to stick around and see what would happen with Mike's case. Dina knew that Naheema was going to need some news to cheer her up. Ms. Weaver stayed because she found out that Mike was responsible for assaulting her nephew and she wanted justice for him. They walked back into the courtroom hand and hand, following Randy. He sat behind the lawyers' seats, with Dina and her mother sitting to his left.

"I hope that bastard gets what he deserves," Ms. Weaver whispered to her daughter.

"Me too."

While Naheema was on her bus ride to Riker's, Mike was about to face the judge.

The court officer called the docket number for Mike's case. Since Mike was broke and his lawyer had bailed on him, he was shuffled over to the defendant's table to his legal aid attorney. He stood with his hands cuffed behind his back and chained to his waist, which was linked to a chain that led to his ankle cuffs.

Mike had a big smile on his face until he saw Naheema, Dina, Dina's mother, and Randy sitting in the back of the room. His face turned into rage when he saw the gold badge around Randy's neck. He couldn't believe it. His right-hand man was a fucking cop, and a detective at that.

Randy met Mike's eyes and smiled at him. Randy saw the rage and disappointment on Mike's face.

Mike turned around as the judge spoke.

"Okay. Let's see what we have here." The judge looked up and asked who was representing Mike Williams.

The legal aid stood up and recited his name. Then the prosecutor got up and did the same.

"Mike Williams, you are being charged in the City of New York, County of Kings, with murder in the second degree . How do you plead?"

"Not guilty, Your Honor, by reason of mental defect," the legal aid answered.

"Give me a break. He's not mentally unstable in any way shape or form," the DA screamed out.

"Counselor, I will not have that in my courtroom."

"Sorry, Your Honor," the DA said.

The judge asked, "What are the people asking, in terms of bail?"

"No bail. We're asking that the defendant be remanded back to Rikers."

"So noted."

The judge looked up at the legal aid, expecting him to fight, but the legal aid attorney looked distraught. The judge felt pity for the first-year lawyer.

"Counselor, are you in agreement with the DA?"

The legal aid finally looked up and spoke. "No, Your Honor, we are not. We're asking the people to be reasonable. My client has never been arrested for any crimes. His record is clean. He is a pillar in his community. He owns a salon in the community and employed a lot of the youth in the community to work at his salon. These charges are nothing but some kind of vendetta against my client."

The prosecutor argued, "Your Honor, Mr. Williams did have a salon in the community. However, there are no records of him supporting any youth in his community through employment. Mr. Williams is a very violent man who uses intimidation tactics to scare the youth in his community. Let's not forget that he violently broke the neck of a witness in open court."

Before the legal aid could speak, the judge said, "People, we are not here to fight the case. We are here to set bail. This is a bail hearing only. I have made my rulings. The bail application has been denied. Mr.

Williams will be remanded to Rikers Island where he will undergo psychiatric evaluation."

"Your Honor, may we approach the bench?" the DA asked.

"Come forward."

The DA went on to explain the situation concerning the previous case and about the new evidence that was given to them. He also explained that this was the case that the new evidence was concerning. Mike's lawyer didn't have too much to say because he was just issued this case two days ago. The judge looked over at Mike, then at both attorneys.

"Okay, step back. I'm ready to give my decision."

Both counselors walked to their tables. Mike looked at his lawyer like he was crazy. His lawyer had the stupidest look on his face. Mike couldn't tell what was just said because they were whispering but from the looks of it, his lawyer didn't have much to say.

"Mr. Williams, please stand. Due to new evidence that was discovered from a previous case, this case is being postponed until Thursday July 29, 2004, at nine a.m. Is that good for everyone?"

"Yes, Your Honor," they agreed at the same time.

"Very well then, court is adjourned."

"What?" Mike screamed.

He looked at his attorney like he wanted to kill him. He expected his attorney to say something but all he said was "*Yes, Your Honor.*"

"You dumb motherfucker. That's it? That's all you have to say?" he screamed.

"Bailiff, take the defendant away," the judge ordered.

"Fuck you too," Mike screamed at the judge. "Fuck all of you bitch asses."

"Order in the court. Counselor, get a hold of your client."

As the bailiff grabbed Mike to escort him away, Mike hocked spit on the judge's desk.

"Get him out of here. Now!" the judge screamed.

The legal aid packed his briefcase and left the courtroom. Mike was escorted back downstairs, strip-searched, and escorted on the NYCDOC bus headed back to Rikers. It was at that moment that Mike realized that he was really fucked. He knew in his heart that Naheema turned his books over to the DA's office to save her ass.

"Fuck, fuck, fuck," he whispered to himself.

Everyone filed out of the court room. Dina and her mother thanked Randy for talking to them, then they left. While they were standing at the curb waiting for the light to change, Dina decided that she was going to go and see Shaquanna in the hospital. She wanted to be the one to tell her about what was going on. She gave her mother a hug and a kiss before walking in the opposite direction toward the A-train on Jay Street and Borough Hall.

Before Dina got to the train stop, her stomach growled. She stopped in Pizza Hut and ordered herself a personal pan pizza. After she finished her food, she stopped at the pay phone in front of the store to call Naheema's boss to let her know what happened. *Damn, this is going to kill Naheema. At least she can resign instead of being fired.*

While Naheema was being processed in the Rose M. Singer Center, Dina was just exiting the train station at Van Wyck station, and jumped on the Q24 bus. When she got off the bus, she looked at the time. It was now twenty after six p.m. She hoped that visiting hours weren't over. She entered the building, walked to the information desk, and gave them Shaquanna's information. A couple of seconds later she received a pass to the mother/baby unit. Dina rode the elevator to the seventh floor and got off. She walked to room 722 and stopped in front of Shaquanna's room, listening for sound, when she heard her friend crying.

Dina stepped into the room to find Shaquanna handcuffed to the bed and bawling her eyes out. She walked over to her and held her. She whispered, "Let it out."

Shaquanna cried like a baby for a good ten minutes before she calmed down.

"It's going to be all right," Dina told her. "I am so sorry about your loss."

"Thank you, Dina." Shaquanna tilted her head from left to right. She was a little confused. "How did you know I was here?"

"I saw Randy. He told me and my mother."

"Oh, really? Where did you see him at?"

"At the courthouse," Dina said, sitting down to get comfortable. "We have to talk."

"All right, but where is my sister?"

"That's what we need to talk about."

"Okay. What's going on? Why do you look like you just lost your best friend?"

"In a way, I did."

"What? Oh, my god, what happened to Naheema?"

"Shaquanna, calm down. Listen, your sister was arrested this morning."

"What? Why?" Shaquanna asked, interrupting Dina.

"Can I finish?" Dina waited a minute. "Like I said, she arrested at three a.m. this morning. The Feds and NYPD broke her door down. They found some marijuana hidden in her room."

"That's bullshit. Naheema don't smoke weed. Why would—oh, my god. That sorry motherfucker! I'm going to kill his ass when I get out of here."

"From the looks of it, you don't look like you're going anywhere yet."

Shaquanna lifted her arm a little and looked at the handcuff, "What, this? This is just a simple misunderstanding."

"Look, your sister is in Rikers right now. Her next court date is in one month."

"Damn. Will you see her before her next court date?"

"Yes. I'm going to visit her on Thursday. Why?

"What's today's date?"

"It's Tuesday June 1, 2004.Why?"

"I feel like I've been out of it for a couple of days."

"Okay."

"When you visit Naheema, please tell her, that I am sorry for what I did to her.. Tell her I don't know why I did it, and I am so sorry."

"I will. Now on to you, what the fuck were you thinking?"

Shaquanna started crying. "I wanted him to suffer like I did."

"What are you talking about? Right now the only person suffering is you."

"This is all Randy's fault. He did this to me."

"What are you talking about? What did Randy do? How is it his fault?"

"Dina, I was pregnant by Randy. I told him, but he didn't believe me. He called me all kinds of names and said I couldn't be trusted. He hurt me."

"What?" she asked, thinking *Naheema will be happy to know this.* "You mean you weren't pregnant by Mike?" Dina began to laugh.

"What's so funny?" Shaquanna asked, getting upset. "Why are you laughing at that? What? You think it's something wrong with that?"

"No, I'm laughing for another reason. I'm sorry, but tell me, how is Randy to blame for you having a miscarriage?"

"Stressing me out, like I said. When I told him he was the father, he flipped out and stormed out of my place. I was so mad that I did some stupid things to get even with him. Then he came back to me, so I thought my plan had worked out, but it backfired on me.

"We started having sex. At first, it felt really good, but by the end, it started to feel like he was raping me. When he was finished with me, I was bleeding and in severe pain." Shaquanna looked Dina in the eye. "That's why it's his fault."

"Okay. I'm not going to ask you about what you did, because Randy did tell me some of what you were being charged with. Do you have any money saved for an attorney?"

"No."

"Damn! Look, let me see what I can do."

"You're going to help me?"

"No matter how crazy you can be, you are still my girl and I will look out for you."

"Thanks Dina. I love you, girl."

"Yeah, I love your crazy ass too."

Dina gave Shaquanna a hug and kissed her on the forehead. She sat with Shaquanna until she fell asleep, then she left to head home.

# Chapter 27

The first night inside of Rikers Naheema had a nervous mess. When she entered cell block D, women were screaming, blowing whistles and catcalling to her. She wished she could be anywhere but there. The corrections officers saw how nervous she was and pulled her to the side to speak with her.

"You need to hold your head up high and show no fear in here or they will tear you apart."

Naheema listened. When they stepped back onto the yellow path heading to the cell she was going to stay in, she did just that. Her entire demeanor changed. That little pep talk put a battery of confidence in her back. She was put in cell 28 with another scrawny woman. Naheema placed her towels, rags, and soap on the bottom bunk, while her cell mate took the top. By the end of the night, Naheema and her cell mate were friends. She found out that the young woman was in for being involved with one of the top drug dealers in the Gowanus housing project. She was charged with conspiracy and facing a ten-year sentence. On top of that, the young woman had just given birth to her first baby girl a few months back. Naheema didn't feel that bad about her situation after hearing that. She and the young woman talked into the wee hours of the morning, trading horror stories, before falling asleep.

While Naheema was having an okay night in jail, Mike was having a rough time. He was in the gym lifting weights when another inmate walked in and saw him. Mike didn't remember the guy from a hole in the wall, but apparently the guy remembered who Mike was.

Some years ago, the guy and Mike did some business, which led him to think of Mike as a friend. He started inviting Mike into his home and before he knew it, Mike was fucking his wife and his side chick.

When the guy approached Mike about it, everything went to hell and he got shot a couple of times. He ended up in jail on a six-year bid for a stolen gun. While he was inside he found out that Mike was sleeping with his seventeen-year-old daughter and had gotten her pregnant. The part that made him want to seek revenge on Mike was the fact that when his daughter told Mike that she was pregnant, he wanted her to have an abortion. Mike gave her money to get the abortion, but she didn't. She went shopping with the money. When Mike found out, he beat the man's daughter to within an inch of her life, then burned her insides so that she would never be able to have any children.

As Mike was putting the weights on the barbell, the guy came up from behind and tried to choke the life out of Mike. Unfortunately for him, he slipped, releasing Mike and that was it for him. Mike took the weight off the barbell, slipped it into his T-shirt, and whacked away at the man's body. When he was finished, the man was taken out of the prison on a stretcher. He was rushed to the hospital in critical condition. Mike was thrown into the hole until his court date.

# Chapter 28

On Thursday June 4, 2004, Dina went on her visit as planned. Naheema was ecstatic to see her. They talked like that hadn't seen each other in months. Dina was glad to see that Naheema was doing okay.

"Naheema, we need to talk. A lot has happened since your bail hearing."

"What's up?"

"Your sister is in the hospital, and she is being charged with fraud, identity theft, and another charge I can't remember."

"Damn, I'm sorry to hear that, but I can't worry about her right now."

"I have some good news too."

"Really?"

"She wasn't pregnant by Mike. She was pregnant by Randy."

"You're shitting me? Stop playing."

"I'm dead-ass."

"Wow. So the baby is safe?"

"No. She lost it."

"I'm sorry to hear that. Did you get a chance to speak to my boss?"

"Yes. She said that it would be best if you write a letter of resignation, rather than get fired. So I did the honors and wrote it for you. I hope you don't mind."

"Damn. Now what am I going to do? What about housing?"

"I'll check on that when I get back. Where is your mailbox key?"

"I have a spare key in my jewelry box, if that's still there."

"Okay. Don't sound so depressed. At least when this is all said and done, you can still apply for a city job. Mrs. Brown said that she would help with that too."

"You're right. Thanks, Dina. I don't know what I'd do without you."

"Don't stress that."

The corrections officer came over to the table to tell Dina that time was up. They girls hugged and Dina told her what Shaquanna said. Naheema thanked her again before heading off the visiting floor. Dina had to wait until Naheema was in the back getting searched before they allowed her to leave the floor.

While Naheema and Dina's visit was coming to an end, Shaquanna was released from Jamaica Hospital into the custody of NYPD. She was transferred to Central Booking on Atlantic Avenue. Shaquanna was still a little dizzy from the medication in her system, so they placed her in the medical center. As the women were being transferred from Central Booking to court and back again, it finally hit Shaquanna that this was the real thing. She may be going to jail because of her stupidity.

*Now what the fuck am I going to do? My sister is in Rikers, so I can't ask her for help. I hope Dina comes through for me and finds me a lawyer. Shit. I can't believe Randy would do this to me. I wonder if I'm entitled to my phone call?*

As the corrections officer walked passed, Shaquanna stopped her. "Excuse me C. O.?"

The corrections officer turned around and walked back to Shaquanna.

"Yes. What can I do for you?"

"Can I get a phone call?"

"Give me a few minutes. I'll bring it to you."

"Okay. Thank you."

The corrections officer left, and Shaquanna walked back to her bed and sat down. Ten minutes later the C. O. came back with an old black rotary phone. She handed it to Shaquanna and told her she had five minutes. Shaquanna thanked her and made her call. She tried Dina's house number, but got the answering machine. "Dina, this is Shaquanna, they got me in Central Booking. Please see if you can get a lawyer for me. I will pay you back when I get out of here. I'll try to call you again."

She hung up and decided to call Randy, but his pager number was disconnected. She hung up feeling rejected. Her last call was to her mother, but she got the answering machine, so she left her a quick message. She handed the phone back to the C. O. and went back to her bed to lie down. Before dozing off to sleep she looked at the clock, and it was only two p.m.

It seemed like it was only a few minutes before the C.O. was back telling her it was time to go to court. She looked at the clock again and saw that it was a little after five p.m. She'd slept for three peaceful hours. Shaquanna and four other women were escorted to the criminal court, through the back entrance on Front Street. She was scared because she didn't know what to expect. Nobody answered her call, and she wasn't sure if her mother would get the message in time.

They were escorted into the holding room before moving into the courtroom. Before she entered the box she tried to get a quick glimpse of faces in the courtroom, but she didn't see anyone she knew.

Two women were seen by the judge before her. One woman was sent home, while the other was sent back behind the door. Shaquanna's legs felt heavy. She said a quick prayer before she was pushed to a table with a legal aid. She looked around the room, hoping to see a familiar face, but nothing. Before she turned to face the judge, she saw Randy sitting on the far right. She wanted to smile and spit in his face at the same time, but the judge sat down.

Both counselor and prosecutor went through the process of introducing their names and who they were representing.

Everything seemed to be happening really fast to Shaquanna because she zoned out once she heard guilty and felony. The last thing she remembered hearing was being found guilty of an E-felony and being sentenced to eight months on Riker's Island, complete anger management classes, and attend counseling sessions. Then she was removed from the courtroom and was sitting in the holding cell waiting to be transported to Rikers Island.

Dina visited with Naheema two more times before her next court date. On Tuesday July 27, 2004, Naheema's lawyer visited with her. Naheema was happy to see Ms. Lebowitz. She prayed that the woman had some good news for her.

"How are you holding up, Ms. Morgan?"

"I'm doing okay, but I prefer to be doing better at home."

"That's why I'm here. I have some good news and some bad news. Which do you want to hear first?"

"Bad news."

"Okay, you're going to be placed on probation for one year."

"What? For what?"

"First, do you want to hear the good news?"

"Yeah, I guess so.

"The DA agreed to drop the charges against you if you can testify how the books that they received ended up in your possession, which I gladly responded that you'd have no problem doing."

"Are you serious?"

"As a heart attack."

"So, I will be going home?" Naheema asked, silently praying.

"Yes, Ms. Morgan. Also, the reason for the year probation is because although the marijuana was not yours, it was in your home. That is why you were offered one year probation."

"I don't care, just as long as I can go home."

"We still have to see the judge, but that's just a formality."

"Thank you, Jesus!" Naheema smiled. "And thank you, Ms. Lebowitz, for everything you've done for me."

"You're welcome, Ms. Morgan. I'll see you first thing in the morning."

"I'll be there."

As Ms. Lebowitz was exiting the visiting floor, Naheema was surprised and happy to hear that she would finally be going home. She was so thankful to have a wonderful friend like Dina. But she was especially thankful for Dina's mother's support as well.

Naheema was brought back to her cell floor, where she hurried to the phones to call Dina. Dina's answering machine picked up and Naheema left her the exciting news. She hung up and went back to her cell. She sat down on her cot, grabbed a pen and notebook from the shelf and began writing a letter. More like a *Dear Mike.*

On Wednesday July 28, 2004, Naheema was released with one year probation. Tears flowed down Naheema's face as she realized how precious her freedom was to her.

Before she walked away from the table, her lawyer informed her to stop at the court officer's desk on her way out to get the information on where she needed to go to meet her probation officer. She waited ten minutes to receive the information. She was told to go and see her probation officer on Thursday July 29, 2004, at nine a.m. She thanked the court officer and left the court room, running into the arms of her best friend and her best friend's mother.

Dina handed Naheema an outfit that she'd taken out of the cleaners for her and told her to go changed. Naheema grabbed the outfit and left to change in the ladies room.

Ten minutes later, Naheema was dressed in her fresh beige linen summer dress and sandals. The ladies left the courthouse arm-in-arm. As they walked to the corner of Smith Street, Naheema stopped and threw the bag of clothes into the garbage. The ladies headed for Ms. Weaver's car, got in and pulled off, headed for BBQ's restaurant.

Naheema was happy to be home. She stepped into her apartment and a feeling of sadness and joy swept over her. Dina kept her apartment immaculate. She locked the door behind her and began stripping out of her clothes, running to the bathroom to take a nice hot shower. It felt so good to be in her own bathroom using her own gels. She stayed in the shower for one hour, soaking up as much hot water as she could.

She left the bathroom and entered her bedroom. On her dresser was a small manila envelope. She opened it and inside was a letter with a passbook and a key. The letter was from Dina telling her what everything was for. Naheema opened the passbook to check the account and the amount that she saw had her jumping up and down in her room like a crazy woman. Her new bank account had a little over eighty thousand dollars in it. She grabbed everything and placed them in her dresser drawer. At that moment, she knew that everything was going to be just fine.

On Thursday July 29, 2004, Naheema went to visit her probation officer, while Shaquanna was settling into her new life in the medical ward at the Rose M. Singer Center. Shaquanna met a few young women who were housed in her section who were going to the anger management classes as well, and they became buddies.

Mike was brought back to court to see the judge. It was like watching a circus act. He yelled, screamed, and cursed his legal aid out and the DA. As the court officers were about to lock him up in the white suit, he calmed down and listened to the case.

His evaluation came back that he was sane and competent to stand a trial. He was pissed. He'd tried his best to play crazy, but the psychologist wasn't falling for it.

The fact that he had to be placed in the box until his court date made the judge look at him differently. The judge asked Mike's lawyer if his client still preferred to take his case to trial. At first Mike was insistent on going to trial so that he could drag it out, but after he found out all that they had on him, he had no other choice but to plead guilty.

Mike was charged with six counts of murder in the first and second degree, one count of attempted murder in the first, criminal facilitation in the first, and a slew of other serious offenses. For the first time in his life, he had no control over his own destiny. He sat back in his chair, closed his eyes, and did nothing. It was over, and there was absolutely nothing that he could do or say to change the outcome. He was remanded back to Rikers Island to await his the day of his sentencing, which would be on Wednesday August 25, 2004 at ten a.m.

# Chapter 29

After being home for a little over three weeks, Naheema received a phone call from Shaquanna's mother. It had been years since she'd spoken to her, but she was glad that she did. Shaquanna's mother reminded Naheema that at the end of the day, she and Shaquanna were family and they needed to work things out. She also told Naheema that if she had squashed the beef between her and Naheema's mother a few years earlier, just maybe she wouldn't regret all that had happened between them.

Naheema hung up feeling a real loss for her mother and for her sister. She decided that is was time to go and visit her sister, and have a face-to-face. About a month after Naheema had been home, she went on a visit. After going through all of the security at the prison she was finally called to the visiting floor. Shaquanna came out looking a little thin, but all and all she looked healthy.

Naheema was a little nervous because she wasn't sure of what she wanted to say to her sister. Shaquanna was a little nervous as well. She wanted to beg her sister for forgiveness, but she wasn't too sure if this was a friendly visit or something else. She stepped to the table.

Naheema stood up the give her a hug. The sisters embraced, and the love was felt by both. They sat down, staring at each other. As Naheema was about to talk, Shaquanna cut her off.

"I am so sorry for all that I've done to you," she said with tears in her eyes. "I wish I could go back and change everything that I did."

"First, you look good. How are you doing?"

Shaquanna was a little taken aback by that. She paused before answering. "I'm doing OK. I can't wait until my time is up, but I'm good."

"Now, I wanted to come here and curse you out so bad."

Shaquanna nodded. "And you have every right to feel that way."

"Can I finish, please?"

"I'm sorry. Sure. Go ahead."

"I had so much hate and anger in my heart for you, Shaquanna, but I got a surprising phone call from a person I hadn't heard from in years. I mean, since we were pre-teens, and she put some things in perspective for me. That's why I'm here."

"Who called?"

"That's not that important. However, I want you to understand that I forgive you for what you did, but I will never forget it. You will always be my sister, and I do love you."

"I love you too. Do you think we'll ever be close like we used to be?"

"I can't answer that right now, but with time comes healing and closure. I can tell you that I will be here to support you through this tough time and when you're released."

"I am so grateful to you."

"Just answer one question for me."

"Sure, anything you want."

"Why?"

"I've been asking myself that too. The only thing that I can come up with is I let my jealousy get in the way."

"Jealousy of what? Of who?"

"Of you."

Naheema looked at her sister like she was crazy.

"Don't look at me that way. I've always been the proudest of you and the most jealous of you. You always seemed to have it together, and you were the one who didn't need a man or let a man define you, and I was jealous of that."

Naheema was dumbfounded. She didn't know how to respond to this bomb, so she kept quiet trying to internalize it.

"Look, Naheema. I know it is stupid. I know this now. But that was the reason why."

"You were wrong for that. Look what not needing a man got me. My apartment was raided, I had to resign from a job that I loved, and I almost lost my apartment. Everything that I worked hard for was almost taken from me by a man that I didn't need, but wanted—so badly that I accepted a lot of bullshit from him just to keep him."

"I know, but I was on the outside looking in. I wasn't looking at it that way."

"Well, now you can. I almost lost everything. But I am starting over again."

Tears fell from both of their eyes as the reality of their lives hit them both. They cried and talked for another half an hour before the visit was over. Naheema promised to send money to her, visit more, and write her. They left the visit feeling like a weight was lifted off of their shoulders.

As the months flew by, Naheema kept her word and visited her sister faithfully. Shaquanna was happy to see her sister, but she was really surprised when she started getting visits from Randy. It was like Naheema and Randy were playing hide and seek, because on the days Naheema couldn't make it to a visit, Randy would.

# Epilogue

On December 1, 2004, while cleaning her apartment, Naheema found a letter hidden inside of the Bible that she'd written to Mike from jail. She placed it inside of another envelope, wrote the address on it and mailed it to Rikers Island, praying it reached him before his death.

On Wednesday, August 25, 2004, Mike Williams, a.k.a. prisoner 04A1586, was sentenced to death.

On Tuesday, August 31, 2004, Mike was transported to United States Penitentiary in Allenwood, Pennsylvania.

On December 28, 2004, after receiving and reading a letter from Naheema, he was escorted to the showers, where he was left alone.

Twenty minutes later, four inmates snuck into the shower stalls with him. One inmate threw a pillowcase over Mike's head, and hit him with a barbell, knocking him unconscious. The second inmate stuffed a pair of drawers inside of his mouth, taped it, and held him down, while the other two held his legs apart.

Each of the four inmates took turns beating and raping him. When they were done satisfying themselves, they turned him over and cut his penis off.

Before leaving him lying in a pool of blood and feces, one of the inmates removed the tape and drawers from his mouth and stuffed his slit penis in its place.

An hour later, two correction officers stumbled upon Mike's battered body. To this day, no one has ever been charged in connection with his death.

Shaquanna's mother met and fell in love with Randy. She felt he was good for her. Shaquanna's mother and Randy picked her up on Friday, February 4, 2005, and took her to her surprise party Naheema and Dina had planned at the Sugar Hill club. They partied into the wee hours of the morning.

Randy and Shaquanna left the party en route to his apartment, where they had passionate sex.

Randy was promoted to Detective First-Grade because of his work involving the case with Mike. Shaquanna and Randy became a couple. As time passed by, they got engaged and moved in together. They are expecting their first child.

Life for Naheema was wonderful. She started going to church to get her life right with the lord, and she was no longer in a rush to find a man. She eventually took the city exam to be a housing assistant and was back at work with her old manager.

In May of 2005, Naheema was released from her probation with a sealed record, and a new attitude on life.

In July of 2005, Naheema moved out of Red Hook. She and Dina put their money together and purchased a two-family house on Staten Island. They had a housewarming and invited everyone they knew. Shaquanna and Randy helped with the preparations. Although Naheema and her sister were hanging out more, Naheema still had some trust issues with Shaquanna, so they decided to go to counseling together and get the help they needed.

Dina met and began dating a corrections officer that worked in Rikers. They met during her visits to the sisters. She is now engaged to be married and is expecting a child in the winter.

# Discussion Questions

1. Should Naheema have told her sister about Mike? Why or Why not?

2. Is there really love at first sight, or was Naheema so desperate to find a man that she allowed lust to guide her relationship?

3. Did Mike really lie to Naheema about what he did for a living, or did Naheema allow herself to think otherwise?

4. After catching Mike and the woman in the act, should Naheema have gone back to find out who the woman was? What would you do in that situation?

5. The first time that Mike beat Naheema, should she have ended the relationship then and there? Why or Why not?

6. If you were in Shaquanna's shoes, would you have slept with your sister's man? Why or why not?

7. The minute Dina knew that Naheema was messing with Mike, should she have informed Naheema about her old relationship with him? Should she have warned Naheema about Mike as a person?

8. After finding out that her sister was sleeping with her man, did Naheema react the right way, or did she take the punk way out? What would you have done if you found out that you sister was sleeping with your man and may be pregnant with his child?

9. Mike did a lot of horrible things in their relationship, but was he to blame for his actions or was Naheema to blame because she continued to forgive and allow him to do it? Why?

10. A lot of women out there have been in this same situation and stayed. only to be destroyed in the end. Have you been in this situation and how did you get out of it? Should have the characters in this book have done anything differently? Would you have done anything differently?

# Melodrama Publishing Order Form

WWW.MELODRAMAPUBLISHING.COM

| Title | ISBN | Qty | Price | Total |
|---|---|---|---|---|
| Drama with a Capital D by Denise Coleman | 1-934157-32-5 | | $14.99 | $ |
| Cariter Cartel (Mass Market) by Nisa Santiago | 1-934157-34-1 | | $ 6.99 | $ |
| You Showed Me by Nahisha McCoy | 1-934157-33-3 | | $14.99 | $ |
| Return of the Cartier Cartel by Nisa Santiago | 1-934157-30-9 | | $14.99 | $ |
| Who's Notorious Now? by Kiki Swinson | 1-934157-31-7 | | $14.99 | $ |
| Wifey by Kiki Swinson (Pt 1) | 0-971702-18-7 | | $15.00 | $ |
| I'm Still Wifey by Kiki Swinson (Pt 2) | 0-971702-15-2 | | $15.00 | $ |
| Life After Wifey by Kiki Swinson (Pt 3) | 1-934157-04-X | | $15.00 | $ |
| Still Wifey Material by Kiki Swinson (Pt 4) | 1-934157-10-4 | | $15.00 | $ |
| Wifey 4 Life by Kiki Swinson (Pt 5) | 1-934157-61-9 | | $14.99 | $ |
| A Sticky Situation by Kiki Swinson | 1-934157-09-0 | | $15.00 | $ |
| Tale of a Train Wreck Lifestyle by Crystal Lacey Winslow | 1-934157-15-5 | | $15.00 | $ |
| Sex, Sin & Brooklyn by Crystal Lacey Winslow | 0-971702-16-0 | | $15.00 | $ |
| Histress by Crystal Lacey Winslow | 1-934157-03-1 | | $15.00 | $ |
| Life, Love & Lonliness by Crystal Lacey Winslow | 0-971702-10-1 | | $15.00 | $ |
| The Criss Cross by Crystal Lacey Winslow | 0-971702-12-8 | | $15.00 | $ |
| In My Hood by Endy (Mass Market) | 1-934157-57-0 | | $ 6.99 | $ |
| In My Hood 2 by Endy (Mass Market) | 1-934157-58-9 | | $ 6.99 | $ |
| In My Hood 3 by Endy (Mass Market) | 1-934157-59-7 | | $ 6.99 | $ |
| In My Hood by Endy (Trade Paperback) | 0-971702-19-5 | | $15.00 | $ |
| In My Hood 2 by Endy (Trade Paperback) | 1-934157-06-6 | | $15.00 | $ |
| In My Hood 3 by Endy (Trade Paperback) | 1-934157-62-7 | | $14.99 | $ |
| A Deal With Death by Endy | 1-934157-12-0 | | $15.00 | $ |
| Dirty Little Angel by Erica Hilton | 1-934157-19-8 | | $15.00 | $ |
| 10 Crack Commandments by Erica Hilton | 1-934157-10-X | | $15.00 | $ |
| The Diamond Syndicate by Erica Hilton | 1-934157-60-0 | | $14.99 | $ |
| Den of Sin by Storm | 1-934157-08-2 | | $15.00 | $ |
| Eva: First Lady of Sin by Storm | 1-934157-01-5 | | $15.00 | $ |

# MELODRAMA PUBLISHING ORDER FORM
(CONTINUED)

| | | | | |
|---|---|---|---|---|
| Shot Glass Diva by Jacki Simmons | 1-934157-14-7 | | $15.00 | $ |
| Stripped by Jacki Simmons | 1-934157-00-7 | | $15.00 | $ |
| Cartier Cartel by Nisa Santiago | 1-934157-18-X | | $15.00 | $ |
| Jealousy the Complete Saga by Linda Brickhouse | 1-934157-13-9 | | $15.00 | $ |
| Menace by Crystal Lacey Winslow, et. al. | 1-934157-13-9 | | $15.00 | $ |
| Myra by Amaleka McCall | 1-934157-20-1 | | $15.00 | $ |

***Instructions:***

*NY residents please add $1.79 Tax per book.

**Shipping costs: $3.00 first book, any additional books please add $1.00 per book.

Incarcerated readers receive a 25% discount. Please pay $11.25 per book and apply the same shipping terms as stated above.

***Mail to:***

MELODRAMA PUBLISHING

P.O. BOX 522

BELLPORT, NY 11713

Please provide your shipping address and phone number:

Name:____________________________________________

Address: __________________________________________

Apt. No: ________________ Inmate No: ______________________

City: ______________________ State: __________ Zip: _____________

Phone: (         ) _____________-______________________

Allow 2 - 4 weeks for delivery

## Drama with a Capital D by Denise Coleman

Available Now!

Lonnie, a strong, independent, career-minded sista isn't one for drama or unnecessary bull. In fact, she's not even sure if having a man in her life is worth the trouble it can cause. However, when she meets John, everything changes, and her comfortable life as a single career woman goes flying out the window. She's in love, and things couldn't be better. Then all hell breaks loose.

cartier
Cartel
The Saga Continues...
cartier
Cartel
NISA
SANTIAGO
RETURN OF THE
cartier
Cartel
2
NISA
SANTIAGO
Book 2 Coming in October 2010

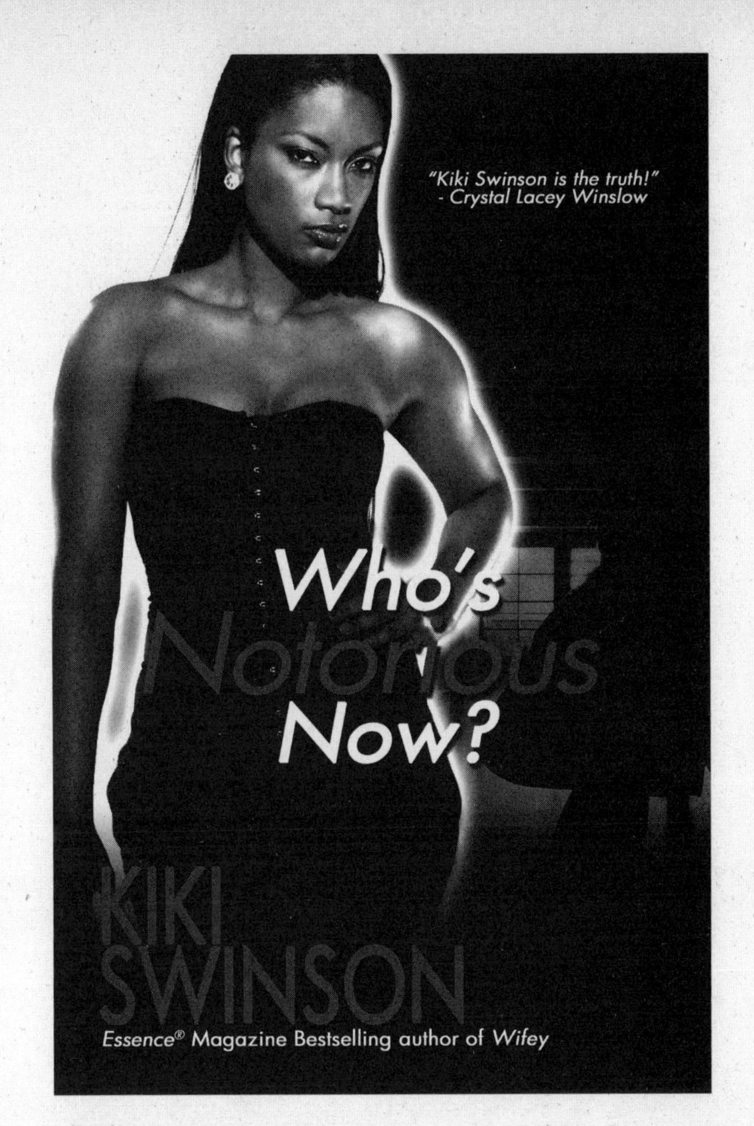

"Kiki Swinson is the truth!"
- Crystal Lacey Winslow
Who's
Notorious
Now?
KIKI
SWINSON
Essence® Magazine Bestselling author of Wifey


## Who's Notorious Now? by Kiki Swinson

November 2010!

Criminal defense attorney Yoshi Lomax finds herself on the other side of the bars in the third book of the riveting Notorious series. While Yoshi tries to prepare herself to face the music once she's extradited back to Miami, the ordeal she encounters en route is more than she could have anticipated. Knowing deep down in her heart that she isn't equipped to handle all of this strife, she has no other alternative but to play the game to save herself.